BRAND OF JUSTICE

A NOVEL

by
CURT RUDE

This is a work of fiction. Names, characters, businesses, places, events and incidents are either the products of the author's imagination or used in a fictitious manner. Any resemblance to actual persons, living or dead, or actual events is purely coincidental.

BRAND OF JUSTICE

Copyright © 2014 by Curt Rude
All rights reserved

Edited by Carolyn Sween
Cover & interior design by Indie Author Services

This book or any portion thereof may not be reproduced or used in any manner whatsoever without the express written permission of the author except for the use of brief quotations embodied in critical articles and reviews.

ISBN 978-0-9884319-2-8

DEDICATION

To incarcerated innocence and loved ones they've left behind.

PROLOGUE

He stood staring up towards the top of a prison wall. No way had he wanted it to work out like this. The clouds rolled in bringing rain and a coyote got to yipping in protest. He had too much going on in his head to care in the least about rain or hail for that matter. This whole thing got going because some cops messed up. He had to tend to matters because they screwed up. How in tarnation could he just stand by and let a lady get thumped? Anyone can boo-boo, he figured. It's when a fella keeps it up and up that it gets old really fast. The bumps and bruises, the looks at school and ma.

He figured he didn't start out hating 'em. Ended up, he hated some of 'em *p-len-ty*. And he didn't figure he was a one-a-them serial killin' jobs. No Sirrree! He knew he was going to probably forget some of it as he hashed it over in his mind. Ahhh, he had made everything better, the police department, court and saved his friend from getting killed. Oh, he hadda do some killin' for sure. But ya gotta pay the fiddler if ya wanna dance.

Plenty of folks in these parts figure things out from the news. He had seen them do it. Not a good way to go near as he can tell. Before long, good, decent, honest types get to being blood-thirsty hounds without even a knowing it. Slip him the needle. He ain't nothing but a waste of taxpayers' money. He heard it all. Pretty hard not to. He knew though. He knew he was innocent. He knew a whole lot. People were remarking some as to dying being easy and living being tough. It's folks who ain't strapped down on a cold steel table waiting on a needle to drip poison into 'em who say such nonsense. He couldn't live with himself if he let someone do any dying on account he had went and screwed it up. Some folks can look the other way and not do a good goddamn thing. Maybe they already been beat down and figure what's the use. Maybe they know, they too fat, stupid or something. Well, he was still just in his teens and he wasn't fat, dumb or stupid. He'd heard tell of boys as young as sixteen going to war. It felt like that to him, he just felt a duty to do something, anything. He figured he was what they call desperate to put a stop to a ma being beaten. He was too involved to look the other way like the cops had done.

He didn't see any guards up in the tower slowly massaging their weapons. What's the deal? Budget cuts. Where the hell is the ol' sharp shooters? Nope. They're up there for certain. Probably bored with the routine of prison life. Most of the guards never get to pop a round off at any of the prisoners. That's just in the movies. Besides the wall look to be twenty- five feet if it's a foot. It'd take some doing to get over that puppy. He could do it though. Anyone can do anything; they set their mind to it. He was gonna pull it off. Oh yeah, he was about to conduct a li'tle ol' prison break by using his noggin'.

He gave the laughing guards a polite nod as they headed towards the parking lot. Suppose they put in their eight hours and now it was time to tackle some choices that come with freedom. A beer?

Girlfriend? Then showing up for the wife and kids. Anything they damn well please. No rules. No bars. No twenty minutes for chow with a bunch of nut job skin heads. Doing time can dull the brain some. After the prison break he hoped things could be like they always were. Living in a cage eating what's dished up and standing in lines can probably dull a guy. Make him numb. Never even having the warm touch of a woman to settle things. How does a guy go about quieting death row nightmares? Some things can't be changed.

Well then, how many needed to be dealt with — huh? If he hadn't been such a good ol' boy he'd a killed more of them lying assed badge pinner-on-ers. He heard it, and seen it. Guys doing time for nothing they ever did. Every once in a blue prairie sky it'd come out 'bout how somebody done gone and got railroaded. Cops somehow got it all wrong or witnesses were yammerin' their way out of a jam. Snitches they're called. Lot of folks doing time because of people who go and lie their asses off for one reason or another. Maybe cops think they see something or a witness wants someone hauled off. Suppose there are as many reasons as there are people. How about DNA? The truth can come back and haunt all those hoity-toity bastards parading around their brand of justice.

Nobody seemed to give a good goll-damn, but he did. Most folks too worried about their own pie hole. He had more things to worry about than just himself. He learned how the human animal can make good, honest things look just plain bad. Friends turn on each other at the snap of a finger. Cops get all worked up with handcuffing and herding criminals around for the cameras. Then the news stories get the whisperers revved up. 'Didja hear the latest?' 'Ya know what I think!' Well they're innocent until proven guilty. Yeah right, he'd seen and heard it over and over. Fact is, you're innocent until you're accused of somethin' is how it works. Then herds of stupidity start demanding justice, law and order and even the death penalty.

Sure I kilt 'em, ain't takin' exception to that. It has to be done sometimes. The law goes and calls it justifiable. I've had plenty of schoolin' regarding law enforcement to know I'd landed right on the mark there. Come Sunday the preacher is always going on and on about doing right. The human animal is too scared to do anything right. I gets the feeling if I didn't kill 'em it would've just plain been a sin, a mortal sin, the kind you can't be forgiven for.

There're plenty of okay cops. It's the ones in the business for all the wrong reasons he took exception with. It's them twerpy lil' bastards that chaffed his hide. They the type always somehow screwing up but who get really good at covering up. They look good because they get lots of practice.

Another thing irked him. Just because a feller dressed up like a lawman, didn't amount to diddlysquat. Persons gotta earn it. Hmmm he thought. Nope, they ain't nothing less they earn it. It's on them to prove their mettle, to turn that costume into a bountified uniform. Yesssiree, nothing but clowns till they get ta proving themselves worthy. Can't change a pole cat just cause you paint over its stripes. Folks change plenty when they commence to sporting the badge. It ain't always for the good neither.

So what's a guy to do when a cop commences to be bad, really bad? Put him down cleanly and completely is what he got to calling it. He'd come up with a plan and stuck to it. No need having anyone suffering needlessly. That kind of stuff would bother him. Nope. Just kill 'em completely and cleanly. Just a tiny bit of using thee' ol' brain and presto, the police force goes and gets a whole lot better! Cops come in a whole lot of shapes and sizes. They come with all kinds of different abilities, he figured. Some were good at it. Copping. Some weren't. Usually the bad ones were good at one thing, covering their tracks. He'd seen what complaining got a person. A ton of cops lying and not seeing things. He remembered discussing in school the code of silence that cops duck behind.

Another thing 'bout them coppers—they always use your first name, like you're friends or somethun'. It didn't work on him, he was the kinda model came with an ounce of sense. He prided himself in the ability to smell a tall tale upwind a mile away. It's like cops and used car salesmen sprung out of the same place. When car salesmen ain't no good, when they can't sella car, they get canned. Do bad cops ever get dumped? Naa. Unions, rules, policies and procedures keep 'em around forever. The system protects them. He knew this. He'd seen enough of it and studied on it some. Bad cops like houseflies … they eat shit and bother folks. They hard to swat though.

Town folks all considered him a good fella. He never turned a blind eye on anyone needing help. After the killing started it got bothersome that so much death was called for. He didn't put much stock in serial killers. He killed when it was called for was all. He was just doing what the preacher always calls on folks to do. To stand up for the right things. It's like weeding a yard. About like getting dandelions outa the lawn. Ya keep pulling and weeding until there ain't no yeller in the yard. Then before long ya gotta get after 'em all over again. He figured bad cops, the yeller types, is a whole heap like dandelions.

He knew yammering about not taking the law into your own hands was a crock. He felt like his life would have been easier if I could have just looked the other way. He was good enough not to believe in something that wasn't right. Whoever figures ol' cops and lawyers only folks that can get it right don't know squat in his book. Anyone with any sense know when things need to be put back in order. He could smell badness rolling in with the tumble weeds clear across the plains. When he smelt trouble, he did something about it.

He thought about how much he hated criminals. About as much as anybody. His hatred ran deep as an oil well on the plains. When he did his killing he had to worry about having nasty dreams. Killing bothers good old boys but sometimes there is no other way. Born of good Wyoming stock they'd say he was. He was one of them good cowboys for sure. The bright sun suddenly peeked out between storm clouds hung low over the prison. The light blinded him back to where he was. Standing next to a cold, grey, prison wall that separated the fortunate from the damned. Varmints, vermin and lowdown cops that damned innocence into this place had to be dealt with. Can't have 'em messin' up perfectly good lives. God had a plan. God wanted people to squash bad deeds. He musta wanted someone to put a stop to them Casper rascals…

CHAPTER 1

KILLIN' & DYIN'
"HALLOWEEN (THÉME PRINCIPLE)"–DANIEL CAINE

Ahhh, yes, he thought. There he is. The headlight was bouncing and weaving towards him. The drunken bastard! On time for the last time…and there won't be a next time. He shivered into his thoughts about how much the feller kept getting away with. Now you see him, now ya don't.

He was slouched back onto the garage wall, hugging shadows, listening to his heart pounding a steady, strong, cadence on his ear drums. His feet shuffled in the dust threatening to haul him away from his fears. What if he couldn't do anything? he thought from behind, unblinking owl like eyes. Then what? It wasn't like he'd ever done anything like he figured he might have to do tonight.

The car slowed, timing the opening garage door perfectly. Only one headlight. The garage needed a light as well. The boy figured it was probably pretty hard to keep the lights on when the mechanic is drunk all the time. A thin, quiet smile slipped across his face revealing a thought. The mechanic was having a hard enough time keeping his lights on as the boy was planning on putting his lights out but for good.

He was hoping. He was holding onto his wits as tightly as he clung to the knife. It was razor sharp and held low in his latex gloved hand. He was not a killer. What if Rogers laughed at him? If he turned tail and ran would it only get worse? Sweat started appearing at his hairline in the chilly night. He wavered in his thoughts. The sweat seemed to wash his resolve down towards his chin line leaving only fear in its wake. If things worked out right may be he didn't have to use the knife. May be he could just scare him a little. What should he do it? His voice would probably announce how scared shitless he was. His tongue was housed in a very dry environment. He was paralyzed and frozen in the darkness realizing he didn't have to do anything but be invisible.

Mr. Rogers pulled himself out of the car onto unsteady feet. He started trying to figure out where his keys were hidden in his pocket. He was drunkenly mumbling something under his boozy breath. The keys were already in an unsteady hand but he didn't know it until he heard them clatter onto the sidewalk. This new issue presented another dilemma. The keys were on the sidewalk but how was he gonna pluck them back up without a nasty fall? Rogers was lost in an alcoholic swirl of confusing thoughts and unsteady feet.

The boy smiled as he made his move "H-Hey—" before realizing he did it. It just happened.

Rogers attempted to focus on the surprise as he watched it snatch the keys from the sidewalk and drop them in his shaky hand. The fog clearing apparatus in his brain wasn't up to snuff tonight resulting in a numb, beery stare. It was the boy, Rogers somehow guessed.

"T-t-tanks—boyee." Rogers grunted, not totally knowing, but hoping he wasn't looking as drunk as he was.

"Ahhh shucks, nuttin' to it sir."

"Look goddamit—if I wanted whisky waters I'd buy da-damn whiskeys. I-I mean waters." He knew the boys been stealing his whisky for a while now and watering it down to hid their crime. "Damn you fellers…st-tealing good whiskey and l-la-leaving me watered down stuff. Didn't figurer I'd catch on…di-did-ja?" Rogers leered towards the boy with scorn pushing all friendliness out of the way. He was rubbing the whiskers on his chin with an oil and grease smeared finger and thumb. The boy had been stealing the booze figuring it wasn't really stealing. He had to do it 'cause he couldn't buy it. So it wasn't like he was bad or anything. Whiskey waters had somehow taken over his thinking before he got back on track. Rogers pushed the boy back telling him he needed a good ass kicking and swung at him before staggering into the house. He did not trust his feet to keep his nose from touching the door.

The guttural breathing increased with the anger. The beery breath was expected. The knife digging into his throat was unexpected. The boy watched from a hazy fury as the cold steel disappeared into the five o'clock shadow. He froze, it happened that fast. He could only see the handle of the blade. That meant the blade. The entire blade? He wanted to run, somewhere, away from the handle sticking out of Rogers' neck. The boy figured correctly that stabbing and throat cutting…if that's what he'd done…would cause blood. But so much *blood*?

Bubbles gurgled and rode the bloody mess out of the gash. Between the continued flow towards Rogers' chest steady jets of blood super-squirted out towards the boy and wall. The spurts were strong enough to hit the wall at first. Rogers didn't really do anything. He seemed intent on figuring out why he was fading. He stumbled around some, digging his hands into the opening that was blocked by the knife. His Adams apple thing-a-ma-jig slid to the side but was hung up on meat and stringy stuff. Blood pushed chunks towards the floor and then…BANG! Rogers tumbled onto the yellow linoleum, followed up with some kicking and twitching. His hands were balling up into tight fists and then relaxing before balling up again.

"Mr. Rogers, y'all okay? Mr. Rogers?" The knife turned a punch into a reddish mess. Rogers had swung first but missed. The boy hadn't. Rogers on-no goddamn account should have swung at him… maybe, just maybe, he wouldn't be bleeding out if he hadn't. The boy wondered if what he'd done was really an accident. When Rogers swung at him the boy quit thinking and just swung back is all. He swung back and was holding the knife but wasn't thinking on it as much as he should've.

Blood oozed out of Rogers' neck. He was blowing and sucking air in and out at the same time. Not knowing much about dying caused the boy to dig out his cell. Dammit, he thought, should I call 911? Maybe or maybe not. Maybe I am a murderer. Was Rogers kicking around 'cause he was dying? If he did go off and die, what did that mean for the boy? If he died that meant no more bumps and bruises in school. No more thinkin' 'bout what others were thinking. Nope, things sometime just happen, it wasn't his fault. Besides he didn't figure he really did it. Now if Rogers would just die and be done with it. The boy suddenly realized that he'd be in big trouble if Rogers didn't die and told the cops. He also realized he couldn't stick knives in anything dead or alive again.

The kicks started to slow. The legs just seeming to stretch out. Rogers' chest lost its steady rhythm; he'd take a big breath, like he was going underwater, then let it out slowly. The big breaths started giving way to smaller more subtle attempts at air before giving up completely. Rogers was going through all the dying motions about like a stuck hog. His fingers were slowly giving up their last attempts at making fists. He made a snoring sound before making a huge yellow puddle on the floor. Good. It seemed to blow by in a flash but yet take forever. Dyin' on a kitchen floor is sure a lot more grosser than in the movies he thought. He stood over the mess, held tightly by his thoughts, like a Blue Heron froze up, waiting to strike at a minnow.

Killing didn't have to take much effort. Not if a guy was cutting into a drunk. He'd been in wrestling matches in school that had tired him out more. The knife slid in like a sharp knife would slice into Cherry Jell-O. For a brief moment he thought he'd have to tug the knife out using both hands. But once he worked it free, it slid out smoothly. His eyes were locked on the skin and meat clinging to the silver blade as it worked free. It thoroughly disgusted him but he couldn't look away. He stared intently, watching the blade pull stuff like what looked to be the windpipe partly out with it. The science teacher called it something. Bronchial tube sounded right. The pink thing must have been the food tube, he didn't remember the name. He quickly rubbed the blade across Rogers plaid shirt. The boy was torn between staying and making sure no clues were around to just bolting for the Honda. He realized thick blood was all over his gloved hands. He couldn't hurl, that could be evidence. The cloud of nasty smells engulfed him. His stomach had tightened up in protest over what his nose was encountering. The only thing he wanted to do was race into the night. He wanted to leave the blood, stink and dead old Rogers behind.

He watched the macabre spectacle as if it was in slow motion. The body kicked and twitched itself into a corpse. Rogers bitching days 'bout watered down booze was a thing of the past. The boy wanted things to change. Once the cold carbon steel found its way into his hand, they had. When the talking turned into doing, blood started flowing. The gurgling had stopped; the puke was just dribbling outta the pink tube. Then headlights hit the fast-forward button.

SHIT. Oh shit…out of here! Gotta get my ass on the four wheeler. Where is the key? The boy dug into both pockets as if he was going to push his hands clear through 'em. Dammit. Really bad. Ahh Christ, I left them in the ignition. Christ, he thought, as he jumped on the four wheeler and fired it up. Ol' Dub had the best four wheeler around these parts. He had to scoot and damn fast, but nothing seemed fast enough. Thinking on what to do got trampled by doing anything fast. The screech of the starter took first place in his thoughts over a beating heart, breathing and already running engine. Why didn't I hear the damn thing start in the first place? The grinding noise of tires on crushed rock closed in, causing a big-time desire to go-go-go! The unexpected car noise kept getting louder and louder, jolting the boy as if it were a cattle prod.

God, why now? Nobody ever swings by here in the dead of night. Why? The trusty old Honda raced forward in an instant, putting distance between its rider and a corpse and car. The darkness settled in on him. The Honda couldn't leave the yelling thoughts in his head behind. Where was the helmet? A bigger thought jumped up and demanded to be heard, like a kid who is the first one to come up with the answer in a classroom. The knife, the knife, where the fuck *was it?* Then thinking flooded in on top of the raging river of fear in his head. Oh sure he thought… it started out good. He didn't know he could do it, but he had. He put a stop to Rogers. Then the head lights ruined everything. He was hoping he hadn't done anything stupid before running off. Did they see him getting the hell outa dodge? The knife and helmet ain't everything. Whoever knifed Rogers could have easily stolen the knife and helmet. No big deal. Or was it? He just didn't get it.

Then it dawned on him, he was wearing the helmet and the knife was penned between his hand and the handlebar. Why hadn't he pissed himself? he thought, as a sinister poker player smile landed on his face. He breathed slower on purpose. He didn't figure he had to keep on breathing like he'd just ran down a calf. He was casting glances back behind his shoulder into the darkness but saw nothing.

His stomach had unknotted itself without puking. The fresh air, unpolluted with the stench of death, was a relief.

The slower breathing helped spit return to his parched mouth. His pounding heart also started settling in his chest. He had gotten away with murder. So what? he thought, anyone could mess up like he did tonight. What mattered was he got away. That counted for something. It hadn't all worked out the way he thought it would, but whatever. Now if he could get stuff cleaned up and spend the night along the North Platte, life, his life, would involve more things like school, girls, friends and homework. There was just something about a night out under the Wyoming stars. The North Platte River splashing its way downstream, the highways sounds and banging of freight cars from the Burlington Northern yard. That was what his Wyoming was all about.

Asshole always came home after having a couple. Yeah, right, a couple. He could remember the bastard laughing about his drinking. A bartender had asked Rogers what he drinks and Rogers had said a whole helluva a lot. The drunken bastard! Then the change would appear out of nowhere. No more mister nice guy. A beer, little bump, whiskey usually, and then bang. It would start up funny and end up miserable. Usually two, maybe three cold beers chasing whiskey down the hatch. Then the exploding heat would roar back up from the stomach into a whole lot of wrongs. It always was about the same thing. Where the hell was she? With somebody else-huh? Well…fuck it then. I'm going to Australia. You're a good boy, why don't ya come with? Australia. Yeap, ya don't have to put up with mouthy women when you're in Australia. He remembered it all and knew there wasn't much wrong with putting a knife in ol' Rogers.

It's pretty hard watching a fella like Rogers call a lady bitch and follow it up with a beer in her face. That's just plain wrong. All the screaming and hollering. Usually pushing. Some shoving. Cops called. Did they ever do anything? Course not. Just a little jaw jacking and back slapping. People cooled down and Rogers never landed in the slammer. Never. Same thing, every time. Cops headed out the door and then BANG. It would start over again. That kinda stuff gets old even quicker when it's a mother on the business end of a fist.

Rogers was a mechanic. Damn good one too. That's what they'd be saying at his funeral. He fixed the squad cars for the City of Casper. When ol' Glen fixed something, he fixed it right. Except for his drinking. He'd get to drinking and then everything went wrong. Some knew the worse stuff was always saved up for the lady in his life. Name calling, pushing and even worse.

Tonight he had been driving his Caddy all fucked up with a headlight out. He must not have been as drunk as ten men cause the cops weren't giving him a ride home. He'd just been out doing a little drinking and driving is all. Not too god awful late, so he probably didn't stop by the little lady's house to punch her into sunglasses tomorrow. Chronic drunk. It just needed to be stopped and by Christ I got the job done! When the cops play a disappearing act with the law then it's up to the good folks to get the job done. Rogers seemed to be too much for 'em. Well I just mighta done better than all the lawyers and judges in the world. I cut Rogers life short and he hadn't suffered much. Rogers made perfect filler for a six foot hole. The young assassin, riding the Honda, smiled.

He already had his pack tucked away in the garage. He had planned to kill but realized he couldn't and then he'd gone off and did it anyways. What was going on back at Rogers place now? Did Rogers die? He had trusty latex gloves on. That always works on T.V. He figured he'd sleep some even if stampeding thoughts seemed to resist that notion.

He shut his eyes but his brain was still open for business. Who the hell was in the car? What did he leave back there? Fingerprints? Nope, he had gloves on. Man—he had blood all over his gloves but no one would ever find 'em or the knife. He'd ditch them in the garage wall. The evidence would havta be scrubbed off the handle bars. He couldn't be sneaking around in the garage without waking her up. He'd havta check out the Honda tomorrow, making sure he got all the blood off of it.

Things should work out just fine and dandy. What if they don't? Nope. Can't freak out. Cool as a cucumber. Gotta be cool as a cucumber. He figured he did good tonight. He actually cut Rogers life short. He got the job done. He hoped so anyways. Nobody seen nothing and there was no way the scoundrel was going to live. God he hoped not anyways. Hospitals can work miracles, but he went and stuck him good. Really, really good. Now if shadows of fear and doubt would leave him be, why he just might get some rest.

Tormented thoughts exhausted the boy and he finely slipped into the dark corridors of something resembling sleep. A worried soul made for an exhausted boy.

What he didn't know were off-duty cops in the approaching car thought they had seen more than they did. Bolting the scene with lights on was a big-time mistake. It was going to change everything. Change everything in a big way. The rider would havta kill, kill and kill again. It was the only way to right the wrongs he'd cut open under the dark, peaceful, Wyoming sky.

CHAPTER 2

TINKEY & DUB
"FAST CAR"—TRACY CHAPMAN

I go by Tinkey. Scott Tinkersley is scrolled on my certificate. Wasn't long before it was cut down to Tinkey though. It didn't mattered none to me. I do the usual stuff…church to keep mom quiet, hangout, pick up the yard for pa. Stuff like that. Everything is special when you're living in Wyoming let me tell you. Shit happens though, like school. School is a problem everyone has to mess with I guess. Ain't much to do if ya went and dropped outa school, only way to a job they say. I don't get much oudda it though. All the grab assing and prom business. Wouldn't go, no how, it wasn't for mom and Sheila. More Sheila. Really. Work puts cash in my pocket but I just don't plan to cook the rest of my life.

So there you go. I hang low around school so I don't get fucked with. Just kinda stare down the clock and smile when it's called for. 'Bout the time I go and get used to a schedule then it seems like things get changed around. With prom on the way it's like here we go again. How do I stand, so as to not look like a dumb ass? Then when do I get to take my flowers off? Don't rightly recall fellas belonging in flowers. Gotta do what ya gotta do.

The long hand finally landed on the six. I stared down the last two minutes and they felt like hours. Math sucks if a guy don't give a rat's ass for the square root of nothing. Finally. Time to escape the dungeon of 'time standing still' and skip to the cafeteria. Funny thing, lunch hour always blows by in a couple of seconds. The food was dished up as I shuffled towards Blanche, the ticket taker. The food was good. Sometimes it would look funny though, like hotdogs having the parts sticking outa the water turning grey or something. Sheila always stared down her food and tossed the rejects my way. Picky eater. 'Ain't never been hungry is her problem' granddad would've said if he wasn't taken' a dirt nap.

The only benefit, near as Tinkey could tell, regarding math, was it was just around the corner from the chow line. That usually landed him near the front of the line. Sheila was usually hung up more towards the middle. Her look, or presence, claimed frenzied attention from the boys around her. She had emerald eyes which sparkled in a warm, radiant face. Folks lucky enough to be near her never wanted to escape the wonders of her laughter. Sheila was considered thoughtful, caring, and kind, even if she wasn't. Her whispering and giggles drew 'em in like sharks to a bleeding seal.

"Did ya hear who Bonner is taking to prom?"

"I don't give one iota, really, not one iota. The world isn't gonna end. He likes 'em big hearted and empty headed. All-righty then, who is Bonner the boner taking to Prom?" Tinkey was nowhere near the conversation. His thoughts lingered somewhere outside the school and Sheila knew it.

She stared at him and pronounced the conversation dead. Period.

"I'm outta here. Ya know it wouldn't like hurt you to not be such a durr. Really. Can't you ever like act interested—in maybe one thing—I have to say?"

She was pretty. She had a point. Maybe he figured he should get better at pretending. It couldn't hurt any. Just look like he was into it.

"Oh god, totally sorry. Don't be pissed, really." He didn't mean it of course…and she somehow knew it.

"God…I mean really. Can't you look at me when we're talking? Like I'm here." She stared into a distracted face and snapped fingers in front of it. "A-D-D Tinkey, is what it is called. You have Attention Deficit Disorder."

Call it what it was, Tinkey couldn't keep his eyes off of the grand entrance of Dub. Tall and gangly. A nose that hung clear down past his chin, ears, from over the top of his head clear down to his chin line. One had to wonder if they'd slap him silly he got caught in a windstorm. His face, even in high school was ancient. Looked leathery and worn, like chaps that'd done been drug through prickly pear. Unbelievable. The hair, kinda mangy, wiry and never in place. Then his walk. He'd put a foot out and flop it down. None of that heel to toe thing going on. Just reach his foot out and flop it all down at once. The arms seemed to hang clear down to his shins. Tinkey wondered some if Dub could tie his shoes without bending down.

"God you're like totally doing it again?" She said through clinched teeth.

Jeez, he thought as his eyes landed back on her. "All-righty then, whose Bonner taking to prom—*really?*" He was talking to her as his eyes slipped back towards Dub. She got up and stomped out of the cafeteria, or at least towards a destination that contained no Tinkey. She had to figure out how to buck this cowboy into her world.

Dub landed on a chair and stared down his tray. His knees seemed to bend up clear over his head as he made the chair appear small. It always got quiet when ole' Dub showed up. He was just there. Never gave anyone problems outside his looks. Tinkey figure'd if ol' Dub was headed to prom his date probably be just plain muttley. Not that he'd ever say such a thing. If Dub did pick something up for prom, Tinkey figured he'd go out of his way to be polite and funny. It'd work out better for him if he had his buddy to hang out with at the dance.

Dub lived with his ma just on the outskirts of town, rail thin, tall and just plain looked like he didn't know if he was on foot or horseback. Dub always somehow made Tinkey feel better for what he had. Today, Dub was sporting a shiner. He was usually black and blue for some reason but a black eye? It'd been some time since he showed up with a shiner.

Tinkey couldn't help himself… "What's sup Dub?"

Dub's face moved in different directions and his Adams apple slid some distance in his scrawny vulture like neck. A grin creased the vacant leathery mask.

"Godda g-g-good one for t-t-today Tinkey."

"Car full of-of lawyers hit our ba-barn… Y-You listening, Tinkey?" Tinkey nodded and continued to watch Dub light into the joke.

"Yeah, yeah…I'm listening." But he knew the joke wouldn't laugh his thoughts away from the shiner.

"Well i-i-i-it was a bad accident; we hadda bury the whole bunch of th-them lawyers." Dub's eyes sparkled, his voice remained low but his face seemed to be younger after the start of the joke.

"Cops show up an-an-an ask us what happen an-and we havta tell 'em w-we went and b-b-buried everyone in the accident. Cop asks us if there were any survivors an-and we tell 'um that some were claiming to be alive but you n-know how lawyers are, always lying!"

Tinkey laughed. Not the pretend being polite laughter, but the real deal, "How'd'ja get the shiner? Somebody haul off and whack ya? Were ya talking when ya should've been listening?"

"I g-got another-another one for you…twwwo lawyers," Dub whispers but Tinkey shushed him.

"All-righty then…cut the bull…I'm serious…how'd ya get the black eye? I'd be much oblig'd if you'd be straight with me." Tinkey was not going to let it go. Somebody had hauled off and popped Dub good.

Dub concentrated really hard towards the distant wall as if he was attempting to make out what kinda tiny spider was clinging to it. "Not g-gonna. Not wanna say…" as he pushed his vittles around with his fork.

"Look man, who's messing with Dub? They keep messin' around they gonna be laying around!" Both of Tinkey's hands had bunched up into rock solid balls as he cast a burning glare across the crowd.

"Not I, dude…" one of the guys on the football team demurred and nodded.

Tinkey was adamant. "Man, somebody is messing with Dub!" He stepped towards the crowd waiting for the school bus "I wanna know who the hell is dicking with Dub."

One brave soul stepped into the Tinkey glare and cleared his throat. "I don't get—"

"Shut the fuck up, I've had it with this bullying! Dub don't mess with anyone, ya know. Do you guys get it?" Tinkey stared down the crowd. He could. His nasty play on the football field insured nobody wanted to mess with him. He was all-conference as a defensive lineman.

Sheila stepped towards Tinkey, "We gotta talk." She commenced to herding him away from the crowd, kinda like a child leading a plow horse on rein.

The bus bounced to a halt and the mumbling crowd grabbed for the rail and escape. "Come on Tinkey." Sheila turned and started walking. "You're pissed and a good walk'll do ya good."

"I don't get it, look, Sheila, Dub shouldn't be messed with, ya see that shiner? Near as I can tell…there ain't no call for anyone to whack him. He looks goofy…I know, but come on already."

"You don't get it…he came to school with it. I got him in first hour."

His mouth fell open but didn't produce words. Sheila poured her words into him.

"I think his ma's boyfriend, that Rogers guy, is the one is a doing it. I'm totally serious here. That's what I think…why don't ya ask him yourself? Call the cops or something. That's what they call domestic abuse and that's breaking the law."

Tinkey thought on it. She was making sense but why wouldn't Dub ever come clean? He had asked him something like a zillion times about it. Made sense though, Tinkey hadn't ever heard of anyone getting after Dub in school.

"Why not let him fight his own battles? Really. Serious." Sheila walked faster when she was using words that angered her. "God, if ya cared half as much about me, we'd get along a whole lot sweeter I 'spect."

After leaving her, Tinkey bee-lined it home, but the matter had been welded to his thoughts. All things Dub tumbled in his thoughts like a tennis ball in a dryer. Sheila could be right, it could be Rogers. Why such a big secret? Tinkey was breathing deeply as his thinking angrily haunted him. Black eyes on a high schooler were plain wrong. Dub had a flat look in his eye, like a dolls. It wasn't right, Dub needed help.

"Trains a coming." Tinkey left his pole laid up in a 'Y' stick and raced Dub to the top of the bank. The Burlington Northern ran plenty of trains into the Casper yard. The roar of the ginormous engines accompanied by the high pitched whine of protesting wheels never failed to elicit a thrill in the guys.

"Man, these babies got kick. We'll be a runnin' 'em soon enough Dub!"

Dub clumsily nodded and gently rubbed a bruise on his bicep as if his was scratching a mosquito bite. Said he had tripped up, but Tinkey knew better.

"The B and N is always hiring. Ya gotta go to like Kansas City for school, math and all that crap and then…we the man a laying on the horn…you and me, brother. Just you and me."

Dub had snuck into the big units when they were out of service. He'd even rode on one once with Tinkey. They'd been making small talk with a crew member and he let them board for a run around the yard. An enormous, humming diesel throbbing towards the horizon would be his escape. From ma, Rogers, the works. For now, his arm hurt. Dub was sure he'd had enough of Rogers, even when they were getting along, because the bad side never went away for good. He had thought and thought on it. He'd figure Rogers just needed a swift kick in the ass but when the time came he stalled. If pa was around things wouldn't be like this. No sir, but pa tangled with a semi when he was in a little bitty Volkswagen and lost. Maybe Dub thought things could be right better for Rogers and his ma if he was out of the picture. May be Rogers would quit using her for his punching bag. Maybe, just maybe, she wouldn't have to be going out evenings with dark sunglasses on.

Tinkey stood next to the lumbering, rocking rail cars as they picked up speed towards the setting sun. Both of them knew it just wouldn't make much sense to hop it going west. Douglas towards the east was even too long a ride for how late it was. Fishing was slow. Boredom finalized its grip on the boys.

"All-righty then, what'll you say we break for the Rock?" Tinkey was wondering as he said it. "Too late my man, to hop trains, fish ain't biting, nothing else ta do."

Dub never thought on matters much… "I r-r-reckon it'll be a-okay."

"Ahhh wait, it'll be getting dark I suppose, maybe we could mess with some rattlers." Snakes always were the answer to boredom. Even if they were being messed with just for the sake of messin' around. No bounty, nothing but forked sticks and pictures to see how big a one you could come up with. "We could head straight away towards Rattlesnake Hills ya know."

"Suppose we could p-p-poking around…some and come up with 'em." Dub didn't mix much excitement with his words. Messin' with rattlers was the sum of all his fears. They went and caused him more concern than 'bout anything, not counting Rogers. What he didn't know was Tinkey was well aware of his fear of snakes even though he'd never let on to the fact. His face had betrayed his secret a long time ago.

"Come on man, you want to hunt up an old mine or something? We could bird dog snakes and dig around some for dynamite." That would kick old Dub in the backside for sure. Old mines in lower elevations sometimes came chucked full of snakes and maybe if you were lucky, a stick or two of dynamite.

Dub thought some on it. "Don't know if snee-snee-sneaken' around an old mine full of snakes is my idea-err of fun. Where She—Sheila at anyways? You guys a-a fighting or somethun?—"

"Oh, come on, man. I'm yapping about rattlers and you're thinkin' some on Sheila! She's up in the high country with her Quarter Horse." Sheila did have a mighty fine horse for trail rides and barrels. Wouldn't take a million for it she had said. Tinkey didn't like the idea of Sheila spending more time with her horse than him. He wasn't even too clear on whom she loved more…him or Fiona.

Dub never let on to his way of thinking. He always went along with Tinkey whether it made a lick of sense or not. Before long he was picking his way around boulders towards an old mine shaft they both knew was there. Only boredom and youthful enthusiasm would land someone at its entrance. Towards the front, boulders were piled in to keep youthful stupidity from entering. These blockades, however, harkened youngsters to trespass. These boulders demanded attention, followed by reckless activity. Others had actually completed many hours of work breeching the barrier. Digging was evident and some of the stones had been wrestled out. Tinkey realized the amount of work expended before their arrival. The bigger boulders that refused to budge were simply dug around.

"All-righty then, me first." Tinkey said while brushing his hands together as if to warm them.

Dub stared on… "D-d-donut know if this make a lick of sense. Cr-er-crawlin' around like a-sn-sn-snake when there'll be plenty of the real v-v-varmints in there!" Dub stepped back clearly, no longer bored, as his heart picked up its pace. It was getting harder to continue playing his not afraid of nothing big man game.

"Oh come on…I'll go first. I'll clear it with my trusty stick. Those ol' prairie rattlers ain't a match for me and my stick…I tell ya. I drag this defensive lineman carcass in there be nothing for you to make it. What'd are ya scared? You afraid of the dark?" Tinkey commenced to speaking with a carnival gamer's voice… "Step right up folks and see a real, in the flesh, girlie boy."

Dub forced reluctant feet to carry him towards the dreaded event. He was sweating some in the chilly evening air as he got belly down and started for Tinkey's feet. Tinkey had already disappeared into the darkness knowing full well Dub had to follow.

"SLOW do-DOWN some SO as I can catch up. Don't figure I-I-I'm taking much of a shine to this. That's all I'm a-a SAAYING…"

"SNAKE!" Tinkey hollered causing Dub to back up faster than he'd been creeping forward, smashing his head into a rock.

"C'mon, just kidding ya. You didn't believe me, did ya? Christ…I gotta tell ya, Dub… you crawl into tunnels 'bout like a girl would." Tinkey about choked on cave dust some as he thought of the shuffling sounds Dub kicked up at the mere mention of a snake. No doubt about it, he thought, Dub was a friend. Fun to be around.

"Don't suppose this makes any sense tat-tat all to me. Then-en you go and star-start hollering 'SNAKE' for no good reason. I don't 'spect, expect-favoring-crawling around any nasty old mines with you having to holler like that. Bah-bah-blooie…na-na-not a lick aaah sense to me no how. I banged my head but good on-on account of you."

"Aaa come on—come on, just kidding for Christ sake and then you gotta get all worked up. Quit hollering, Christ y'all gonna get us busted." Tinkey had crawled through and pulled his stomach between two cool stones and managed to get up off his belly into a crouch.

Tinkey knew clowning around Dub was just a fringe benefit to their friendship. Besides, he no way wanted Dub to take out the rock with his gourd, but accidents happen.

"All-righty then, I'm in." Tinkey spoke as he realized he'd not be standing in this old mine shaft unless someone, anyone was with him. Then he remembered snakes, thought some on bats and spiders and quickly flicked his flashlight on. Only thing the light indicated he was in danger of was spiders, or actually webs. Reams of webs floated in the damp air of the dank shaft.

Dub pulled through and worked himself into a crouch next to Tinkey. His light added to the light being cast by Tinkey's. Mines weren't places to be without light. After walking some into the depths of mother earth they came to a pile of dried boards and pilings at an intersection to another shaft. Being expert 'miners' as the boys thought of themselves they remembered to scratch an arrow in the dusty floor and wandered towards the right.

Tinkey stopped and Dub bumped into him. "Hit the brakes already, dude. What'd ya tryin' to do, man, like give me whiplash?"

"Wh-wwwha is it?...snake?" Dub urgently whispered.

"No, no, settle. I'm mean—really, snake this...snake that. Every time you open your mouth it's always snake this...snake that. Get a grip, dude. You losing it, cowboy?" Tinkey pointed his flashlight up towards the upper reaches of the shaft. He looked away from Dub not wanting him spotting any encroaching fear on his face. "See that? It's some kind of ventilation shaft or something! It's blocked off and you can see ain't nobody been messing around with them rocks. Not until now, buddy. You up for a little work? Ya ain't scared, are ya?"

Dub was staring at the area lit up with Tinkey's flashlight. "Don't s-sss-suppose there snakes up in there do-do ya?"

"Oh darn it, I think my flashlights broke?" Tinkey pointed his light he had conveniently switched off into Dubs face. Dubs leaned towards the light inspecting it for damage.

"Na-no it don't look—"

Tinkey flicked the light on suddenly, blinding Dub. "Dude, only did it to get your mind off of you know what."

"Fu-fu—" Tinkey walked up towards the newly discovered shaft, leaving Dub befuddled and frustrated with the bright flash burned into his eyes and the word fuck stuck on his tonsils.

After working his stick around the rock pile he hoped it was clear of snakes as he declared the area completely snake free. "Don't hear 'em rattling do ya?" Both of the boys started pulling and tugging on stones and at times quickly jumped out of the way as sizable stones bounded unevenly downward before settling on the dusty floor. After some doing they impatiently would point lights into the clutter of boulders but could see nothing. Gravity aided greatly in the clearing of the boulders. The dust they continued to kick up placed a right nice tan on the boys. Both Tinkey and Dub finally pointed beams of light into the tunnel after pushing a remaining stone out of its resting place into the darkness. It was theirs to be had. Treasure. They both felt like Long John Silver. Pirates of the prairie. Busted up wooden crates, along with rope, lamps of some sort and fascinating long forgotten garbage from what the boys were hoping were the cowboy and indian days.

"Fuuuck me! Ain't nothin' but old treasure in here from the good old days. You best stay put! Might be a rattler in these parts. Score baby. Look at all this stuff will ya?" Tinkey picked up some old rope and started absently tying a hangman's noose while coughing mine dust up. "Good rope. Good shape. Oh, don't move…ya got a spider on your sleeve!"

"Sh-Sh-Shoo you spy-spy-derr," Dubs said as Tinkey swatted it off for him.

"You shoo flies, dumb ass." Tinkey smiled before convulsing into fits of excited giggles.

Dub swung over towards one of the wooden crates with a top sittin' on it and tapped it with his snake stick. "Whoa, buddy; you want this place to blow? Whoee, you keep fucking around and we're gonna be laying around. Come on, quit the kids' stuff. What gets tapped and goes freaken kaboom—huh?"

Dub pushed gently on the crate carefully realizing from the weight it was not empty. Actually it was heavy. He carefully untwisted wire, holding the top of the crate in place, they both peered into it. Many leaky old reddish sticks of dynamite were resting in its damp musty confines. They both stared on their find, it was the Comstock Lode. They'd mostly talked about finding dynamite until tonight. Tonight, they scored big-time.

"Shiiiit man…will you look at that?" Tinkey said, pointing at it excitedly.

"How ya-aaa-ya figuring on we get-getting it out-ta-ta here… here?" Dub figured the next thing to do after finding a load of dynamite was getting it out of the mine shaft.

"Very carefully, one stick at a time. See that white crap on them sticks? You mess with that and its ka-blooie big-time. It's like nitro or something, you know that…"

Dub stared on some. "I-I know. I wha-was born at night…but notta born last night!"

Both boys cradled a stick after having gingerly lifted them out of the crate. Neither boy wanted to be the one to have to touch the sticks but they feared letting on that they were scared even more. Hanging onto high explosives blew all the boredom out of their Wyoming night.

"I best carry the dynamite, Dub, you scared to death of snakes, man. You gotta be ahead of me checking for snakes. Okay? Put your stick back man. You even think you hear a rattle or buzz, be cool… least we both get blown to smithereens. Ya have ta use your stick on the bastards. You'll blow our asses clear to the moon if you back up into me. You got it?" Dub nodded in a slow thinking fashion while gently rubbing some whiskers recently sprouted on his chin. He was not one to ever argue. Not with Tinkey or anyone. Before leaving they piled rocks back into the opening to keep their cache of fun hidden.

"All-righty then, time for our great escape, let's make like a tree and leave…" Dub didn't laugh because outside of his lawyer jokes he never got them. His attention was locked on the forbidden escape route he had to shimmy through.

Tinkey held the stick of dynamite lightly to his chest while keeping all thoughts of it out of his head. He slid into the excavated opening between the rocks suppressing any urge to hurry.

"Easy-easy-easy does it…easy-easy-easy does it." Tinkey slid up out of the opening and stood a bit waiting for everything about his body to slow down. He slowly exhaled. Life was suddenly gonna explode into more fun than the boys ever thought they'd own.

"Check this out, dude." Tinkey smeared some of the white goo off of the dynamite and tossed it against a rock with a resounding boom. Both guys snickered nervously under their breath as they prepared a spot in the prairie sand to ditch their dynamite. Now they had to consider their good fortune. Camaraderie is born, of the mother, of all good luck.

CHAPTER 3

SENIOR YEAR
"HOME ON THE RANGE"—BREWSTER HIGLEY

"**H**ey, dick breath." Tinkey knew enough not to havta ask Dub if he told anyone. "You gotta work come Friday?"

"Yeah, I'm o-on the fry-fry-fryer, aren't you working?"

"Oh yeah, I'm on the grill. We should be out of there by two after we get done with the bar crowd." Tinkey wondered what to do about Thursday. No school on Thursday or Friday. "Ya know Sheila is headed to Cheyenne with Fiona. Barrel races. You wanna hang out down towards Alcova? Swim, camp or something down on the Reservoir?" Tinkey cast a glance in Dubs direction realizing his hollering snake had caused the knot on Dub's head. No mystery this time regarding Dub's bumps and bruises. "Come on dude…you got a headache or what?"

"N-N-No…Imma figurin' it be a good time…I-I best checkup on ma-ma though." Dub was thinking hard while falling over his words.

Tinkey was thinking some, too. "I expect she ol' 'nough to go and take care of herself."

Dub was already plodding down towards the bus stop. Tinkey watched him take steady giant strides, reaching out with one foot and putting the entire foot down and then pulling his weight up on it before working his other foot out into the next step. Dub always, but always, stooped forward with the same old dead zombie look pasted on his face. Tinkey smiled some and thought about how hollering snake could blast that look off his face. Tinkey knew a bunch of folks around Casper and surly couldn't recall anybody plain 'fraid of snakes like old Dub was.

"All-righty then, call me dude, Dub…give me a jingle, soon as you check up on your ma, I'm a waiting on your ass, big buddy!"

After fooling around with the tent and camping gear Tinkey was annoyed with himself for forgetting his sleeping pad. This necessitated a quick u-turn and return to his house. He had the Coleman cook stove, sleeping bag, lantern, the works, but blew off the pad. That wouldn't do, Wyoming ground is mighty hard and full of rock to boot. You sleep in your bag without a pad and you'd be feeling it for a month of Sundays.

"Mom…forgot my pad. Where ya figure it is?"

"In the garage, where it always is, dear. Where you headed?"

"Oh, I left ya a note, figured I'd spend the night down at the reservoir, Pathfinders."

"You aren't going alone are you?" Mom asked.

"No, Dub, Dub and I are gonna head down there. He's checking up on his ma. I mean he's always kinda worrying on her some. You know they live over there alone since Dub's dad died. I think his ma's running with a fella that can be mighty hard on her. Dub gets banged around too. I don't get it. Why his ma run around with a fella who would do stuff to them…like that?"

"Dub go and tell you that, honey?"

Tinkey thought some... "Well, ahh, no, but all them bumps and bruises godda come from somewhere and why else does he gotta go running home to check up on his ma? I don't get it. But his ma and that Rogers, the mechanic, are dating or something."

Mom thought about Rogers. She knew that Dub's ma ran around in sunglasses all the time, even on cloudy days. She also was mighty careful on the words she went and used around Rogers. "Oh, I don't know about that Rogers, seems he drinks too much. When he gets to drinking he can be just plain ornery, let me tell you. I think your friendship is a very good thing though for Dub. He's probably plenty worried about his ma you know. Now before you head off you remembered your insulin and you are going to eat properly—right?"

"All-righty then mom, oh, I almost forgot, I havta call Dub before I head to his place. Yeah...I got everything, no need to worry on my account."

Dub plodded in his usual humped-over gait towards Tinkey's truck in the driveway.

"Got ever-everthing," Dub pronounced as he stuffed his gear into the bed of the pickup.

"All-righty then...let's see. All we gotta do is pick up our dynamite and we should have a pretty damn good night—huh?"

The boys headed towards Rattlesnake Hill and the hidden dynamite. Dub had bought along his rifle. Everything was set for a nice, quiet evening, sleeping under the stars in the wide open solitude of Wyoming country. Tinkey had checked his blood and his levels were good. After setting up camp they hiked up towards the rim overlooking Pathfinder Reservoir to settle in and watch the sun lose out to the moon.

The walk up towards the ridge had held a surprise. After some walking Dub surprised Tinkey with a rattlesnake discovery. Tinkey had poked some with his walking stick as he stepped over a dried up limb busted down across the trail. Dub, bringing up the rear, for whatever reason musta poked more than Tinkey had. A steady, angry rattle, more like a buzz than anything, resulted from the pokes of the stick. At first, he couldn't see the rattler before it gave up its hiding spot along the limb and started off quickly towards Dub. The snake wasn't any more than a couple of feet long. It had its head held up slightly as it bore down on Dub who side stepped it and flipped it with his stick. The reptile started to quickly serpentine downhill before pausing, as if to get its bearings. It then headed into sage brush.

"Been a while since I saw one of 'em out and about. Christ, I stepped right over it. I could've gone and got hit. Not good, not good at all. Kinda pisses me off that I went and missed one of them little bastards." Tinkey didn't like the idea of having stepped over a snake without so much as boots on. He knew he'd gotten lucky on the plains which wasn't always a commodity you could count on.

After the boys had arrived on the ridge and landed on suitable rocks to gaze on the disappearing sun, Tinkey asked how his ma was doing.

Dub skipped the question and mentioned the railroad future they had discussed. "Yea-yeah, they hire folks, because of all the-tha-that coal ya know. Someone gotta get th-tha-that coal east. May as well…be-be … us."

Dub noticed Tinkey eyeing his bruise. It was a nasty deep purple more than blue, depending on the angle. It was a new one added to his collection and it wasn't caused by Tinkey's going off and hollering snake. That one was on his head and it had hurt plenty but this one was on his shoulder. Dub knew a long sleeved shirt would have kept it from Tinkey's prying eyes and thought it was stupid to have grabbed a short sleeved one instead.

"What da ya-ya call a lawyer with an IQ-Q of a hundred?" Dub didn't wait for a response. "Ya call him your on-honor. What do-do you call one with an IQ of fifty?...Senator—Haa, good one, huh?"

"Look man, Dub, I know stuff—you know…"

For some reason Dub didn't shush Tinkey with a joke but just stared on the newly revealed stars and moon. He gave the appearance of being nowhere near the conversation.

"You wanna live over with me?"

"Na-na-no…ma, she'd a be-be needing me."

"Call the cops or something! You don't have to take this from Rogers. It ain't right. I'm telling you. Call the cops." Tinkey's eyes pierced into the very place the jokes sprang oudda Dub.

"Na-no…he knows them cops, all ahh-of them. They are always drinking and ca-care-carrying on. They a know to-to. I don't tell 'em but they know. If I-I did go and tell 'em it'd be light-lights out. No I don't tu-tell. We gonna be-be run running freight trains before y-ya know it. All of t-this go away." Dub sat back, using a rock as a backstop, staring out across the reservoir with his knees clear up pert near over his head. He rocked his head to and fro pulling a grin out of what was a grim demeanor only a split second before.

Tinkey couldn't ever quite believe how long Dub's legs were. Dub seized the melancholy moment and lapsed into the safety of silence and no jokes. Nothing but staring, lost in whatever was going on behind his eyes. Tinkey had come to expect these moments and backed off, concentrating his efforts at tossing rocks.

After long he got to talking again. "Why Dub, my man, if you ever got a blister on one of your feet I bet it'd take a long time for your brain to know it. Damn ya got long legs."

So peaceful on the outside. So miserable on the inside. The peace came from everything around the prairie as the day light things fell back into soft, silent darkness that claimed everything. A calmness born of shadows reaching out at the fading light whispering bedtime to the boys. Dub knew Rogers wasn't about to mess with him as long as he was safe and sound under the Wyoming sky.

Tinkey was miserable and confused about everything Dub. No amount of anything ever seemed to clear it up for him. He tossed things around in his thoughts. Dub wasn't talking. Rogers was nothing but cantankerous when drinking. He drank most nights. Sometimes he was known to have barley lunches. A beer, a chase and then new bruises for Dub's collection and sunglasses for his ma. None of it made a lick of sense. Not at all.

"All-righty then. Come on man, it's time for a little fireworks before we die." Tinkey had picked the pace up and started the descent, though he was more careful with his poking and prodding as he headed to camp. Dub followed closely, not much wanting to be alone in the darkness. Tinkey didn't want to do anything as stupid as he'd done walking towards the rim. Missing a snake and getting hit could have put an end to his crawling up into a Burlington Northern engine and throttling it over the tumbleweed crowded prairie.

The brisk walk, with thoughts of what was soon to come, snapped the boys back awake. Tinkey wanted to tend to his insulin needs first. He took out his kit under the watchful eye of Dub and loaded up a syringe. He then removed an orange cap off the tip of the hypodermic syringe and quickly buried the slender needle into belly fat just above the belt line. The needle slipped into Tinkey as his thoughts were locked on dynamite. Dub chilled some, then looked away while figuring he was too afraid of needles to be a diabetic. He rubbed his biceps and thought the word fuck over a couple of times.

"Th-th-that hurt?"

"Nope! All-righty then, let's see if we can't do something about that dynamite." Tinkey, without picking up the dynamite, carefully rubbed some of the white paste off the stick and rolled it up between his fingers into a ball the size of a marble. "Okay…are you ready?" Dub's head bobbed up and down. Tinkey let fly and the resounding boom along with flying sand provided the adrenaline rush so longed for by boys of all ages. They both were laughing quietly, realizing the thin line between safety and accidents. It was a blast sharing a dynamite induced moment of laughter.

"Fuckin' A—A—A…" Tinkey was grinning like a bulldog shitten' barbed wire.

Dub had all but forgotten his struggles and misery. "N-now we gonna do the whole stick?"

"Yeah, we'll sit it up over yonder," Tinkey was urgently pointing at several rocks. "Load up the rifle and I'll lay the dynamite down." Tinkey handed Dub the rifle as he bent to pick up the paste covered reddish black stained stick. He wanted to shoot at the dynamite but figured Dub deserved the honor more. "Go ahead, my man…ready, aim, fire!"

Dub squinted best he could while Tinkey light up the sights with his flashlight. He leaned towards the intended target and squeezed the trigger. The resulting explosion roared across the evening stillness, blowing sizable chunks of rock, sand, and dust into the night sky. After some time, Dub pulled his fingers out of his ringing ears and laughed along with a dust covered Tinkey. "Son of a bitch…we blew the fu-fuck-fucker…aaa-up good." The laughter didn't stop for some time. Then, when one of the boys even mentioned it, laughter would again roll across the prairie. The dynamite grand finale. It had blown both boys away from Rogers. It had blown them together on the wind swept plain. They were truly brothers in arms. Two cowboys against the world.

"I hate r-r-Rogers. Ma sees good in him. Don't know a-a reason whu-why. I don't expect to see any good in him. N-Not no how.

Things a-always bad. He derr-drinks. Beer. Then bad care-carrying on. Real, b-b-b-bad really. R-r-Rogers don't like me cause ma sa-say I make him get to thunk-thinkin' on my pa. He ornery as a buh-bull. One of these days I-I expect I-I should just kill ol' Roe-Rogers. That'd serve him right. D-don't put much stock in him tat all. He-he-he ain't good to m-m-ma. I hate it pl-pl-plenty. He make m-me feel plain bad."

Tinkey nodded slowly. He was startled and lost. He'd never heard Dub blabber on. His words left no doubt he carried memories of every ass kicking Rogers had laid on him and his ma. Each boy finally crawled into the warmth of their sleeping bags surrounded by their own troubled thoughts.

Dub beat Tinkey to work. He was already in his apron and was straining oil for the fryers. Tinkey tied his apron on and fired the grill up. They avoided any mention of the success of their camping experience the night before.

"Order Up." Tinkey read it out loud and the boys found their time taken up deep frying, grilling and plating up.

"Dub…your dad or whatever, Rogers is out there with that tall drink of water, that blonde cop. They both having steak sandwiches," the waitress mentioned with a harried expression. Tinkey watched the jawbone tighten involuntarily as Dub shuddered from the word… Rogers. Tinkey understood and felt like he would shudder, too, if Rogers was his mom's boyfriend. Both boys knew that Rogers was drinking. It was a Friday night after all.

"Sheila is hounding me about prom. I hate this time of year. Wanna go together?"

Dub thought some. "I-I-I did-didn't go ask anyone to pro-prom, can't ri-rightly figure out who'd wanna be caught dead with me. I-I-I don't dress up good. Be-besides somebody gonna have to man this play-place if you and Sheila are out on-on the town."

"Suppose that's right…" Tinkey realized he felt like something but wasn't sure what. He was going to prom with Sheila. He had a mom and dad. He didn't ever show up at school with bumps and bruises and embarrassed expressions. Tinkey had no idea if Dub wanted to go to the prom or not because so much of him was hidden. He wanted to do something for Dub, but was stuck. He knew Dub hated Rogers. Who wouldn't? Tinkey also knew Dub's ma would show up tonight for whatever reason, drink some, and end up fighting.

"Two more cop buddies are out there with Rogers. He sure thinks he's a ladies man. He tips like he's homeless or something. Oh, sorry, Dub…isn't he like your daddy or something?" The waitress was too busy to wait for an answer. All that was left of the hurried question were swinging doors. Dub never made like he was going to answer. He only stared down on his project, cutting onion rings. Tinkey always marveled at how something that appeared so clumsy could perform so well. Dub was an expert with a knife. He could even sharpen them on a steel. It was like you couldn't see the blade when he was working with it. Near as Tinkey could tell, Dub was completely self-taught. Tinkey always had Dub put an edge on his blade for him.

"All-righty then, you wanna hang out after work? We could pick up a movie or something, ya know."

Dub hesitated, then mumbled straight away… "No, I-I-I best be home."

Tinkey knew Dub didn't have much to get off work for. He knew Dub didn't have much of a reason to go to prom, let alone home. Nothing ever seemed to be there but more bumps and bruises.

"Whoa dude, slow down with that blade. You already cut enough rings for tomorrow night." Dub slowed some, staring down on the mound of fresh cut rings, wiping his eyes as he took his apron off. He then looked at the blade that was still in his hand, as he slowly laid it down. "Ga-ga-gotta run to the john, be right back."

"All-righty then, got ya covered; I'll put the rings away. Only fair, you cut the entire load on your lonesome."

Dub left the kitchen in his usual style, walking with enormous strides. Never any heel to toe deal with him. No matter if he was in a hurry or not, he just lumbered forward. Tinkey had to take three steps just to keep up with one of Dub's.

Orders had slowed as the restaurant crowd seemed to have eaten its fill and moseyed into the bar. Tinkey watched his hands going through the motions of putting the onion rings in a five gallon plastic pail full of water. Sheila had Dub figured as nothing but gloomy. But she just didn't get how much he could laugh. The night before they had laughed their asses off. Tinkey figured Dub just needed a break and it'd work out.

A waitress slipped into the kitchen and in a conspiratorial whisper told Tinkey, "That asshole Rogers, mixing it up with Dub and his ma again. Thinks he's big time 'cause of—" Tinkey wanted answers, cutting her off mid-sentence.

"What are they fighting about now?"

"Oh, who knows…you know they never need a good reason to get into it. He's raising hell about wanting to go to Australia 'cause she looked at another guy out there or something. He's like…such an asshole…total durr." The waitress was staring at the swinging French doors, with disgust plastered on her every expression. She tossed her head back after being satisfied that she had figured the bill out right and stomped out of the kitchen saying… "Last time I screwed Rogers' bill up by a dime and he still bitches about it."

Dub came back into the kitchen in his usual unhurried manner and rolled the mop out of the closet. He seemed to be at a loss to even come up with a lawyer joke. His Adams apple was bouncing more than usual, but no words got outta his mouth. Tinkey thought some on telling a lawyer joke of his own but then thought better of it. Sometimes silence was the better alternative.

After a wordless clean-up, Dub vanished. Tinkey had scooted to the bar for change and returned to an abandoned kitchen. That wasn't good. Something was up, but what? Tinkey wanted answers, but wasn't sure he even knew where to start. Rogers and his crew had left the restaurant and weren't in the bar either. Dub had disappeared. Everything kinda just got real quiet after everyone split.

Tinkey put his jacket on, pulled his keys out, and slumped behind the steering wheel wondering on what just happened. Well, 'now what?' he thought as he drove to Dub's place. He slowed as he drove past the house noticing lights on. After parking, he slipped up to the house in the darkness and he heard thuds, loud thuds, and furniture getting banged around. Screaming and hollering and a lot of swearing coming from Rogers. That was for certain in an unsure evening. They were at it again. Where was Dub? Tinkey couldn't hear him, but figured he was in the house taking care of his ma.

The anger came up from some place and choked Tinkey. So many wrongs for so long. Dub didn't go and mess with anyone and then he has to put up with this. How many more days would he havta parade around school with bruises? The howling and cowering silhouettes behind the shades caused an involuntary clenching of fists.

After the door was flung open by a raging Rogers, he got in his red Cadillac and stomped on it, showering the area in gravel. In a second or two he jumped on the brakes and skidded to a rockin' stop. After putting it in reverse, Rogers stomped on the accelerator and roared to a stop in front of the house. "You can have him, I'm done, I'm headed to Australia, bitch! Do you hear me? You and that goddamn thing you call a kid can go straight to hell. I'm done, BITCH!" Then, when nothing but silence came from the house, Rogers stepped on it and fishtailed into a peaceful Wyoming evening.

CHAPTER 4

CAMPING

"WRITING WRONGS"—THE MONKEES

Morning came and morning went. Motions were in order. Tinkey was lost and strangled by his thoughts. He put together a paragraph about the previous evening. He didn't want to go all over it again. Usually, whenever his thinking was getting away from him, he could kinda rope it back in by putting it on paper. It helped him to understand his thoughts, when they were in sentences on paper. He found by writing a wrong, it helped him make it right.

> Rogers was fuckin some with them again. what can I do? Call the cops till mom Talk it over with Dub i don't know i don't put much stock in Rogers is all If Dub gos and mixes it up with him I got his back

He kicked around the garage, getting it in order. Not so much to get on his dad's good side as to be doing something, anything to escape the relentless sounds from last night. Tinkey knew his dad would never go and call his mom a *bitch*. What was waking up like for Dub? Mister Aldinger got in Boysen's face big time in gym class. He told old Boysen that it ain't right on no account to go and call a gal a name. 'That ain't no way, no how for any cowboy to act! You can just take it out of my gym.' No matter Boysens' girl went and flirted with another guy. No way, no how, Mister Aldinger had said. He stared us all down and told all of us it weren't right!

"Tinkey…Tinkey you haven't had breakfast. How about mom whips you up something that'll stick to your ribs—huh?"

"I don't know, Mom…I'm not hungry."

"OHHH dear, are you feeling okay?"

"Yeah, I'm okay I guess, just not hungry right now." Tinkey was thinking he should've just ate and got it over with. His mom worried too much if he wasn't eating. "I'll be in, in a bit, just thinking some, I guess."

"Uh-oh…you and Sheila go and get into it, oh dear, just before prom?"

"No, no, it's not that. But I guess I went and got a burr under my saddle blanket … I suppose."

Mom cocked her face around to face him and rubbed his shoulder.

"I just feel awful, that's all. I mean I wandered over to Dub's place after work. Dub don't know, but I showed up at his place and it was terrible. Old Rogers was getting after 'em again pretty good. I don't get it, all that hollering and name calling. I know it ain't right on no account. Mister Aldinger even went and got in Boysen's face for name calling his girl, ya know. I don't get it, Mom. Not at all."

"Well, I don't know what to say, dear. I hate to hear of this stuff going on. He didn't go and hurt them any, did he?" Mom was speaking very hesitantly, clearly as lost as Tinkey was.

"I know he went and hurt Dub plenty, even if it ain't account of bruising. He was dishing up some horrible words, ya know?" Tinkey shook his head slowly "Can't reckon as to why Dub's ma goes and lets this stuff keep on a happening. Don't make a lick of sense to me, I tell ya."

"Come on, come on, we can talk some over pancakes and your favorite…Jimmy Dean sausage." Mom was confused but had figured the only way to get to the bottom of this once and for all was to get the law involved. That was what they were for, after all. She wanted to put this to rest, for the sake of Tinkey and Dub. The way she had it figured, the law was there to wrestle problems like this down. She had a feeling things could be made right with a simple phone call. She didn't figure she had to go and share this with Tinkey. He had enough on his mind the way it was.

Tinkey finished up breakfast and was feeling a great deal better just having been able to unload on Mom the way he did. She was what he expected every mother to be and that's what was even more disturbing about Dub and his situation. Dub had a ma that needed help. That just didn't seem right at all. Tinkey knew that Dub was hurting plenty. He never went and said as such but Tinkey knew none the less. No matter how he looked, Dub wasn't dumb. He knew the difference between come here and sic 'em. He mustered up as much courage as possible and strolled yonder towards his pickup.

"Good morning, ma'am…Dub around?"

Dub's ma considered the question some while touching her chin. "No, I 'spect he headed out on the range for some camping. He surely does like the peace and solitude of the wide open spaces, y'all know."

Tinkey had immediately directed his gaze away from the bruised chin and nodded in agreement. He figured a prairie full of twisters was more peaceful than this place.

"Boy, why don't you wander out and fetch old Dub. 'Spect he might be hungry as a bear. I'd be much obliged."

The voice had come from within the dark confines of the house but Tinkey knew straight off it was old *Rogers* himself. He was suddenly frozen up some. How can this happen? How can this happen?—a voice was asking him over and over again.

Tinkey had never expected to find Rogers at Dub's house. Not after last night. He thought his morning was going to be full of bumps, bruises and lawyer jokes. The only good out of it would have been if Rogers actually left for Australia. Now Dub had gone off, his ma had gotten smacked around some, and Rogers was yacking as if he didn't have a care in the world. Didn't nothing make sense at all to Tinkey. He just stared towards the horizon some and then heard a car pulling up.

The officer got out of his cruiser, stretched some while putting on his Stetson, and pulled up his belt while strolling towards Tinkey.

"Top of the morning to you, son and ma'am" as he tipped his hat towards Dub's ma. "Just swinging by…got a call regarding a ruckus out in these parts last night. How y'all doing ma'am?"

"Oh fine—just fine, fit as a fiddle. Tripped on that crack in the walk and bumped my chin some. Other than that, no, I 'spect I'm just fine. Ruckus, oh dear, now where you suppose such talk comes from?" Dub's ma had a false doll smile pasted to her face, hoping it would help to hide her shame.

"Ahh, don't go and get all worked up on account of some folks not knowing enough to keep their respective noses in their own beeswax. Don't never, I tell ya, help anything to get all worked up over nothing." The deputy was smiling ever so sweetly as a dejected Tinkey was thinking it over.

"Why, Rogers is just a fixin' to kill a powerful hunger…you are sure invited in for coffee or eats, Ed." Dub's mom musta already went and met Deputy Gein through old Rogers himself, Tinkey was thinking.

"No, no, already coffee'd up, gotta go and check on a prairie goat went and got hit by a truck out on I-29. Prong Horn always loses them battles. You be good now." Deputy Gein touched his hat and raised his voice some, "You be good, Rogers, I'll swing by the gay-rog later."

Rogers voice, tired but stained with falseness, sounded from the darkness, "Yeah, Ed, be down there before too long."

After the squad had swung back towards the highway Rogers showed up alongside Dub's ma. He was rubbing his yet unshaven face. His left hand was wrapped up in gauze like a boxer's. He looked out towards the disappearing squad and was thinking some. He started to talk, then started thinking all over again. He was wearing boxer shorts imprinted with horse heads and a wife beater shirt, which could have been white once upon a time. He stank of used motor oil and stale beer. His hair was greasy and going off in all directions like some kind of renegade bird of paradise. He had a finger in his belly button clearly lost in thought.

"Aren't any folks around these parts, not near enough…to go and call the *law*. Suppose Dub is acting up some and looking for trouble. Yeap, I'm afraid this time he went and gone too far. That's why he ain't around. He's yeller, damnit, yeller like his pa was."

"Ah, now let's eat some. You can't be a knowing now it's Dub went and put the law on your tail."

"Well, I know Dub ain't around, the law shows up and goes and embarrasses me on no account. It just don't strike me as right, not no how…I tell ya."

"Such talk, now Tinkey, let's say you go and fetch Dub, so as we can fix him up with breakfast…everything'll be allll right. Now go on." She put a hand on Rogers to guide him to the table and hopefully away from thoughts that no good would come from.

Tinkey knew the morning had gone really bad for Dub. Rogers wasn't the kinda feller to let something like that pass. Nope, there'd be hell to pay. It just never seemed to end. Absolutely, the more he went and found out, the more confused he became. His confusion evolved into panic as his thoughts wandered from Deputy Gein, a missing Dub and Rogers. Why would Dub's ma go and tell the deputy she had tripped on account of a crack in the sidewalk? Why didn't the cop ask some questions on the matter? Isn't that what the law does? Ask questions knowing full well that folks take to lying some when they ain't up to no good? As these thoughts galloped in his mind, Tinkey figured the only solution to his world turned upside down was to get ahold of Dub and warn him.

Tinkey started hitting the usual spots. Wasn't much of a problem finding Dub. He was out in the vicinity of highway 220 near the abandoned bridge south of Casper some miles. His Honda four wheeler was parked down towards the public access. Nope, finding Dub was the easy part. Telling was harder.

Tinkey saw Dub before Dub saw Tinkey. Dub was whittling a branch with a razor sharp knife. Near as Tinkey could tell, in the approaching noon sun, there wasn't much left of a pretty good sized stick.

"How's it hanging—Dub?" Dub startled but stared some on the wood chip pile and thought some.

"G-g-Good, it'd be right n-nice out here without the likes of y-you hollering snake. Peaceful, I gots ta say."

"You ever gonna forget that? Look, we gotta talk."

Dub didn't bat an eye… "H-h-how does a-a lawyer sleep? First he lies on one side. Then-then he lies on the other side."

"Look, I think…" Tinkey started but was interrupted with another joke.

"W-What's the difference between a l-lady lawyer and a p-p-pitbull?"

"I don't get it…I'm trying to be serious here!"

"Lip-l-lipstick stick. Get it?" Dub sounded more desperate than silly.

"All-righty then...camp, let's camp. Let's break for Muddy Gap. We can score some beer down there. Willy, he's always good for a box of Coors. Then we can swing back to The Rock. Independence Rock...just hang out...right nice and peaceful out that ways. Neither one of us has to work. Sound like a plan, Stan?" Tinkey realized his voice had crackled up an octave or two.

"G-g-got check on ma-ma I suppose."

"I swung by your place and *Rogers* was there. Then that deputy...that Gein guy showed up and was asking about trouble. I think Rogers figures you went and sicced the law on him. Did ya? Did ya go and call the sheriff on Rogers?"

Dub stared, moving his turkey egg sized Adams apple up and down. "N-n-now...why in tarnation would I g-goes and put-put-ta the law on him? Don't see ha-how i-it would help."

"I don't know, but he can get downright ornery. Crazier than a bull round cows at calf making time. Right?" Tinkey was suddenly relieved that he had been able to push past the lawyer jokes. Dub seemed to be getting it.

"W-w-was he at all riled when y-ya was there?"

"Kinda, dude, but not 'drinkin' mean. He was still on coffee," Tinkey said.

"Yea, I'll s-s-swing by ma's...ma-make sure everything is okay with-with her. Who knows...maybe r-r-Rogers hit the road. May be he-he-he headed to his place." Fear was forcing its way into Dub's actions, like lava is forced out of fissures. After a while of hard whittling and no talking, the fear seemed to have solidified into solid scorn. "I ought to stick this puppy in the sonofabitch, treat him right!" Dub sunk the razor sharp blade into the crust of the sandy soil. "Serve him right. What'd the deputy go and say?"

"Nothing Dub...why he went and just didn't say nuttin' at all...I tell ya. You know how it is. Just like laughing and hanging out. Your ma said something about tripping on a crack in the sidewalk last night."

"Tripping? Tripping? She said she tripped? Why?"

Tinkey was trapped, "Well, it wasn't much, she ain't hurt—"

"Ain't hurt...Whatcha mean? Ain't hurt? Huh?" Dub demanded.

"I mean...if you'll let me finish ... she just had a little bruise on her chin, may be a mouse on her right eye, I'm not sure. I didn't wanna stare or anything."

Dub pulled the knife from the crusty sand only to plunge it into the hard Wyoming sand again and again. "I hate that bastard. I tell ya, I hate that bastard through and through. That bastard. I oughta stick him but good. Serve him right. Then he'd leave my ma alone." With each word he stabbed the sand harder and harder. After sometime, Dub's usual gloomy nature, stole back onto his outward features.

Tinkey okayed the plans with his parents, packed the supplies, tossed them in the back of the pickup. He hit for Dub's place. En route he called Sheila to see if she could make it to The Rock. Everything was working out good. Now he figured if he could somehow swing by Dub's without a hitch, it would be smooth sailing from there on out. At least he was hoping so. He had noticed that Rogers' truck was parked along his shop, so evidently he was working. He and Dub would be safely tucked away by a campfire some fifty or sixty miles from Mister Rogers by the time he closed the garage. That was the plan anyways.

"Ya-ya-yeap. Yeap...ma plenty mad, l-let me tell you. She's got it in-in her head that I went an-an-and called l-l-law on him. I know b-b-better. She don't wanna hear it no-no how. She plenty worked up c-cause I'm the only one. W-w-well me and her and Rogers. We the only ones know how b-b-bad it gets when he's d-d-drunk. Now she all d-d-down on me. I-I-I know plenty…but…I was born at night, b-but I wasn't born LAST night…I tell ya. I know b-better than to go and c-c-call the law."

Tinkey figured he should keep quiet. He had been around the place and saw a thing or two but it'd only bother Dub. Besides, he knew he didn't call the law. He knew the cops hung with Rogers. The whole town knew it. Some folks even had it figured that's why Rogers hadn't been nailed for drinking and driving. He heard 'em talking some at the counter on account of what they called professional courtesy. They'd said Rogers and the law were thick as thieves. Thick enough to keep ole Rogers outta the hoosegow. Some of the folks even talked some on Rogers getting rough on Dub's ma. None of 'em ever claimed to have done nothing about it. Not a one of them. They just chicken shits is all or don't know if their ass was punched or drilled. Tinkey didn't know what to do either. The law though, they are supposed to know and do something about a man beating his woman.

"Well now, is it the Gap for Coors or should we swing by Rattlesnake Hills?"

"N-N-Naw, don't figure I-I-I wanna go crawling round some ol' mine. Be-be-besides…drinking and exploding d-d-don't mix u-up well. I-I-I still kin-da hurt from the last time we went and crawled in tha-that mine, t-too. Saa'nake. Yeah. Funny, real-really funny." Dub turned his face toward Tinkey.

"You ever, I mean seriously, ever gonna let it go? Ahh man, cops. Cops on our tail. Don't go and look. Christ—Dub!"

The squad closed in on the pickup, leaving no doubt that the reds would be on in a minute. Tinkey squeezed the steering wheel and wondered how his speed had got away from him. That had to be it. He glanced down at the speedometer and was actually just under the speed limit. He musta got on it a little, crawling up out of the valley south of Casper. Dammit, he thought. Dammit all to hell, and then the lights came on, and he ducked in on the shoulder, crawling to a stop.

"Howdy, officer." Tinkey wasn't sure if he was allowed to turn towards the officer so he just stared down 220.

"Is…this…vehicle…registered…to…you…young…fella? Let's kick up some ID, pronto. Come on. You, too, boy." Dub started digging for his wallet also.

"We can make this easy, or we can make this h-a-r-d. I have asked you a simple question and you'll be so kind to as to start answering. Okay? Or don't you speak Wyoming?" The officer had slowed his speaking down to a crawl and was lowering his voice with each word. He was putting on skin-tight black leather gloves, the kind without fingers.

Tinkey's thoughts on how to be nice had rendered him deaf for the moment. The sudden opening of his door woke him from his fear induced numbness. He was plenty scared all right, but even more, he was bound and determined to catch up to the situation.

"Who is the RO of this vehicle? I need ID. Registration. Proof of Insurance. C'mon! Let's go. Let's not act as stupid as we could be. I don't wanna repeat myself. Come on, you boys is dumber than a scoop shovel, I swear—let's kick up some ID, on the double. Any weapons I need to know about in this vee-hick-all? Any bombs, drugs or alcohol? Have you been drinking, boys? Or are you both always deaf and dumb?"

"No, huh, no, we got nothing like that stuff in this…" Tinkey was cut off by the menacing low whisper.

"Can I search this veh-icle? Come on, OUT!" The officer made a swiping motion with the right side of his body towards the ditch. Tinkey and Dub both scrambled to where they were directed.

Only then did Tinkey's voice somehow catch up to his thoughts and he whispered… "All-righty then…you're the man, just between you, me, and the pissin' post. Godda say I'm surely glad we ain't running around with dynamite. That's gotta be 'gainst the law. Can you imagine five-oh finding a stick of die-no-mite in the truck? Christ, we don't get high, no dynamite. Yeah, we're cool man. Cool as a cucumber. Why ya figure he pulled us over?"

"Boys, I don't recall telling you to stand over there and yap. Didja go and get your story straight?" the cop was saying as he approached them, adjusting his gun belt.

"No, we don't got no story…" but Tinkey was interrupted by the officer taking their IDs from them.

"Do you know why I stopped you?" He then proceeded to blow a small, pink bubble, before sucking it quickly back into his mouth.

"Maybe speed?" Tinkey guessed.

"Brake light, boy. Thirty one, five, nine, fifteen. Two or more stop lamps and then, and only then, are you complying with the regulations of the Superintendent of the State of Wyoming. Do I make myself perfectly caa-lear on that point…*b-o-y?*" The officer appeared to be very upset until his growl started working itself into a possible grin.

"Y'all that fella, Rogers's boy, ain't chaaa?" He stared directly through Tinkey into Dub.

Dub was in tip-top Dub form. "Y-y-y-yeah, I-I'ze r-r-Rogers feller."

"Relax…and spit the crap outta your mouth when you address me, boy. Well now, you boys strike me as being right smart enough to know the importance of having brake lights. Don't figure I need to go writing you up for the statutory violation now do I?"

"Tell me boy, old Rogers, he go and set your momma straight last night? Word is, around the station, they got going again…huh?"

The officer had fallen into a conversational tone and winked, slowly chewing on his wad of bubble gum.

"Don't know much ah-on that, SIR, I was out along the North Platte last eve-none."

"Oh, I suppose you don't know nuttin' about that then, huh? Well, you just tell Rogers you met Deputy Dylan Klebold." The officer winked at Tinkey and elbowed him as he gave each of the boys their license back, without calling them in. "Well, I do declare you boys are fit fiddles. Have a good evening. Oh…you know what you call a woman with two black eyes?' Tinkey and Dub were too frightened to venture a guess. "Hard of hearing. Now scoot before I change my mind and write you up for the brake lights. Ya hear?" Officer Klebold spit his gum out, spun, and laughed his way to his squad before zooming off in a cloud of dust.

Only after heading south down 220 past Alcova and the Pathfinder Reservoir did any conversation commence in the truck. Lighter at first, before getting plenty heavy.

"All-righty then…just between you, me and the pissing post, let me tell ya. Those cops know more than meets the eye about old *Rogers*. Damn." Tinkey was lost on the thought of cops knowing stuff and not doing a single thing on account of it. "I tell ya, Dub. Ain't right in my book. Not right at all. Cops knowing how wrong it is and I mean, doing like *nothing*."

"I'd like to pu-put-putta blade in the b-bastard," Dub mumbled.

"Fuck that dude…you can't go around knifing cops, Christ, you and that knife all the time. You take a knife to a gun fight you end up dead—dude."

"N-no-not cops, I-I ain't discussing cops, not at all."

CHAPTER 5

ALL BETTER

"ANOTHER SATURDAY NIGHT" – SAM COOKE

Tinkey pulled into the Muddy Gap convenience store. Nothing much else in the Gap. Just the store, couple houses, ancient log cabin and that's all she wrote. Skirt the Granite Mountains some and next town would be Rawlings. Plenty of Union Pacific trains, The Hole in the Wall saloon and of course, the prison. Old Frontier Prison, complete with the gas chamber, bars and all.

The truck bounced across the lot. Tinkey parked on the side of the place and waited for Willy to make his grand appearance. Had to have Willy if your plans involved underage drinking.

"Rabbit didn't know how see that coming…I'm headed in, gotta take a leak, you want anything?" Tinkey had glanced at a jackrabbit splattered on the road as he was climbing out of the truck.

Dub was digging dirt out of his nails, swinging his head back and forth. Tinkey pulled his face back from the open driver's window and headed towards the store. After a couple of steps he heard Willy. Had to be him. Who else runs around Wyoming with Johnny Cash blaring

"Ring of Fire"? He stopped and kicked some asphalt chunks around with his boot. William Bonin swerved around the rabbit carnage on the road. The messed up rabbit led Tinkey to an unpleasant memory about like a toddler is pulled to an unwanted nap. He was on a family drive and saw a cat get nailed on an off ramp. The mushed cat was squashed onto the road, but its tail frantically flicked up and down. Tinkey's mouth was frozen into an 'O.' It didn't make sense to him how fast something could leave the world. Mom had taken pains to explain how it was the way of things. Everything and everybody dies. He shook his head no, but knew mom was always right about such things. He still hated and was scared of death.

"Yo, my man…Mister Tinkersley…what'll it be today? Christ, ya get a load of that rabbit? I thought it was a deer, for god's sake. Didn't know rabbits had that much blood in 'em." Willy put on like the rabbit business was funny, and Tinkey hid behind a smile.

Tinkey quickly voiced his order to forget about the rabbit mess.

"Hey, I suppose a case of Coors and some wine coolers, the red ones."

"Oh, you gonna be drinking with the ladies tonight, my man? Let me fill your order and then it's later for you." William went by 'Willy' or 'Pimples' because of his herculean struggle with acne. Once money exchanged hands, Tinkey didn't know what to really do, so he slouched towards the store with Willy.

Tinkey hung near the chips, acting plenty interested in which flavor to score as he shot a glance towards Willy. He was acting plenty smooth, laughing and joking with the girl behind the counter who was chewing a large hunk of gum.

"Hey li'tle lady…" Willy pulled his floppy lips back revealing a yellowish smile with specks of chew stuck on his teeth. "My lady is a demanding some of the sweet red coolers. Wild Berry, I believe hon. You got that? The red ones?"

"Hang on, havta check," she enunciated somehow around the gum while rolling her eyes.

After she vanished into the darkness of the back room, Willy slipped a bottle of the hard stuff into his oversized jacket pocket along with some Copenhagen he fetched quickly from behind the counter.

"Well like, God, they're red ones right there, like totally, right there." She pointed to them, then changed out the warm ones with the cold ones.

"Whoee, sweet lord, how you figure I didn't see 'em. Thank you very much, my little lady."

"Whatevvver. You want anything else?"

Tinkey couldn't believe it. Willy was at it again. It was just plain wrong, but it didn't bother Willy. Stealing and breathing both came naturally to ol' Willy. The bible didn't hold much sway with him. Like he'd pointed out to Tinkey in the past, 'God don't go and help those, ain't got no sense, than to help themselves.' Tinkey held up a plastic rattlesnake and looked past it to Dub, sitting in the pickup. He wanted to toss it in Dub's sleeping bag, but with everything happening lately, he wasn't so sure it'd be funny. He picked up a bag of chips instead and dropped them on the counter.

The girl stopped chewing… "Any gas today? Just chips, no salsa?"

"Yeah, just Doritos."

Willy slid up to the counter behind Tinkey "Yeah boy, you a needing salsa for dipping them there chips? What kinda cowboy are ya!"

"Okay, put me down for salsa then." Willy flashed his yellow know it all smile, "You from around these parts?" The girl answered with a roll of the eyes. Willy wasn't getting anywhere but it didn't bother him. His forever yapping insured he was a smooth operator. The world was Willy's stage; he was getting more out of the shopping experience than some cash and an opportunity to shoplift.

Before long the boys headed back north to meet up with the gals. Dub was still in a funk. The cop's comments, his ma, the bruises, and Rogers seemed to cling to him like stink onna skunk. The only thing Tinkey could come up with to improve the mood was girls and a sore head in the morning. If a party behind Independence Rock didn't get the job done, nothing would. He was doing his best with smiling and making like nothing was on his mind. Just as cool shadows fall behind buildings on warm sunny days though, dark thoughts lingered behind his smile.

Wyoming was full of hazards. Not just snakes and cougars. Things more dangerous. Things like drunks slapping women and kids around, while cops looked the other way. Things like guys with yellow teeth ignoring the bible.

The wind would whip up and whoosh through the mesquite, sending smoke into the huddled crowd around the campfire. Many a pioneer had eyes stung with campfire smoke as he struggled with matters of life and death. It was all about getting covered wagons to places bounding with opportunities. Many years after the disappearance of early travelers, two boys stood on the Oregon Trail. They secretly found themselves concentrating on obstacles that seemed to threaten mutual desires. The pioneers had pushed on, always towards the west. The boys would return to Casper. It was there, in Casper, where hopes in the soul would be kindled.

"Now did y'all have a grand ole' time out there on the plains?" Mom asked, Tinkey.

"We sure did…after a cop pulled us over."

"Oh dear, didja get a ticket or something?" Mom asked as she stopped sweeping the floor to look up into her son's eyes.

"I don't know, I mean no, we didn't get a ticket or nuttin'. We got stopped for a brake light out is all. Man, that cop was worked up though. Ya know, he figured out who Dub was. So the cop goes off on how bad it gets between Dub's ma and Rogers. It was like he *knew*. He like thought it was funny or something. He joked about it. Tossed it right in Dub's face. Dub made like it didn't get to him or anything. It did. I could tell. He just got moppy."

Mom looked at Tinkey as she crossed her arms... "Oh, I'm sure they know. I called the authorities and let them know in no uncertain terms. Oh, dear...it's the only right thing to do. I called them after what you went and told me. I figured it was the only right thing to do...dear. We havta do something—"

Tinkey froze with the realization his big mouth had gone and made Dubs' life more difficult. Rogers was plenty pissed about having a cop land on the steps that morning. Tinkey hadn't the foggiest notion his mom would go and sic the law on Rogers. Dub's ass would be grass as soon as Rogers caught up with him. Tinkey wondered what he could do about the mess he caused. Could he head to Dubs' place and tell Rogers what he'd done? It was him and not Dub. Would that help? Rogers didn't ever need a good reason to swing. He'd probably pound on Dub because Dub hung around with him.

"Oh, dear, did I upset you some, honey? I didn't mean to—"

Tinkey, attempting to stare clear into the grass roots in the yard outside the window. "Ahh shucks, Mom, maybe it'll make it right somehow. Don't go worrying on it no more than ya already have."

The difference between how bad things really were, as opposed to how he wanted them, pinched into his thoughts. He felt some like a coyote caught up in a pan trap. No easy solutions seemed to be in the offing.

Tinkey drove aimlessly across the plains, heading towards Douglas for no reason. He was alone in his pickup and wanted it that way. He drove past the enormous coal fired plant and escaped back into his past. He could remember driving with his folks to Lusk to meet up with his cousins. Those times seemed so easy now. They'd hangout by the old wooden water tower, waiting on trains or go swimming or something.

He headed back west and ended up pulling into the Fort Casper parking lot and gazed across the street towards the fairgrounds. Barrels today but he just didn't have the stomach for crowds of any sort. Cheering Sheila and Fiona on wasn't a priority. He sat back, checked his blood levels and realized he was in need of some insulin. He had completely blown it off, which didn't happen much. He quickly took care of it before pulling his journal out.

> how could I have been such a blame fool????was Dub sporting bruises because of me and my big mouth. How fair is having a friend got no sense????law gos and get paid to take care of Mister Rogers and then all they do is laugh on account of the mess Dub in.Mr Aldinger done said it aint proper to call gals names   why that cop got enough time to mess with me for a brake light and do nothing for Dub????

Tinkey jumped out of the pickup and slowly walked along the walk path, annoying an occasional goose or two, forcing them into North Platte. He walked with no direction in mind. Concern yielded to frustration which now, in turn, seemed to be giving way to scorn. He knew Dub, as was his manner, would have buried everything he was feeling by now. They had gotten back fairly early from the Rock. They both had to work tonight. Tinkey recalled seeing Rogers' Caddy parked alongside the garage. At least he was working, anyways. The walk resulted in Tinkey being none the less confused, but somewhat refreshed. He wasn't sure what he had to do but got to feeling he was going to do something. If not for Dub, for himself.

Tinkey jumped in his truck and got the finger for pulling out in front of a car. A black one. He wasn't sure how he blew it off. He wasn't sure if the light was red or what. He did get the finger, though. That much he knew, as he started concentrating more on his driving. A finger and horn had provided him with a much needed boost of adrenaline and flash of embarrassment. He took the bypass around the fairgrounds, never once thinking of checking up on how Sheila was doing. His thoughts were well past Sheila and any possible trophies that might come her way. His thoughts were pushing him in another direction.

After pulling up to Dubs' house while laying on the horn, Tinkey approached it, only to be told Dub's wasn't around. He wandered with interest to the opened garage and noticed the Honda was gone. May be he headed to work early. Who knew? Tinkey didn't figure Dub would want to be hanging around waiting for Rogers to get off work. Tinkey didn't know which way to point the truck, so didn't even start it up. He just slouched back and wondered how long he should wait for Dub. They usually rode to work together.

Tinkey had snoozed into his thoughts until he was snapped back too by the humming of Dubs' Honda headed in his direction. A little patience was all it took. Patience and a healthy dose of fear and loathing. Tinkey was back out of the truck and in the garage in no time. They needed to haul ass. He directed his gaze towards the back of the garage onto the trail rutted into the sand. Yeap. Ain't no mistaking Dubs on a four wheeler. Knees seemed to go clear up over his helmet. He leaned into the handlebars with his head drooping in vulture like fashion.

The four wheeler skidded to a stop in the garage and Dub tugged the helmet off with what looked to be foot-long fingers. He was looking down, giving his eyes some time to adjust to the sudden darkness. He was clearly startled upon having his name come at him from somewhere in the darkness.

"We gotta roll, Dubs, Saturday night, we're gonna be busy, ya know. God…where were you—"

Dubs shot Tinkey a look of surprise, which was returned by an expression of shock. Tinkey had plummeted from thoughts about work to a blank stare and gurgling sounds. He was gagging some, like people do who they accidentally suck something down the wrong pipe.

Dub's right eye was completely swollen shut. It was just a watery slit with some reddish tears towards its corner. The eye was a horrible, swollen mess. Dub's eyebrows managed to maintain an arch of surprise but no lawyer jokes were tossed out to fill the void. The crimson, purplish, ugly thing drilled onto Dub's face stuck a sense of rage into Tinkey. He owned a part of the reason. He had talked, and it got back to Rogers. The rage fueled blackness accelerated across his thoughts. He wanted to stomp it out, the reason for his feelings. It worked on the gridiron. After he screwed up and missed a tackle, he'd come back stronger on the next play. He was surging, but had no idea how to aim his heated intent in a proper direction.

He walked towards his pickup and started kicking the rear tire hard. Hard enough to rock his beloved truck. He kicked hard, with the fury of a riled bull. His eyes were slammed shut and he was breathing hard.

He heard a door slam, his door. He stopped to look into the truck. There was Dub, staring straight ahead. Tinkey pulled the door open and drove. He slowly looked towards Dub, who quickly looked off in another direction.

"Yeah, I'm r-r-ready as I'll ever be, I g-g-guess."

"Let's hit her, then." Tinkey thought how stupid it sounded only after he had gone and said it. On the ride to work, no mention was made of the shiner. The silence was uncomfortable.

After getting set for the night, Dubs found he was an unlikely center of attention for sympathy overloaded waitresses. They were all running around speculating and wondering some on how and why it had happened.

"Dubs, why ya just gotta plain learn to be seen and not heard… Honey."

"Yeah, you musta been talking when you should've been listening!"

Dub's knocked around looking at the floor trying to stay busy. He'd start with something, then spin around to do something else without even looking up. He was about as trapped as a calf being dragged out of the herd for branding.

"Damn stallions, should be de-nutted when they goes and kick like that. Christ, that damn horse could've kilt Dub. I saw it plain as daylight and no reason for it. Shoot, man…could've happened to me. Nice one second, then bang! Dub's, he one lucky dude…man—"

"Lordy he don't look lucky to me. Old man Bailer caught one to the noggin' and he was never right. Every time his daughter went and hit the garage door opener, Bailer pissed himself. That's what they say." She was rubbing Dub's shoulder in a 'get better' fashion. "You gonna be fine, just fine."

Tinkey spun on the comment… "Come on already, really? If you just took a hoof to the head would you wanna havta go and hear that—*huh?*"

"Oh sorry, already." She picked up her tray of salads and worked under it before straightening up for the dining room.

"All-righty then, it's you and me. You gonna be just fine, my man."

Dubs looked into the fryer with his one open eye. If he kept his distance from Rogers who'd steer him clear of ma? If Glen Rogers got all worked up and ma went and caught a punch she'd probably end up as goofed up as Bailer. He didn't like the idea of having his ma hurt. She'd be in a world of hurt without him around. He didn't like it one bit.

Tinkey had his own dust devils spinning across his thoughts. Both boys went through the motions of putting meals together in silence. They were using words like 'excuse me' which they'd never done before. No lawyer jokes or talks of running trains tonight. Just polite unnatural discourse. Dub appreciated Tinkey's horse kicking story. It helped.

"Order up, Dub…the fries, let's roll." The work load provided relief from gloomy thoughts of things getting worse and worse. The clatter of plates, the grill sizzling, and orders being shouted out provided a refuge from the pain. After concentrating on the relentless pace of orders, the late afternoon darkened into a cool Wyoming evening. The daylight changed into what evenings were all about, but the eye stayed the same.

After the frantic dinner rush, things around the kitchen started rolling on a more even keel. Waitresses gathered and whispered on tips, the young dishwasher banged around the Hobart and flirted with the bus girls. Dub preferred alone time to consider things, figuring Tinkey would want some answers. No answers were available though.

The silence was too awkward for Tinkey, who commenced to sing… "It's another Saturday Night and I just got paid"… before having to hum the rest of the melody.

"What we gonna do, Dub? The night's young, my man. Wanna go hang out down by the diesel yard, fish some, kill the rest of the Coors?"

"Don't expect to do much, I suppose. Got a d-d-dern headache. Best wander ya-yonder, check up on Ma. T-t-take it easy."

Tinkey was used to running the show. He had become so used to ruling the roost that he was stunned into silence and had to grapple with the loss of control. Didn't make any sense for a fellow in Dub's shape to be alone. They hadn't even hashed it out as to what really happened. Near as Tinkey could tell, they both knew the horse that went and kicked him was none other than Rogers. He felt in some strange way he was owed something like the truth. But he realized he wasn't gonna be paid. He just sat back and listened as the screen door slammed shut in the suddenly lonely kitchen.

Tinkey was stuck about as tight as last winter when he hit a drift. He was spinning thoughts around in his head but not getting anywhere. He was about as surprised tonight with nothing making sense as he'd been with the drift causing his wheels to spin. He wanted to dig himself out of the current mess, but wasn't coming up with any solutions. 'Ahh, the hell with it,' he mumbled mostly in his thoughts. 'I'll just swing by Dub's place. Make sure he's okay, is all.'

He pulled up to the house and moseyed up to the door. Dub's ma was home and had said... 'Dubs isn't home and musta hit out for the Platte. He liked to sleep under those Wyoming stars.' Nothing was said about why he liked it so much. Nothing was said about why Ma figured Rogers had a decent bone in his body after all the beatings. Nothing was said about the sunglasses being worn in the dead of night. Nothing was said about the grief caused by her actions.

It was after Tinkey left that the blackness of his thoughts over took the kind side of things. All the goodness dribbled away and seemed to get carried downstream like feathers on the Platte. Dub had apparently slipped off to spend some time alone with his headache and that hurt some. Tinkey and Dub were friends and were supposed hang out in bad times. Why was Dub deciding to be along tonight of all nights? What was he up to? Why'd he leave the restaurant so fast?

It was dark, the occasional rustle of this or that in the night was expected. The helmet was gathered up, a knife, a very sharp knife was secured to the belt. Dubs knew how to sharpen a knife, that was for damn sure. The night was clear, the night was still, and the night contained a whisper of impending death. He pushed the Honda to the path behind the garage. Couldn't wake her. He pushed the four wheeler with patience and regard for a plan that had taken over his every moment. Dreams dashed by a nightmare fueled his struggle to push the Honda towards deliverance.

After pushing some, he put on the helmet, started the Honda and thought some on the evening. It made him nervous to do what needed to be done. Life could be good again. Beatings could stop. No more sunglasses, no more lies and no more jokes. Life could be 'bout tomorrows bringing on good things again, instead of black eyes and bruises.

The Honda found its way to Rogers place. It had been there before. Once upon a time things seemed to be good. When did the drinking do Rogers in? Had it always been this bad? Why did some carry on drinking when only bad came of it?

The time spent in the night, surrounded by the glory of its sounds and warmth, was only shattered by the sound of Rogers' red Cadillac as it headed down the road. The heart quickened some as the time was nearing. The sweat formed on the brow as Rogers pulled himself up and out of the Caddy. How can a drunken sonofabitch punch as hard as he could? Didn't make sense no how. When the keys clattered to the sidewalk it was time to step from the darkness of nothing and work on something.

He smiled as he made his move "H-Hey…"

Rogers focused in on the newcomer and watched him snatch the keys from the sidewalk and drop them in his hand. The surprised apparatus in his brain wasn't working this evening, explaining his inability to get surprised.

"Tanks—boy," Rogers grunted, not knowing, not caring.

"Ahhh shucks, nuttin' to it, sir."

Then there were words. Rogers wanted to put the bastard in his place.

The guttural response was expected. The beery breath was expected. The knife digging into his throat from the side was unexpected. His throat burned and his bloody hand caused him to open his mouth, but no scream came out. The screaming apparatus was not working.

The blood was expected by the boy, but so much *blood?* That wasn't expected. Words were supposed to be used, but a *knife?* That wasn't expected. Not at ALL. It tore into vile flesh aided by a loathing for anything Rogers.

CHAPTER 6

BUSTED

"WANTED DEAD OR ALIVE"—BON JOVI

After racing down off the road onto the path that led to the back of the garage the engine was killed and the Honda coasted towards a silent stop. Prior to a complete stop the boy had already jumped off and was putting his weight into it. It didn't take much pushing; it was only slightly uphill to the garage. Once the Honda was parked, clean up started. It was dark. Occasionally, a furtive peek was cast out the window. Everything was quiet.

The Honda was rubbed down quickly in the dark. The helmet was hung from the steering wheel. The knife had gone somewhere tonight where it had never been before. There was blood on it. Maybe it belonged on the bottom of the Platte. Ain't no way cops would find it there. He didn't have time for that now though. He knew where he could reach up behind the wall. That was the best place for the knife for now. He chugged a bottle of water to kill his thirst. The rustlers moon didn't provide enough light, but it was helpful. He did the best he could. Finally he decided he should hit for the range. The insects buzzed and a bird or something, screamed off in the distance. He walked off quickly without realizing it. He ran his hand through his hair shaking his head. Why couldn't he settle some?

The car load of cops had gotten together down at the watering hole after work. Music, Hank Williams, which nobody seemed to get sick of hearing in the company of long necks and dancing. Great times with some laughing and plenty of bitchin'. There were always lieutenants who didn't know their ass from a hole in the ground. There were plenty of officers who were getting promotions they didn't deserve. Sergeant Shit for Brains always was worthy of boozy bitchin'. This stuff had to be tossed around in the Honkey Tonk. The beer flowed smoothly and last call usually happened entirely too fast. The officers hadn't gotten off work until eleven which only provided them a couple of hours to gulp down some comfort. The cops got treated to some extra minutes of drinking. Other patrons were shown the door first.

Rogers had slipped in after the arrival of most of the officers. He always seemed to get called at all hours for roadside repairs. The life of a mechanic was a twenty-four hour proposition, no doubt about it. He had given one of the senior bitchers, tonight, assistance with a faulty battery. The officer had swung by a friendly dispatchers place to as he put it…'check her oil.' He had hooked up with her prior to the end of his shift. Her husband got off work same time he did, necessitating the earlier get together.

A City of Casper vehicle parked in the garage with a dead battery would have raised eyebrows. The lady of the house, complete with a hot headed husband and set of twins, could've made things really…unpleasant. Rogers always provided much needed backup for the communities' officers. He carried his duties out fast while exercising his right to remain silent. He'd actually had his metal tested once and passed with flying colors. The dreaded internal affairs had called him only to discover he couldn't remember nothing.

The officer ordered drinks for Rogers with a broad smile on his face. "Gads...you're the man, Rogers, You...golldern friggin' A-Okay in my book! You one helluva cowboy... pilgrim!" All the officers laughed as Hamilton Fish toasted Rogers in his best John Wayne voice. The off-duty crew understood Rogers had once again come through for one of the brothers in blue.

The beer poured down Rogers wide open throat. He craved the bubbly place alcohol floated him to. Once the beer set up shop in his stomach he got the feeling he was more than he could hope to be. The beer released him from the garage, greasy hands, and spark plugs. After a couple, whiskey was always in order. Boiler Makers. A shot of rot gut washed down with a cold beer. These were two things that never failed him.

The music, backs slaps, and important kick-ass friends made it complete. They were important, they were the law, and drinks made him feel like one of 'em. Important. His hair was disappearing. He even dreaded showers because the drain always seemed to get clogged with his precious hair. It wouldn't be long before he was not only a grease monkey, but a bald one to boot.

After Rogers drank enough to somehow secure passage from what he was, it always ended too soon. Usually on account of *her*. He fell back into himself and choked on his words. The booze felt good but it also replayed her words. He knew she wasn't around cause she was out looking for another man. After several more quickly downed drinks, he wanted to do what he hadda do. Set her straight. Laughing at him. Calling him a drunk. 'Just a little bald grease monkey was all you is.' He looked down at the bronze twinkling liquid in the shot glass, before downing it. It hit his stomach and burned back up with anger into his thoughts.

"She's a cheatin' bitch for damn sure."

"What's that you say, cowboy?" Fish was smiling. He'd gotten laid and got out of Dodge before her old man showed up. That would have been messy. He wondered if he should give up on married pussy before dashing the thought.

Rogers stared at the empty shot glass and heard Fish order him up another.

The next shot of whiskey hauled the word whore into his stomach. That's all she was. A whore. She was just a salesgirl. Fifteen bucks an hour was all she was worth. He was a businessman. The whiskey told him he was better than a whore. He paid more in taxes than she made, all told. The booze always flowed to an awful end regarding her.

"You whore…you're just in here for the men. Slut," Rogers whispered in a soft voice after she landed on the bar stool next to him.

"Uh-oh…somebody piss in your shot glass…*dear?* Yeah…you're right…*h-o-n-e-y*…I'm just in here for the men!" she snarled quietly.

He knew he couldn't put up with her bitchin' without more drinkin'. No amount of slapping had got her to shut it. He had a caddy, red, white leather interior, shiny, money in the bank, big belt buckle. Woman with any sense would know he was a man. His first wife didn't get it. He ordered a shot and tossed it back. The drinkin' wasn't working. She was still there.

Several bottles of liquid courage pushed Dub's ma down an angry slope as quick as if she was on skis. "Well, big guy. I ain't don't have to put up with this. I should've had Dub kick your drunken ass a looongtime?" She felt good. She had said it. She took another anger driven gulp of her liquid courage.

"You open your trap—"

"And what?" It felt good. He had to behave. They were in public. "Did you hear me? You touch me and Dub'll ki—" The beer was dishing up all kinds of delicious words but then he jumped into the conversation.

Rogers stared hard at the empty shot glass wondering if he needed another one. His mood had darkened as quickly as a fast moving thunderstorm steals sunny days.

"Ahh come on...lighten up, buddy." Fish rubbed Rogers' shoulder. He then smiled and turned toward Dub's Ma. "Now come on, lady...you don't want to say anything you'll regret tomorrow, besides, it's just the beer talking." He spun his head back in the direction of Rogers. "How about we head to your place for one?" Fish had silenced Dub's ma.

Rogers concentrated on looking sober and nodded yes.

"By God...I believe that's right...let's head to my place, then." Rogers wasn't sure how many shots he'd had but talked very deliberately so his whiskey secret remained just that.

"My man, Rogers, you're a good man." Gacy smiled and put his arm around Rogers shoulder.

"I'm headed to the Quick Stop for chew. Anyone need anything?" Rogers took in the crowd around him. A stumble would be embarrassing. He wanted to walk to his Caddy, get to the store and make it home before his buddies. Nobody responded to his question so he headed for the door very carefully. He refused to even look at her. He was done. The hell with her.

The lawmen were content with helping Rogers break out of the bar without her. They surrounded her while being very attentive.

"Ahh hell...let him go. Everything'll be better come morn'un, ma'ma."

"Well—" She was getting up as she grabbed her purse.

"Look. Get some sleep. Look up Rogers in the morning."

"Well...I suppose I could swing by Shorty's and have Dub put together a bar burger for me." With that she was allowed to finally push herself out of the door, into the parking lot, to her car. Rogers had already sped off.

"That Glen, Ol' Glen Roger's…good guy, I tellya. Who all is headed over to his place?"

Fish started talking in the urgent manner of a used car salesman. "Come on guys, ya pussy whipped or what? Just one. One nightcap ain't gonna kill ya."

Three of the revelers jumped in one car. The driver was Detective Gacy. John had taken the cure some years ago. Waking up with a heart that was threatening to pound his head clean through the floor with a wife waving bye-bye had brought on sobriety. It was agreed upon, long ago, that Gacy did the driving. His partner, Hamilton Fish, jumped in the passenger seat. His hair, streaked with grey, had lost some of its luster over the years but yet, was a perfect mullet. A roundish nose, called Roman by some behind his back, could've been cut from a fleshy ball. It was a large, red, pitted object. Noticeable protruding tuffs of black hair escaping from the nostrils completed the ensemble. White flaks of stuff, like powered milk, clung to the hairs. Officer Corll, off-duty, slouched across the backseat semi-comatose. As manager of the department's fleet, he'd had a hard day tending to the needs of the squads and immediately lapsed into an alcohol induced nap.

Hamilton 'Albert' Fish pointed towards the headlight that suddenly appeared from near the garage, "Ahh, what's he doing over yonder on that there four wheeler? Trying to get himself killed for Christ sake? Oh wait, it's not Rogers."

Gacy leaned forward over the steering wheel to get a better look as he squinted. "Who in tarnation is it, if'n it ain't…" Only bouncing taillights could be seen as the four wheeler slipped into the darkness.

Fish, cleared his throat. "Na, that's that kid of hers…he's always beating around on that thing. Ain't he supposed to be working?

Didn't she go say somethun' 'bout haven' him whip her up a burger? You don't suppose she's *here?"*

Corll woke up on the words, ashamed somehow for having slipped into his boozy nap and missing a moment of shared camaraderie. "Yeah, yeah…I saw him; it's that kid of hers all right."

Fish answered himself. "Yeah…she musta not had it figured right. Lookit that jack leg go, driving like he ain't got a brain in his head!" He stopped talking long enough to down the last of the beer in his can as the taillights disappeared.

The car pulled up and the back slapping, pushing and joking guys laughed their way to the house. "You finally awake, sleeping beauty?" They banged on the door before pushing it open and spilling into the carnage on the kitchen floor.

"Oh *fuck*, oh *fuck*…" Gacy was suddenly all in the moment. "Oh *fuck*, his throat, fuckin' throat's cut. Christ…he gone?"

Fish started poking fingers around the exposed meaty gash in a futile effort to find a pulse. "No…PULSE, CALL it in. FUCK!" Without thinking, he lip locked on Rogers' bloody lips and provided a breath. He only managed to blow foam out of the severed bronchial tube. It splattered the wall with slimy red spittle, along with bloody, thick, clots. He looked up… "Call, goddamit, get the cavalry rolling. NOW!" Fish tasted the foul business on his parched lips and wished he hadn't done the CPR thing.

"That tall drink of water…her kid, what's his name…went and sliced ol' Rogers throat," Gacy hollered. Backing out of the scene was probably in order. "We can't go fucking up the crime scene, guys."

Corll was wide awake… "It was her kid! I sawed it with my own eyes, I did."

Sirens were approaching. "Yeah, he kilt him…damn sure. That lit'le fucker'll pay for this. That's why he was all gassed up to giddy up outta here. Ol' Rogers didn't deserve this." Fish's voice had slipped into a sinister cadence. He had a score to settle.

"Don't see him none since yesterday afternoon sometime. He didn't have to work...kinda just laying low, I suppose." Ma wasn't at all sure why the detectives showed up on her front step. Fish was so friendly last night and now he was all cop, sticking a badge in her face. He kept at her with questions. She wondered what this pomp and pageantry was all about. Last night, they were all buddy-buddy and now they're prancing around all full of themselves. All the questions had something to do with Dub.

"Ma'am...we're with the Casper Wyoming Police Department. This is Detective Gacy and I'm Fish. Could we come in, please? Is your son home?" She noticed one of the cops had his hand down resting under his blazer where she knew a gun must be.

"Well, now what in tarnation is this all this about? Dub, Dub's okay, ain't he? Why you two all worked up? Acting all high and mighty? Why, JW? Why, Mister Albert Fish?"

"Just relax, ma'am...your eye, how did that happen? Did you and Dub have a problem? It's just you and Dub...that call this place home. Is that correct, ma'am?"

"We have a warrant, ma'am, but first where is your son?"

"I already done told you he off on his lonesome, didn't I?"

"You were...out and about...last night, as I recall. Didn't ya think Dub was going to fry ya up some late night vittles? Correct, ma'am?...Is that correct...ma'am? You didn't know where Dub was between the hours of say...one and two, though, did you? That correct, ma'am? Is that correct? I heard you last night threaten Rogers with my own ears I did. You said you were going to have Dub kill Rogers is how I heard it. You should answer unless, of course, you wanna be an accessory. Is that what you want? We already checked… Dub was *off* last night. He wasn't working."

"Well, I don't rightly know—" Ma was confused as she attempted to talk. She wanted answers, not questions. The detectives worked words into her mouth. They weren't confused and knew what they had to hear. Her thoughts raced. Gacy and Fish dog talking her for no reason. It ain't no crime in her book to be off work, so why were these detectives all worked up? They came with a warrant and nothing was making no sense to her. She wondered why they wouldn't stop talking and give her a chance to straighten them out.

"Please step outside now." One of the detectives had her by the arm, kinda ensuring she was in fact coming out of the house as they wanted. "We would like you to have a seat in our vehicle while we search the premise."

"Why won't you listen to me? I told you Dub ain't home. You got it all wrong. Dub didn't do anything. Dub I tell you isn't—"

"Oh…I don't recall telling ya Dub went and did anything wrong. Where'd you come up with that notion? I had my way, I charge ya with aid and abet, ma'am!" The detectives both told her this as if they were a singing duet.

The door slammed shut on her pleading, leaving no doubt they'd heard enough. She was confused and wished she could just talk to Dub. Nothing seemed out of the ordinary last night. Dub had been off work. He'd told her as much but she'd forgot. Ain't no law against forgetting. Those detectives wanted Dub though. They didn't say why, but she felt as if something was going on. But why? Then she noticed two things.

The first thing she noticed was that a young fella, a cop the others called 'Nicky New Guy,' was standing back behind her, leaning on the trunk. Oh, yes, she thought, it's that rookie. She couldn't think up his real name but seen him picking up cars down at the garage after the oil changes. She swung around and knocked on the rear windshield and hollered. She wanted answers. She didn't want to sit in the back of a squad.

"LET ME OUTTA HEREEEE—" He just looked at her dumbly. "AM I UNDER ARREST?...LET ME GO!" The officer just bobbed his head like a parrot carefully following a treat just out of its reach.

The second thing she noticed was Dub. He was walking with purpose towards her. Relief swept over her. At least Dub was okay. The relief was fleeting, though. She didn't want the cops manhandling him. Why was she locked up in a car with detectives digging around her place? How come Fish and Gacy and turned so official and mean?

Dub was practically on top of him before the young cop spotted him. Ma was hoping Dub could talk some sense into the young whipper-snapper and get her butt outta the car. Then her morning got even stranger. The young fella went to fumbling and pulling on his pistol before finally pointing it at Dub. He was also hollering.

"DOWN on the ground—hands up...DOWN on the ground... DOWN—DOWN...NOW!" Dub looked at the kid officer with an expression conveying the fact he'd never had a gun pulled on him. He wasn't sure if his hands went up first or if he should sprawl out on the ground then stick them out. He froze up on the dilemma. He never was much for questions and certainly wasn't going to start asking them with a Glock pointed at him. The confusion was suddenly cleared up. He was tackled from behind by the detectives from the house.

"Hands up, asshole...now...hands up. Keep that gun on him." Then he felt punches or kicks. "Quit resisting, scrot. Now, hands behind your back. You hear me, scumbag...hands up noooow!" Dub was hearing it all. He just wasn't sure how to do anything with his hands due to the fact they were pinned under him. He wanted to say something but the words couldn't be gurgled out under the weight of the two detectives crushing in on his back. The punches hurt. Then the prying started and before he knew it one of the detectives had painfully pried his arms out from underneath him.

"Okay, asshole, you just added a resist to the charges…do I make myself clear? Resisting, buddy boy!" Dub was hauled to his feet after being cuffed. Then it came to him, the young cop was Dylan Klebold, the same feller who stopped Tinkey out on 220 for the brake light. He had no idea why that little piece of useless information popped into his head, but it had.

"Okay, big guy…your ma already went and told us that you hauled off and whacked her good. Didja feel good doing that, asshole? Huh?" Dub was thinking some on whether his shoulder or wrists hurt worse. The handcuffs had been clamped down plenty tight and his fingers were tingly.

"C-c-c-can. C-c-c-can. My hands. C-c-c-c."

"Look, you always talk like ya got shit in your mouth? Stutter box? Haul off and hit a woman. If you'd do as you were told…you little piece of shit…just maybe I'd loosen 'em…if'n that's what your whining 'bout. If it was up to me I'd tighten 'em some is all Im'ma gonna say. You hear me boy?"

Dubs figured he wanted to certainly do as he was told. He knew in his heart it would be a whole lot easier talking if the cuffs could get loosened some.

"Look, we know what you went and did. There ain't no denying physical evidence son. We have the evidence and I just want you to know only the truth will set you free. Life is like that, son. Right makes might and the best policy is always to tell the truth. My momma always says that, son. The truth will set you free. You ain't gonna lay there…say my momma got it all wrong now…are ya? You listen to your momma? She want you to kill Rogers? We're going to get to the bottom of this, sure as this damn day is going to end! We gonna figure this out…the easy way. Or the hard way. Your choice, shit bag."

Then, suddenly, like the unexpected meadow lark melody after a downpour, he heard kinder words. It was how the fella went and said them. Dub wasn't currently thinking much of anything except the awful pain burning up his arms from his wrists. They was a hurting, a mighty some, for sure. The kinder voice provided hope that the fire in his wrists could be doused.

The kinder-sounding words were asking the younger officer for his key. Dub was lost. It was only after the first one was loosened, cutting the pain in half, that Dub opened his eyes, "Th-th-thank you k-k-kindly, sir. That sure is a m-mighty-powerful relief." Thoughts started to trickle in upon Dub. The other cuff was loosened bringing on a wave of relief. Only then did he give some thought to his predicament. Had he understood one of the detectives to say he went off and hit his ma? That didn't make no sense at all. None whatsoever. Why did the detective go and say that? Dub, no way, no how would hit Ma. She wasn't no liar. Why did he get bull rushed, beat on some, and cuffed? All the detectives had to do is go and ask him to do something. He knew enough not to mess with cops. They scared the beejeebers out of him.

"E-e-e-is ma hu-hurt? Shee okay? Ca-caaa-can-can I go and…and ta-ta-talk with her?"

One of the tackling detectives, who was clearly still worked up some, approached Dub. "Yeah, she'll be just fine, no thanks to you… lady hater. If I meet the likes of you off duty, first thing I do is kick your ass up the street. Then you know what I'd do, stupid? I'd kick your ass back down the street. That's about all stuttering boxes like you deserves. Good ass kicking. I'd give anything to lose a boot in your ass…you tall drink of no good for nothing piece ahhh crap."

Dub listened and wondered if cops were supposed to say things like that. Didn't seem somehow right. Then he felt his arm being grabbed from behind and felt himself leaving the ground. Even before landing on his feet properly, he was pulled and pushed towards a squad car. It was only then he heard the words that ground his thoughts to a sudden stop. Arrest was one of the words. Murder. Murder in some kind of degree. Booked. He was going to be booked or something for a homicide. His ma was already in the back of a police car. He was jammed hard into the back of another squad, hitting the side of his head on the door jam. His ear hurt, but not nearly as much as his wrists had. The car started for the station and Dub wondered some on whether his ear was bleeding. Even though his ear hurt, he knew both were working just fine, when they registered words into his overworked brain, stutter box, lady hater and the worst word—*murderer*.

CHAPTER 7

TWO DOWN
"IN THE JAIL HOUSE NOW"—JIMMIE RODGERS

Tinkey stretched some in his nylon tent. About the time a feller goes and flops down out in the open in a sleeping bag, sure as thunder there'll be a cloud burst. Nylon tents kept the prairie rattlers at bay also. Wouldn't want one of them snuggling up with ya in the evening.

Tinkey thought some on rattlers and how they got under Dub's skin. He surly didn't like the idea of rattlers, and Tinkey supposed it probably meant any snakes. Truth be told, Tinkey didn't much care for snakes himself. He hadn't seen anyone go and get bit by a snake but knew it happened. There were signs down by Independence Rock warning tourist to stay clear of them. Barney Thompson had a yellow lab get nailed. Snake bite killed that dog in no time flat. Lot of howling, then the bitten area went to swelling a great deal. Puss got to dribbling out of the black hole bite marks and the dog just whimpered off. Kinda made chewing motions with his mouth. Barney said it was the damnedest thing to havta go through. Tinkey shuddered some upon giving his close encounter with the rattler some thought.

Then recollections started making demands as his sleepy haze faded. He remembered mom wanting help with the flowers. She struggled with holding the water can over her head. Dad needed something, too, but he couldn't quite recollect what it was all about. It'd come to him. Then Dub. Tinkey sat bolt upright and rubbed the crusty sleep from the corners of his eyes. While patting his hair down he decided to keep it all out of his mind. He was at the end of his rope and besides, it was disturbing. All a guy could do is hope things would start looking up for Dub.

The sun blinded Tinkey. He stretched figuring he'd dedicate today as a hang low day, kinda just take it off. Life in Casper made it difficult to lay low. A calamity of some sort always robbed him of his self-proclaimed days off. Sheila and the senior prom were definitely a threat to any idleness. He'd have to do something about it he supposed. Sheila couldn't do all the planning. A riding pal of hers, Sally, was in need of an escort. She wasn't much but Dub didn't exactly strike him as the kinda fellow who could be too all demanding in the girl department. Sally had a good 'nough figure as far as he was concerned. All the guys said she was a 'Butter' girl though. Everything was fine butter face. If anybody could over look that minor problem, it'd be Dub. Besides, like he told Sheila, Dub wasn't like all sexed up. Nope…Dub was a purr-fect gentleman!

The wind kicked up some dust and sandblasted his face just as he made his grand entry onto the prairie. He ran his tongue across his pasty unbrushed teeth as his stomach rumbled. Time to hit for home.

He rolled up his gear in no time and got pointed home. He followed the river while listening to the train yard noises. His home place was near a point between the fairgrounds, along the Platte and the yard. He would've never guessed, as he stumbled along the warming sandy path, how his life was about to be transformed into everything it had never been.

Dub was unceremoniously pulled from the back of the squad, landing in an awkward position. He was leaning on a cop, while being pushed against from behind. The officers were making eager sport of his handcuffed body, like dogs fighting over a chew toy. The detectives were in attendance and followed the pushing and shoving mass down the hallway. One of the detectives nodded his head towards a chair, providing some direction for the uniformed officers who were very energetic in their efforts to be a part of it. A suntanned open hand pushed into his sternum, landing him in a chair.

"Already told ya…boy…what I think of cowboys that pound on the fairer sex, now didn't I?" The detective leered at him some before standing up and clearing his throat. "Whatcha got to say 'bout yourself now? Huh…" The detective was determined to come up with the proper story, as he saw it, to what had happened.

Dub wasn't quite sure just what to say and wasn't comfortable with having to attempt words because he'd strangle on the syllables. He had already realized Gacy didn't much care for speech impediments or stuttering. He knew Gacy from the diner. Everybody called him JW. He felt like a cow with its head stuck in a fence. The more he struggled, the more confused he was getting.

"Godamnit, I knew Rogers. He was my friend. I'll say that. You know that, you work at Shorty's. Rogers was a damn good guy in my book." Gacy's anger had pumped up veins on the side of his head as he reddened. With temper in tow the detective stomped out the door.

The other detective, the one who had loosened his cuffs, was looking off into space, tapping a pencil on the table top. "Oh, now, JW…he just kinda worked up. You don't wanna see him if'n he goes and gets worked up much more on account of *this*. May, just may be, this is all just an accident, I'll hear ya out. You betcha…that's why I'm here, for goodness sake. Can I fetch ya a soda, water maybe? Just trying to be neighborly is all. What da ya say?" He smiled and looked down upon Dub.

"I could surely use the bathroom…is that allowed?"

The smiling, and much friendlier detective didn't think that would be a problem at all. "There are rules around here, Dub. Is that okay, I call you by your first name…*son?*"

"Yes sure-sir, i-it surely i-is, thank you."

"Let me read over some things before we skedaddle to the head. Is that okay?" Dub was nodding some, feeling very fortunate that all detectives weren't like Detective Gacy. If Dub had it figured right, Rogers probably gone and went and filled that detectives head full of nonsense. While thinking on this, Detective Hamilton Fish was reading from a card. It had started something like; you have the right to remain silent. That sounded like a mighty fine idea. Dub didn't want to choke on words today, of all days.

"C-c-can I-I non-n-not say things?"

"Hold on, partner…I'm here to *help* you. Yes-siree. This remaining silent business is just me following the rules, son. I want to help you." He whispered it, then in a cheerful voice while patting Dub on the shoulder he said "enough of that silliness now, let's get you to the bathroom young man…oh, did you want a soda, water? What can I get you?"

He helped Dub gently to his feet and brushed sand off his knees. "Would you believe it? More stupid rules! I have to leave those darn cuffs on, but do they feel better in the front?"

"Ye-yeah, they fee-fee-feel good. Tank you v-very much." Dub was relieved to have someone around who was his only chance at understanding what in his world was going on. Detective Fish had said he was around to help, and just knowing that, felt really good. He knew he could use any help available and besides the pop sure would hit the spot. He figured JW would have let him die of thirst, if it was left up to him.

"More doggone rules, I havta hang out in the facilities while you relieve yourself. Can you believe it?" Dub was uncomfortable with being watched and wished he didn't have to go so long. "I know you from down at Shorty's...ain't that so? You a pretty good cook—huh?"

Dub was still going pretty good, but heard him, over the splashing that sounded louder to Dub than it actually was. "Y-yeah, I-I c-c-cook down to Shorty's, pert-naa-near go-going on a-a year I s-sa-pose."

"Where you get that shiner, them bruises? Were you fighting some with old Rogers?" Fish was rubbing his chin thoughtfully and nodding with the 'I understand look.'

"Oh, we'd get into it some..." Dub was relieved he was done peeing. He didn't do the usual extra push to completely empty his bladder, but just zipped up quickly. It just seemed kinda embarrassing to have to do his business in front of somebody.

Detective Fish seemed to be looking away in a polite manner. "Why, you lose any more weight son, I'm afraid you'd fall through your asshole and hang yourself...but man oh live, you'ze a tall drink of water." He laughed, but stopped when Dub didn't join in. "Sorry, didn't mean that...yeah...why don't we stroll back and get our talking out of the way."

"You run around on that four wheeler...correct?"

"Why y-yes sir, I do." Dub felt like he'd known Fish his whole entire life.

"You ran around on it last night...correct?"

"Why I-I suppose that's a-a fact."

"You own knives like any cowboy does-huh?" Dub cast a glance over towards JW, who had reappeared and was slouched against a table glaring his pissed off look at him. Dub didn't figure he wanted to spend any time alone with him.

"Yes, zz-sir…i-I-gots a-a knife."

"Well, where in thunder is it?" Fish smiled in a reassuring, understanding way while nodding.

"Well, I-I don't r-rightly know. I wreck-reckon I-I left it in the gay-garage—right?" Dub was wondering if this was going anywhere. Fish seemed to be getting stuff so he hoped they could end their little get-together soon. Were the cops gonna get Ma? What'd she know about it? Did she…?

"So you left it in the garage. Is that your story?" Gacy howled suddenly.

"W-will-well…I do-don't recall last time I…"

"Look, cut the bull. We all know what happened! Do we look stupid? Huh?" In a slow high chirpy voice Gacy continued in a mocking tone, "Wha-wha-why i-isn't t-the fuckin' knife in the garage? Because you ditched it, ASSHOLE. Didn't you?!" JW clenched his fists and stepped towards Dub, who immediately pulled his shoulders together and made like he was going to shrink into the chair.

Detective Fish cut in on Gacy. "Are you saying you don't know where the knife is? But you have one?"

Dub was hoping things would not end up with him having the cuffs retightened. He figured Detective JW Gacy would love to do it, but Fish was holding him back.

"Fingerprints. We are going to have to fingerprint you, and I havta tell you, son, we found prints on the four wheeler and at the scene."

"YEAH, how-how-how does that make you feel…" Gacy asked while stepping towards a flinching Dub, grinning like a Halloween creature.

"You want to ever kill Rogers? Remember, we should stick to the truth." Fish fell back into his easy going style. "We'll understand.

We're officers of the law. Believe you me, we have seen it all. Why we heard your ma, just last night, say something about just that." Fish put a hand of understanding on Dubs shoulder and shook him lightly. Dub wanted it all to end. He needed to see his ma and straighten this out. He hadda make sure she was okay. He had heard the word 'murder' or something like that. He started feeling his scraped up knees and elbows for the first time.

"Were you plenty riled with Rogers last night? We already talked to your ma. She's a waiting on you to get this over with. She needs to talk to you. She wants that, so let's just get to the bottom of this. She already tell us you didn't get along with Mister Rogers. That eye looks nasty."

Dub thought some on his ma. What in tarnation had she went and done? Maybe she did get mad. Rogers could do that. Was Rogers beaten on her again? Could the cops prove she kilt Rogers? Is that why the detectives kept talking to him? What do they want him to say? So many questions and no answers. If the law knew everything, why were they asking so many questions? Why was he handcuffed? What did he havta say to get outta this predicament? He knew his fingerprints were on the four wheeler. Was that all the cops needed to keep him in the station? Why was Hamilton suddenly *Detective* Fish? He had always been Albert down at Shorty's.

"What y'all want me to say? Yeah, I wanted to kill ol' Rogers at times." Dub looked directly at Detective Hamilton Albert Fish. He didn't want to hash over the beatings and hoped Fish didn't make him.

"How about the truth. We been beating around the bush long enough. Remember…the truth will set you free. Son—" Fish looked at him with kindness and understanding while nodding up and down slowly. "We have plenty of evidence. Besides, you already said you got into it with Rogers. We heard it plain as day, we did!"

Dub told them the truth. He did on occasion get into it with Rogers on account of Rogers drinking and getting low-down mean. He smushed his mouth from side to side. He wanted to let the cops know things but wasn't sure how. He was on the four wheeler last night, but then again, he was on it most nights. Why did the cops think that was important? He didn't know what they were getting at. Why couldn't he just remain silent like Fish had said he could? Why had they put her in the back of a police car? Was she arrested? Why couldn't he ask questions so he'd know how to answer their questions? Why was he thinking up so many whys?

Near as he could tell ma just might be in big-time trouble. He had to see her. It didn't feel good, seeing her bruised up some, on account he couldn't help her any. How long would it take for him to be done with the cops? How many times would they keep asking him the same questions? He knew he didn't know a lot about what they kept asking, but he did know he wanted it all to go away.

"YEA. OKAY I DID IT! NOW LET ME SEE HER!"

"Well, perhaps you could tell us just what you did. You know. From the beginning. Why you went to Rogers' place. Why he got you so riled. That sort of thing." Fish was in no hurry. Dub was. If Gacy would just leave the room that would have even been better.

"I-I did it all, everything. I-I was on the four wheeler. I-I had my knife and I got into it with Rogers. A-and then I stuck the-the knife in his har-heart. N-now can I see Ma?"

"Whoa, we've been at this for a while. Let's turn off the tape and take a break. Restroom break. I'll fetch ya Coke. You want another Coke?" As Fish was talking, Gacy had already turned off the tape and started rewinding it.

Fish left the room for the coke. Least that's what Dub figured. That left him all on his lonesome with Gacy who approached him and got just inches from his face. Dub flinched but the chair held him in place. He smelled the breath that was somehow off, from like, stale, long ago swallowed onions.

"Look, scumbag...you listening? We turn the tape back on and you tell us how you went to Rogers' place. You cut his fuckin' throat. You see a car coming and you got your ass out of there, like the fuckin' coward you is. You jumped on your four wheeler and hauled ass outta there, pronto. *Right?* Do you need me to go over it again for you, only a little slower? Huh? I can do that, Einstein. Oh...and while you're at it, let us know where you ditched the, ah, murder... the knife. Okay, fuck stick?"

Dub wanted Fish to return and wished he'd said he didn't care for a pop. Sounded like Rogers was actually dead. Why couldn't he just see her? What would happen if they went and put her away for a long time? What would Tinkey and everyone think if Ma was a murderer?

"Well...I'm back. I know this is all very upsetting and doggone it, figured a pop would help you out, son. That's why I'm here. Well, why we're both here today. Lordy. We're here to help you out of a pickle. You understand we are here to *help* you out?" Fish's words fell upon a very troubled soul. Dubs nodded his appreciation vigorously. He was ready to put this behind him.

"Now let's just say what needs to be said so we can move on? Do you have any questions or do you need to use the facilities? Anything I can do for you? I just want you to understand. We can get through this together. We can probably make some sense out of this. I just know you're a good fellow. You just had an accident I'll bet. Maybe he caused this. Rogers. But we'll figure this out right fast. Your momma needs to talk to you. I'm here for you. Call me Albert or Ubby, that's what my friends call me. We gotta stick together through these tough times...so Ubby it is. None of that Detective Hamilton Fish stuff. That's for the birds."

Dub felt Albert's kindness about like he felt warmth from a camp stove. He agreed with Fish and wanted it all to be over. He'd just say what they wanted to hear so he could straighten this matter out with her. He had to see her.

"Okay…we are on tape…I, Detective Fish and Detective Gacy, are present, along with Dub. We have fully explained his rights and he has voluntarily, freely expressed his desire to speak with us. Is that correct, Dub?"

Dub nodded.

"No no, that won't do," Fish laughingly said. "We're taping this interview so will you please state you entire name for the record and then I'll ask you some questions? Of course you are free to say anything you want. You understand?" Fish was sounding like a pa and again Dub was glad he was present. Dub just felt like Fish was on his side, whichever side that was.

Dub spoke in even, slow tones, hoping not to stumble much on his words. "Yea-yea-YES, that is r-r-right." Fish smiled and Gacy crossed his arms and exhaled forcefully.

Trapped! Dub felt like a free range cow suddenly forced into a chute. How much trouble was Ma in? Now if he could just remember to say stuff like how Gacy had said he hadda. "I got m-m-my knife. I-I d-d-drive straight way-away to Rogers. I stabbed…I m-m-mean cut him bad…all by my own. Then I s-spotted a car. Headlights. I…I…I got on my H-Honda and d-drove to m-my garage. Is that's where-where it wa-was? Then I-I runned off to-to hide. Ya-Yup…is that how I did it?"

Gacy talked over the question, quickly asking, "Where did you run off to?"

"Oh…I-I stayed…down on-na river."

"To hide?" Fish asked in an understanding voice while frowning into an up and down gesture with his head.

"Y-Yes…to hide from you…g-guys so I-I wouldn't get c-c-caught."

"Was anyone with you? Or were you all alone?" Fish slowed the conversation down in the hopes Dub wouldn't stumble on his words so badly.

"No…Ma-ma didn't now-know nothing. N-n-othing. Nobody b-but me. I'm the only one that d-d-d-done it. She n-no how a t-t-tell me to d-do it."

"So you murdered Rogers in cold blood? Is that what you're saying here freely of your own accord? You cut Rogers throat for no good reason? Why don't you tell us why a seemingly nice fella like you would go and do such a thing like that? Rogers was an upstanding citizen of Casper. You know that—*right?*"

Dub pondered some. Rogers weren't no upstanding citizen near as he could tell. These very detectives had to know something of the sort. Rogers was a low-down scoundrel and the mere mention he was upstanding in Casper was plenty upsetting. Plenty indeed. The detectives had to know some of what Rogers was really like. Anger reared up. "He wouldn't fix my four wheeler."

"Now thank you for being truthful. You'll feel better for it, son." Fish's smile indicated he was doing what they wanted him to do. He'd see Ma soon.

"If he's dead I'm plenty relieved. I havta say." Anger, long last freed from the depths of Dub, spoke up forcibly. "Ya, I'm plenty glad he dead if'en he dead. There ain't no mistaking that."

Hamilton Fish was looking plenty pleased, as was detective JW Gacy. They both smiled benevolently as the words flowed freely from Dub.

"Now are we done? Is that what you wanted? C-can I see Ma? C-can I see her? Oh I-I forgot, I don't na-now where the knife i-is. La-lost."

Fish started acting like Gacy. They both seemed to chill down some as they crossed their arms and looked down on him. Fish was even tapping the floor with the sole of his black shoe slowly swinging his head back and forth like a cobra following a flute.

Gacy spoke up and delivered dreaded words. "You are going to be booked for CAPITAL MURDER, fingerprinted, and put away in a nice cell. A jail cell with bubba. How does that make you feel? Yeap, you're going to be someone's girlfriend. Then you're going to court to answer to this killing business you just admitted to on tape. I was in the car. I saw you jump on that four wheeler and hightail it outta there. Well, it looks like your running days are over, ass wipe. Do you hear me—*boy?*" He was fiddling some with the recorder.

Dub recalled the four wheeler comment. How did he see him on the four wheeler? That didn't make a lick of sense. Not one lick. He was a detective after all, so why did he lie like that? Cops lie? Detectives are like super cops. They shouldn't tell tall tales. There just no way he had seen him getting on the four wheeler.

Fish was looking on him some and nodding up and down. "That tape's off—*right?*"

"Yo!" a smiling Gacy affirmed.

Fish turned towards Dub. "Yeah…you went and done wrong. Not too long ago folks in these parts would have had you strung up by your balls. Yeah…I figure they would have hung you by your scrawny neck until you gooood and dead. Have to find a mighty tall tree so as you couldn't touch the ground. You know Rogers helped me out the other night when my car died? He went and did it on his own dime. That was the kind of fella he was. I had to get home to my wife and kids and he helped me. Then you get all full of piss and vinegar and doggone-it, cut his damn throat because he wouldn't fix your four wheeler. I don't know what this world is coming to when varmints like you are running around pulling shenanigans. Well, I guess all's you got to look forward to is a lit'le rub a dub-dub time in a shower with Bubba. How that make you feel—*Dub?* Rub a dub Dub!" Fish laughed. "Rawlings'll take care of you. Thing called the lethal injection. After Bubba gets done given ya the ol' two ball injection, then POW! the state'll have you put out of your misery in nooo time flat. Whoeee!"

Fish pulled the soda away from Dub and dropped the three-quarters full can in the garbage like it was dirty… "You listening, boy? Huh? They gonna slip a little bitty needle into you." He'd held his forefinger just a bit away from his thumb. "You went and sent Rogers to meet his maker. Well, pilgrim…here's to hoping the needle hurts a whole helluva lot. I'ma thinking folks in these parts are gonna be right smug on the day they plant your ass in a hole. Wonder what folks is a thinkun' on what kinda fella your momma went and growed up. 'Spect they had their ire raised plenty, partner. Suppose your ma'll get run out of Dodge on account of you." Any sparkle of friendship had all but vanished as fast as food left in front of a glutton.

"C-can I s-see Ma, Albert?"

Fish leaned into the question, ignoring any personal space with his teeth clamped tightly. "It's Detective Fish, Boyeee—"

A jailer and deputy came and started leading Dub down a long hallway. He cast a furtive, confused glance over his shoulder and saw Fish high-fiving Gacy in 'done good' football player fashion. None of it made sense as everything suddenly became about being scared, lonely and confused.

CHAPTER 8

REACTION

"I SAW IT ON T.V."—JOHN FOGERTY

It was like he didn't want to really see anyone today. But he'd have to see them sooner than later. Better to just get it done. Who knew, perhaps it would all just be smooth sailing anyways.

"Mom, Dad, I'm home…" he hollered as he fetched a glass and approached the refrigerator. The scent of bacon teased him into knowing he'd missed breakfast. Nobody was home either. He fumbled around in the kitchen putting together a bowl of cereal. The phone rang. It was Sheila… "Tinkey, you there? Pick up, come on. Didja hear, Didja hear? Okay call—" He usually picked up when it was Sheila on the line. Should he answer? Nope. He didn't want to hear who Bonner was taking to prom again just yet. Naw, he figured he'd eat and call her back. He wasn't interested in anything so early in the morning. Just eating.

He sat at the table and aimlessly crunched on his cereal, not realizing he was eating, let alone reading the box. His mind was blank as his mouth encountered spoon after spoon of sugary sweetness. It was after plenty of crunching that he overheard the slamming of car doors. Mom and Dad were home.

"Oh dear, there you are. We've been looking for you." Mom had a hand over her heart as she approached him. She drew in a big breath like it was the last breath needed to fill a birthday balloon.

Tinkey knew something was up and he figured it was show time. "W-What, Mom?Dad? What's going on? Is Grandma—?"

"Oh, no, no, she's okay, thank goodness…oh dear, no, there is no easy way to say this. Lord. Dub. Your father and I know how special your friendship is. You've been a dear friend of his for as long as heaven knows."

Tinkey stopped eating, holding a spoon full of cereal halfway between the bowl and his mouth. "Mom…is…he…okay?" What happened to Dub?

"Well…yes, yes, yes and *no*. I-I just don't understand it. We've talked some on Rogers. Well, I know Rogers was awful hard on 'em. He was terrible in fact. We both know that. We talked plenty on that son. But Tinkey…Dub is locked up. He's locked up on account Rogers got *murdered* last night."

"Murder? Now why would they go and figure that? Dub couldn't hurt a flea, for Christ's sake. I mean really. Murder…Dub?" Tinkey cleared cereal crumbs and phlegm from the back of his throat. "I mean, are the cops just talkin' to him or something? That's why he's in jail, I'll wager."

"You can't see him. Not until he's *formally* charged. He doesn't have any visitation rights, I don't figure. We went down to see if he didn't know about your whereabouts. They wouldn't let us see him on any account. They, the policemen, detectives do need to see us. They wanna do a *formal interview*. They have questions about why I called them I suppose. You remember, about how I called them to turn Rogers in? No...I expect this is more than just asking Dub questions."

Tinkey's spine straightened, "They want to talk to *me?*"

"Yes, maybe some of this will clear matters up for Dub." Mom was confused as to whether it was exciting or scary to give a formal statement. She knew her friends and neighbors were talking about what she was going to be a part of. She wouldn't be able to sleep come night.

She called the station and the detectives agreed to take a statement from them as soon as they could get there.

While piling into the car they heard a news report. They sat in silence. "The Casper Police are investigating what preliminary reports are calling a homicide. The victim of an apparent homicide is believed to be a 53-year-old male resident of Casper. Police are withholding his identification pending notification of his kin. A person of interest has reportedly been taken into custody. Unconfirmed reports indicate this was not a random act of violence."

After the young female voice had read the news report, folks from down at Shorty's were interviewed.

"By golly...Rogers. Why, old Rogers would give you the shirt off his back. Don't make a lick of sense, no how. I hope they string him up, the guy went and pulled this stunt. Ain't right no how."

A girl spoke up..."How awful, this plain don't make any sense. No, sir. I'm at a loss." Tinkey recognized her voice. She worked with him and always had it figured that Rogers was nothing but a low-down scoundrel, who wouldn't let up on her, for not giving him the right amount of change. She had said it plenty. "He was a regular, here, we gonna go and miss him plenty." We are? Tinkey thought. Hell, I ain't gonna miss him, he thought. If that radio announcer went and asked him those questions he'd tell it the way it should be told. He thought back from the vacant place where his thoughts had landed.

He thought he'd say it was high time someone had sense enough to put a stop to what Rogers was pulling. Been right nice to have the drunken, woman beaten' bastard, land in his bottle and float along ways from Casper. Cops wouldn't or couldn't do a damn thing. That's how he'd call it. Damn right!

When Tinkey and his mom got to the station there was a crowd towards the front entrance. After getting out, a reporter, with a fellow chasing her with a camera, approached them in a fast walk. Others saw the dashing, stumbling reporter and gave chase.

"You there, you know Dub? You worked with him. Do you think he murdered his dad?"

Several others closed in asking how long Tinkey knew Dub. Reporters wanted to know if he could confirm the identification of the perpetrator. Had he talked to Dub after the murder? Tinkey quit listening to the reporters. He looked down, as cameras were pushed at him, and he followed his mom's shoes to the door. His mind had latched onto how stupid the word perpetrator sounded to him.

"Back off, back off," a uniformed officer was hollering. But the reporters were starved for tidbits of info, and Tinkey was concerned that he or his mom just might get clonked by a microphone or camera.

After getting into the station, Mom brushed her sleeves and patted her hair down. Dad was looking around, and Tinkey was actually scared.

"Boy oh boy, ya got down here right fast. Otherwise…I'd had the uniforms help you out some. My name is Detective Gacy and I'd like to have a word with you folks separately if y'all don't mind any. Sir, do I require a discussion with you?" Dad explained he couldn't understand why but would help anyway he could. "Well, I'll interview you first, ma'am," and they disappeared through a door. Dad and Tinkey sat down, accompanied only by silence and disturbing notions of one kind or another. Dad couldn't know what to say to help and Tinkey had no idea how to ask for guidance. The detective seemed to be the best and only hope of blowing away the fogginess surrounding his feelings.

"Well, son, you gotta trust them officers to help Dub out. That's what policemen do. They sort evidence out and make sense of it. The truth is always the best thing. Be truthful." Dad had always believed in officers of the law. He'd been one of them in the Air Force.

"Well, thank you, ma'am, and now it's your turn, young man." Gacy shot a reassuring smile towards Tinkey. Before marching towards Gacy, he held the chair for mom.

"Now the reason we have you down here is just a formality. Your momma went and told me you and Dub as near to being kin as possible...without being kin. I want you to know that I realize it puts you in a bind. I surely do, young man. You are a man, son, and men have to man up on occasion." Tinkey was thinking some on what Gacy was saying but also in how he was saying it. Tinkey knew Rogers was a lowlife that went and got himself kilt. Gacy appeared to be enjoying himself too much. Tinkey figured this fella should at least act some like a mortician. Why, them folks is always gloomy and downcast. Then here's Gacy strutting his stuff like an English-style horse proudly showing its form in a ring. Struck Tinkey that Gacy musta contributed some in landing Dub in jail. Yessiree, solving murders must be a passel more enjoyable than chasing down kids snowballing cars. Murders only happened in other towns. Whereas this would generally be considered good news, may be, just may be Gacy was waiting for the big-time. Murders just like on TV!

"Something's just wrong even if'n it's your buddy who goes and does it. Now you know this simple fact, before we talk?" Gacy smiled and winked at Tinkey. "Why, your momma tells me she called the station because you told her something on the order Dub got into it with Rogers. Huh. Is that right, you know for a fact they'd got into—it?"

Tinkey considered the question. He was getting the feeling Gacy was better at putting words in his mouth as opposed to listening. His eyes were entirely too close together on a face that was longer forehead to chin than ear to ear. The hair, what little was left was mostly crowded some around his ears. Tinkey started feeling like Gacy wasn't going to clear things up for him. Tinkey recalled his dad a tellin' him one night what gets folks in trouble…'It's when they get to a believing their own bullshit, son.' In one sentence Dad had done it. Cleared things up. Gacy believed he was a whole lot more than he was.

"Them your words, not mine. You puttin' words in my mouth. Dub might've gone and got into it with that asshole but it don't make him a killer. You're an investigator, so you should be able to at least figure something like that out!"

Gacy's face immediately ditched the smile for something else. "Why, you little rascal, let me tell ya a thing or two. We got us some evidence here. Witnesses. Fingerprints. A confession. We got your buddy on tape goin' on and on, how he pulled that stunt. So son… how 'bout some co-op-err-ration here. I know you work with Dub down at Shorty's. It don't give you no right to impede my investigation into a homicide. You understand? You go and pull that stunt and you'll be charged with being an accessory. Do…I…make…myself… clear?"

"Witness, thought you went and said Rogers is dead. So just how in the hell y'all got yourself a witness? That doesn't figure no how." Defiance flowed evenly from Tinkey about like spring sap from a maple tree. Gacy glared and spun his toothpick around and around in his mouth as his arms scrunched tightly together.

"Look, you little bass—I've said I gots me a witness…so I do. So who the hell gives you the right to come 'round strutting your stuff? Yeah, pretty boy with all the answers…huh? Well, you're picking the wrong fight with the wrong fella. You plenty full of yourself, but you'ze getting on my wrong side. Do you understand, pardner? Ought to charge the likes of you with obstruct. How that'll make ya feel? Yeah…your kin would be right proud of you, I expect." Gacy had stretched the word 'expect' out long enough to make it seem like forever. He was hot under the collar resulting in his face reddening up some. He loosened his neck tie and rolled his head from side to side. His eyes were bugging out of his swollen head like two queue balls with black spots in them.

A skinnier fellow marched in and set down some papers on the desk. "I'm Fish, call me Albert." Fish didn't take notice of the fact his partner's head looked like an over-inflated red beach ball.

Tinkey drew in a deep breath as if he was getting prepared to make a speech. He remained seated and let the new detective's mullet distract him from Gacy and his words. The mullet, baby fat, pudgy face, wire rim spectacles, all made it sooo easy to conclude, he wasn't impressed. This guy was, in fact, a clown who wasn't going to ruin his circus.

Gacy beat a hasty retreat, acting as if Tinkey smelled as bad as the fellow who had went and died in an outhouse one incredibly hot and humid day, and wasn't discovered for several days.

"You get more bees with honey than you do vinegar." Fish laughed easily while Tinkey stared hard at the clock on the wall. "Come on, Tinkey, we just gotta hear you out and then hit for Shorty's. What's the special tonight? Why can't I get ya a soda or something? Come on, buddy." The whole name deal, laughing, sounding friendly as if they'd been buddies their entire life. This only gnawed at his craw. Questions about what the special was. Anybody with half the brains god gave a goose, just plain knew it was prime rib. That, and steak was all Shorty's ever ran as specials. Why, Dosh, the owner, himself would tell anybody that you run fish for a special in Wyoming, why the folks would launch your ass to the moon.

"Witness, evidence, I just don't figure Dub went and hurt anybody...let alone kilt Rogers. Mom did call on Rogers but the law didn't go and do anything. He is dead, Rogers, right?"

The smiling detective stopped smiling and lowered his voice as he leaned towards him, "Detective Gacy said Dub jumped on the four wheeler to flee the scene. He and Officer Dean Corll, he runs the fleet for the department, they both sworn officers, trained to observe criminal activity and they saw it happen. You understand? Dub was seen. Plain as day. He climbed on his scooter and took off. Then we followed the tracks towards his garage. We found blood on the four wheeler. Dub went and owned up to what he did. So we just talkin' some to you as a courtesy. You know, just tying up the loose ends is all."

"I don't put much stock in a fella would go and claim to having seen something in the middle of the night. That when it happened, right? It was dark out. They didn't go and see nuttin'. Just what they wanted to see. Wishful thinking in my book. Them officers was probably drinking some—huh? I've seen 'em pound a few at Shorty's. Follow tracks, how you know someone didn't go and borrow that damn four wheeler-huh?"

Detective Fish started in on the conversation, but Tinkey wasn't in the mood to give up on his end of it just yet. He figured he alone knew what the truth was. He also knew he was on top of the truth without any law schooling or anything. Just common sense was all. He had jumped to his feet.

"Look, we can't both talk and I think you a needing a hearing what I'm a saying. I know Dub didn't kill Rogers. Somebody else plain as day slipped in there and ran over to Rogers place and did the killin'. Why, there a lot of people in little old Casper!"

Fish spoke over him. "You don't see the truth is just as plain as the nose on your face. I know it hurts you some to have to know that your best friend went and killed someone who shouldn't have been kilt in the first place. So were you with Dub last night at all? If so, where?" Fish was using his bored, whatever, lets' finish up voice.

"If I went and told you I was—you wouldn't believe me no how." Tinkey leaned towards Fish, who didn't react.

"Okay...okay, have it your way. I'm done. This interview is over...goodbye, have a nice day. Oh, by the way...I was in the car, got it? I was in the car and saw your buddy on that four wheeler with my own eyes. Have a nice day. Rogers damn sure ain't. Now skedaddle... out with you." Fish was staring at his feet with his right hand making sweeping gestures toward the exit.

After pushing their way to the car, Tinkey collapsed into the back seat. Nothing was right. Cops always get it right on T.V. Then he had to visit with a pair of bumpkins who already had it all figured out. They plain didn't want to hear anything that wasn't to their liking. All they wanted to do was keep Dub locked up near as he could tell. Didn't make no never mind to them that the killer was out and about. That they locked up an innocent feller.

It hurt deep into his chest to think any on Dub. He fixated on the thought of Dub sitting behind steel bars, completely lost. He knew he'd go and see Dub and tend to him as only a best friend could. Seeing Dub was going to hurt some. He'd have to figure a whole lot out before anything got better. Talking to Sheila might help but how? No way had he seen this coming. Rogers was dead. The hell with Rogers. He got what he deserved. Dub didn't deserve nothing though. They were going to score jobs on the railroad and then let life finally, really, begin. They were going to run coal trains from Gillette to god knows where, and now Rogers died, and Dub disappeared from their plans. Cops in Casper weren't the answer. They didn't have a clue as to what their very own eyes were seeing. Nope. They were dead wrong.

The pain ground into Tinkey's thoughts like a boot heel grinding out a cigarette on the sidewalk. He was hurting and lonely. His thoughts had drifted to a place where nobody wanted to be. He felt stuck. Everywhere his thinking went was the wrong direction. He'd think he came up with the solution to only realize it'd never work. Tinkey had it all wrong from the get go. The darkness galloped over his sense of righteousness and belief in human kindness.

Sheila was at the house when they pulled up and ran for him. Her tears were hot and mingled with his. Her touch held him up like a life jacket. How was Dub going to hang on while being pummeled with so much rot from the wholesome, god fearing folks of Casper? His eyes were fixed on Sheila about like a mink with its foot crushed in a pan trap watching as the trapper approached.

"Oh, this is awful. Are you okay? Did you tell the cops stuff? Is Dub in for it? Everyone is talking. You know what Reuben said? Dub is going to get the death penalty. That's what he went and said. I'm yapping. Sorry. How're you doing, baby?"

Death penalty? The notion struck him as absurd. The cops had to figure this out. It was their duty. The cops he'd met today weren't the answer. There had to be smarter ones around. Is that why the Mullet had called him by his first name? To get tricky and look friendly? To use him? Were those detectives in it to kill Dub? But if he was innocent, they'd have to come clean and figure it out. Tinkey remembered getting pulled over out on 220 by an officer full of attitude. But detectives were smarter than the average little uniformed wonders. Were detectives just making like they were a whole lot smarter than they really are? A life is at stake.

"How they kill folks? The law, I mean." Tinkey already knew, but his mouth went and asked the dreaded question anyway. He had no idea why. He just didn't like the sound of silence at this moment.

Sheila looked at him and squeezed him hard in her arms. "Rawlins…they have the lethal injection thingamajig down there. It's on the outskirts of town. Place looks like a school or something on the internet. But that's just Reuben yapping. He's a good contractor but he don't know any more than the rest of us about this. I don't think the state'll go and kill Dub. Neither do you. May be he didn't do it anyway."

Tinkey pulled back out of her embrace and walked towards the house. It was too much.

"Besides, he ain't ever been in any trouble in his life…Tinkey." Sheila whimpered.

The news started reporting that eighteen-year-old Dub Emil Sessions of Casper was arrested and would be arraigned on charges. Capital Offense of Murder was the big one. The different stations were going on and on about arraignments and grand juries and it was all hard to understand. Tinkey had checked up on when he could set up a visitation with Dub. He knew he had to let him know this was all gonna work out in the end. The law wasn't allowing visitors until he was arraigned. The prosecutor was getting the facts together. Tinkey didn't figure it should take near as much time as it did.

Dub was cold come morning. He had a stained mattress, on the thin side and a green blanket with holes in it. The floor was tiled and the door was solid steel with a little window in it. The glass in it was of the unbreakable kind. Dub sat back on the bed, alone, much of yesterday and all of today. He was waiting to be let out after someone got it right. He hadn't seen anyone or heard anything. He didn't know how to pass the time. He switched the light on and off figuring he'd do it until the light went and burned out. Then he got bored. The fellow that gave him his food just left it in the cold cement room and beat tracks.

What was Tinkey thinking? Would he come and hang out with him in the crowbar motel? Did Tinkey have him figured as a killer or something? His thoughts would start up, like a misfiring engine, before sputtering to a halt. The detective said they had prints on the four wheeler. So what. He always rode it and it would be covered with his prints. Would the killers prints be on it? Was that the answer? He said something about his knife. His knife was in the garage, wasn't it? They were doing an investigation. They'd figure it out but then his mind would lose track on where it was.

The only thing that would make sense is when the detectives showed up and said they figured it out and they were sorry for having did what they did to him. Would them detectives get into trouble for seeing stuff they couldn't have seen? How long would it take? Prom had been scary enough until he got put into jail. This fix was lots worse than any ol' prom.

The darkest screams of injustice howled into Tinkey's thoughts. In the blackness, something, a ray, just a sliver of hope cut into the hopelessness. It sprang forth from determination. The determination burned up into a passion, a need to build it up all better again. The system, with its inept detectives and so much ignorance, fanned the passion. A gun. A gun was required even if he wasn't about shooting anyone. A pistol would work. A well thought out plan was in order. There just wasn't any other way to blow away the foggy stupidity that had drifted in. He wanted to do it correctly. So much was riding on him. No half assed attempts. He had to succeed. He wanted a former life, complete with hopes, dreams and prayers that had been snatched away. He fetched his notebook and attempted to straighten out his thoughts.

> I can't go and mess up anymore. it gots to stop and right now it does!!! Im gonna stop them before they do anymore messing around with folks. thats what I got to do and right away to

CHAPTER 9

TWO DOWN
"IT WASN'T ME"—GEORGE THOROGOOD

The whole town was talking about Dub. 'Didja hear?' 'Do ya wanna know the latest?' Everyone seemed shook up a bit but certainly didn't want to hear anything upsetting the balance of their opinions. 'I think the bastard did it for drugs.' 'That Dub was an odd duck, let me tell you.' 'Don't surprise me in the least that he'd do something like this.' 'I always figured he was on something the way he walked. That slow way, he just wasn't with it. He'd always stick that paddle foot out real funny like. Christ, he got arms hang clear down past his knees.' 'That creepy ape was around our kids. Makes my skin crawl, I tell ya.' 'The law gonna take care of that varmint. Some states went and did away with killin' bad ones. Not Wyoming praise be to god. Not Wyoming.' 'Downright wrong, we gotta try the bastard, is all I can say. A waste of taxpayer's time and money. You betcha!'

Tinkey caught the sly glances cast in his direction. He picked up on the notion that somehow folks weren't so sure they knew where he was coming from. Until lately he'd always been the same old Tinkey. Now all of a sudden he was encountering throat clearing and conversations that hit the brakes when he showed up.

"Aw—Tinkey, I can stock the silverware, no need for you to go out there."

"Why you being so nice? Never recall you want'in to lug silverware out there." The waitress's offer of assistance had not come as much of a surprise. She was plenty kind and had heard the yip-yapping at the counter. Her face was scrunched up and she didn't look him in the eye. Tinkey's mom had even used her softest tones in talking to him. 'Honey…how was your…Day…okay?' as she was staring down the plate she was drying in her hands. His Phy Ed teacher and football coach had even become more 'understanding' or something. 'You know, young man, life is tough…then it only gets tougher.' It all amounted to nothing. Tinkey wanted it the way it always had been; he figured once the investigation got going everything would straighten out. Folks could just get back to being what they'd always been.

His thinking and planning had provided him relief from his bruised feelings. Hanging in the kitchen, hiding out, wasn't called for. Dub needed a voice. Who better, Tinkey thought, to jump on the wrongs? He had seen what the flow of stupidity had done to Casper's finest. It had washed a pair of detectives down the drain pipe of ignorance and exposed them for what they were. The news stations weren't spilling any intelligence into the community either. They seemed content to just yammer on about what the police were saying. Determination had welled up and clung to Tinkey like cold metal on a junkyard magnet.

Tinkey picked up the silverware. "No, I got it…you got plenty to do on your own." Stupidity wasn't something he planned to start avoiding. Besides, he had no choice. He heaved the silverware up and pointed towards the door. For a moment, a fleeting moment, he almost wished he could let the waitress haul the silverware out. He knew it was too heavy for her, but his burden was even heavier.

"Tinkey…Tinkey, let me go and take care of your business out there. No need for you to be going on out there. Folks is talking some. You know, about you and Dub." The second waitress bumped into Tinkey as he was motoring for the swinging door. Tinkey appreciated her direct style. It made no never mind to him that she was the one who had been good talking Rogers on the radio. "Why ya go and say all that nice stuff 'bout Rogers? Huh?" She stared at him, "Well… you havta speak kindly about the dearly departed you know." Tinkey shot back, "Oh, I get it…so you're saying you can make an asshole good again by stabbing him—right?" She exhaled and pushed past him without another word.

Tinkey headed for the diner full of opinions. His thoughts were driven by adrenalin and determination. How could a room full of so many different folks all be wrong in the same way? Would anyone be seeing it properly? He wasn't expecting nothing but hoping for something. Anything headed in the proper direction. Folks walking around weren't exactly clear on the matter. Old critters on the diner stools would have it all wrong.

The regulars at the counter lapsed into a state of uncomfortable silence when Tinkey appeared with the heavy tray of silverware.

"You boy…how are you, boy?" Paul Reid seemed to have gone and swallowed a whole slice of toast. He squeezed his eyes shut and made a face to help the dry toast along.

Tinkey sat the tray on the counter and shrugged, as if he could care less. He didn't feel much need to go and shoot off his mouth. He'd already accomplished plenty by just walking out into the restaurant.

Reid wasn't comfortable with the silence. Silence was his enemy. He was a cowboy in the know, and anyone knows, a man in the right has an obligation to spout off. Tinkey's sudden appearance had surprised Paul. He had just been saying how he'd like to put a certain someone in his place before that someone suddenly arrived with spoons and forks. His audience had taken to blowing on hot coffee and sneaking a glance or two at Reid. It was as if they suddenly were demanding something, anything from Reid.

"That, that there friend of yours, Dub, he in a fine mess. What'd ya think of your buddy now? He ain't all high and mighty no longer now—is he—*boy?*"

Tinkey displayed his 'could care a less look' as he gazed towards the encounter, noting the tooth pick in Reid's slobbery mouth and realized how grand it would feel to knock the Stetson off his head. Tinkey knew all along Reid hid a bald head under the hat. Folks know you can't just strut around in buildings sporting a hat. Even a Stetson. Weren't right at all. Common western manners. Old Reid wouldn't like to hear any about what he was a hiding under that hat. Nobody likes to discuss things they pretend awfully hard don't exist.

Reid was thinking some behind a pleased smile. Boy done been put in his place because it had to be done. Wouldn't be right to let young ones lead the herd. Paul continued with the full stomach kinda smile, sitting back and enjoying the silence. He pulled his hands together over his gut and slouched back into the booth. He figured it was high time for the buckoo to take his lumps and be gone. Killing just plain wasn't right no way how you looked at it. Besides it felt good to put a little whipper snapper in his place. Guidance, he figured, is what he dished up and it didn't hurt knowing folks was watching. Maybe even she was watching. Oh, the thought broadened his smile even wider. He'd been sweet on her far back as he could remember and it wasn't cause she was a damn good waitress. Hell no, he just knew circumstances any different, why he could end up with her. She always smiling at him. She'd know him for what he was. A real man don't take nothing from no one, no way. That's how she'd have him figured. Reid had said how 'um-poor-tant' it is to get after little bastards 'didn't know' there place. He'd did it and felt mighty fine.

"C'mon boy, where's your manners?" Ried smiled and repositioned his tooth pick in his mouth and stared hard across the counter at the hang dog expression. "Your friend there...Dub...he in the wrong. You best know that and stop trotting around all full of yourself. So where your manners, boy?"

"Well, I guess I went and left them where you left yours. You the only fool can strut around in here with your Stetson on. Ahh...an old turkey buzzard got more on its head than you do...ya goof." The others laughed, but Reid scowled under the surprise of criticism and scorn. One minute he had the varmint cornered, and now somehow, he was reeling from a sensation of being pushed, into a corner of his own.

"Now, you lookie here...you little snot-nosed—wet behind the ears—nitwit. W'all will havta think on what the big boss man gonna think of you and your mouth. Yes—*siree*, I suppose you think your buddy is really something, cutting Rogers up. Huh? We'll have to see what Dosh thinks on account of your behavior. After all I'm a paying customer. Be right nice for a feller to step in and have a breakfast without have'n to put up with guff. Why you don't skedaddle back into that there kitchen so as I can finish up in peace, Misteeer Tinkersley—*boy?*"

Mr. Tinkersley. The old fool resorted to the 'mister' trick. "Whatever Reid, run and tell on me. I've been really a naughty lit'le bugger!" Tinkey was bobbing from foot to foot while staring down into the floor like a kid'll do when he has to use the facilities. Next he said, using a high whinny voice, known to be on purpose by all, "Oh, I surely been bad. You gonna tell your mommy? Please, not that." All other words were lost under the roar of laughter. Customers were slamming down coffee cups, rubbing tears out of their eyes. Reid discovered an interest in his eggs and pushed them around with his fork, feeling heat peeling off his forehead like heat off a hot poker.

"All Christ, Paul…you went and tail stomped a coyot' I'm ah-feared!" But laughter wouldn't allow any other words. His breakfast companion was forced to take a break from eating lest he spew chewed food onto the table.

Paul Reid wasn't laughing as he watched her, the friendly waitress, disappear with Tinkey into the kitchen.

Prom. The night finally arrived, not counting the afternoon of the grand event. Dad sat with Tinkey recalling proms past. Tinkey had gotten the responsible talk. 'Here are the keys, son. But please treat your old Pa's car with respect—' It was all the usual blah-blah-blah, and Tinkey was wondering about how his picking up the corsages had went. Then there was Sally. Sheila had pointed out she just thought it was imperative, yes, that was the world, imperative that Butterface wouldn't be home alone, missing prom. A sly smile creased his face thinking of the butter face comment. No. Sheila would never use that term. That was for damn sure. Then it struck him as odd. It was really odd that he couldn't go and recall the last time he smiled. Maybe prom was in order after all.

It wasn't though. The florist had just stared at him. Handed him the boutonniere and shot him the 'pin your own damn flowers on' stare. Then back on the deck with dad. He's rambling on and on and Tinkey remembered the butter face thought when suddenly dad says be careful. 'No drinking, son, none. The cops just might be taking some extra interest in you. Probably…got something to do with Dub and all. Yessiree, I'm ah feared that's how it works, son. The law just might be interested in…Ah…making your life just a tad bit uncomfortable.'

Tinkey knew his pa meant well. Still confused him some as to how the law could get going and make some folks lives a heap more miserable just cause they got a notion to. Just didn't seem fair, though he recalled cops at the counter discussing the need for some 'scumbags' needing 'extra patrol' to set 'em straight. Tinkey didn't know how it happened but felt he had slipped into the scumbag category somehow. Besides, pa usually got things right. If he had gone and got branded as a 'scumbag' so easily, how had Rogers gone and avoided it? Using a woman for a punching bag and getting hammered 'bout every night must make one a scumbag. Did the cops get to pick and choose who were and who weren't scumbags?

After picture taking, the grand march, and dinner, it was time for the dance. The night flew by. Guys hanging close to the wall fearing the 'fast dance looking stupid deal' and hiding behind ball-busting conversations. Talk centered on the upcoming graduation, who was gonna do what, and how everyone had to stay in touch. Dub loomed in the thoughts of the entire class.

"Man, dude…how y'all doing?"

"Bout as good as anybody, I guess."

"Man…you and Dubs…you hung out, ya know? The cops talked to you. That have you spooked some? Word is a lawyer is in order. Even if ya didn't do anything. Cops'll put like words in your mouth, dude. Totally serious, Tinkey. Man, you took one for the entire class… my man. Spot on…sticking up for our class like that even if he kilt Rogers!"

"All-righty then, how you come up with the guilty deal—huh?"

"Oh, well, you know. Everyone *knows*. I'd heared plenty already is all I'm saying, Tinkey…not on account I want it that way…is all I'm a saying." Tinkey felt about like he would if he was stuck in a washout during a downpour. It just got to the point that it was near impossible to stop the water from washing him downstream.

Then a gal stepped into the conversation. "I heard he kilt Rogers 'cause he got hooked on *meth*. He got caught stealing money cause he was a-needing a *fix*. That's why, no disrespect Tinkey, but that's why it happened. It's like he was always out of it. Always black and blue. All those bruises meant he was on something. That's what I heard anyways. From Alicia's ma. She's a nurse after all. She knows about stuff like drugs, you know…and that's what she said. Why, I can recall plain as yesterday times when I thought he was high. Yeap. High as a kite, I tellya!" she said sternly. "ALLL…Meth…Heads…look beat up and stuff. We should've knowed it…we could have been in danger or somethun'. My ma said as much. *In danger.*" She crossed her arms and shivered some. "You remember how he'd show at school, like, always a-looking like he just got his ass kicked? That's what I think. Drugs!"

Heads were nodding as everyone seemed to be agreeing on what really happened. They had done a considerable amount of thinking on the subject.

Tinkey cleared his throat. "Even if Dub is a cold-hearted murderer…we should still, like, support him. He was a part of our class after all. You guys know that. He was a part of our class."

The crowd nodded. Alicia finished up with a final troubling thought. "The State, they have lawyers that might give Dub the capital punishment business. I'm like not kidding here. Dub is in for it. I'm scare't for him."

Tinkey had become plenty frightened himself as he wondered in and out of different thoughts and concerns regarding the upcoming trial. The truth of the matter was never given a chance because people just always figured the cops got it right.

It all started with a door opening and a cop in a tight brown shirt stretched across his beer belly strutting in with a 'look how important I am' expression. He had an oversized spotty bald head swung from side to side about like a cow's sack come milkin' time. He had a stern look, and Tinkey was hoping he'd trip on the carpet, but it didn't happen. Behind him two cops paraded Dub into the courtroom handcuffed snuggly to a leather belt cinched tightly around his stomach. He was wearing a blaze orange jumpsuit with white socks and black plastic thongs on his feet. Tinkey didn't figure they had to go and cuff him up and parade him around like a criminal. Three cops were near him making an escape impossible. Where would Dub go if he could make a break for it anyways?

"Mom," Tinkey leaned over and whispered, "why they got to go and chain him up and parade him around like that? Is that part of the deal? To, like, break him down and hog tie him so as folks get to a thinkin' he ain't no good?"

Tinkey stared hard into Dub's eyes, which looked flat and stale, like day-old coffee stains on the bottom of white cups. Dub looked to be running on empty as far as emotions went. Tinkey could see there weren't any lawyer jokes safely tucked in behind his eyes. Dubs slouched into a chair next to a pair of suits who quickly nodded in his direction, before returning to the matter of paperwork. The jailhouse had the same effect on Dub as a closet has on a forgotten potted plant. He seemed to have lost color and wilted back into himself. His head sagged towards the table top pulling his chest down.

The prosecutor had poured her oversized body into clothes that groaned at the seams. Her hair, expertly done up, never looked like she led herself to believe it did. No amount of make-up hid the contempt she felt for anyone sitting in the defendant's chair. She was the daughter of missionaries who somehow copulated on a fateful evening. Their shame smoldered, fueled by her undeniable presence. She struggled to unload the wrath keenly felt for her existence. Whether guilty or innocent, she was not a beast driven by right or wrong. She was a legal creature who only had designs on climbing towards bigger rewards, thus proving her worth.

Dub had the appearance of a fledgling attempting to hold its head up long enough to be fed. He'd push his head up, and it would wobble weakly before landing back in his hands. He appeared to have somehow managed to actually lose weight. His clothes just hung on him. After several hard fought glances around the courtroom, Dub lost interest and buried his face into his hands.

"All rise."

Mom elbowed Tinkey, as she beat him to her feet. He watched Dub, who, as always appeared to never finish getting up. First the head started rising, followed by slouching shoulders and a stiffening of the back. Tinkey missed Dub. All the laughs, the time Dub smacked his head good when he had yelled snake. It was easy to remember all them little things.

The judge had the appearance of the Grim Reaper, all gussied up in a black sheet clinging to some parts and hanging over others. His waxy, grayish head and pudgy white hands contrasted with his black wear. He read and read charges while looking towards Dub. He looked to be bored by the whole matter. Dub didn't look like he was getting it.

Dub was arraigned for murder. Least that's what folks was calling it. The prosecutor called it homicide in some kind of degree. She also had a whole passel of other felonies that musta took a lot of learning in law school to dream up. Burglary was one of 'em. Tinkey tightened his fists and relaxed them during the proceedings. The guys in suits continued shuffling papers around. They'd jump up and ask for permission to approach the bench. The detectives were seated behind a divider. Nothing about fingerprints or anything was mentioned.

Tinkey got to feeling like Dub was being charged with just breaking about every law Wyoming had. Everyone was real quiet in the courtroom. Nothing but ceiling fans could be heard as they whirled and beat the dead air. A mess of folks were wearing pink.

"Mom, why is everyone in pink? Is it the breast cancer deal?"

"No, hon, it's folks wearing pink to support Rogers, is what I heard."

"Why they wanna go and support—"

"Now you just shush." Mom cut him off.

"How do you plead?" Dub just stared on some and the skinnier suit answered.

"Innocent, Your Honor, on all charges."

Then the judge got going, with Dub having a right to remain silent and to have an attorney and asked the prosecutor about bail. Tinkey's throat got dry as the prosecutor ranted on and on about the nature of the crime, how bad it was, Dubs, the defendant being a flight risk. She just didn't want to shut up. Then she used the word death. Not as in Rogers being dead, but in the state demanding the death sentence. Death? Dub? Fair? Both of Tinkey's hands balled up into fists as he rigidly stiffened toward the judge. He never felt his mom's hand rubbing his shoulder.

Dub's attorney had talked some after standing up. He had talked about how Dubs had nowhere to run off to. He went on about Dubs not having a police record and having a good attendance record at school.

The judge rubbed his head and looked down on his desktop while he twirled his pencil. He then said something; the words weren't making a lick of sense to Tinkey. They all amounted to Dub being led off back through the door with Deputy Beer Belly and his two brown-shirted friends. Tinkey was elbowed again after he failed to hear the all rise comment. People started talking and moving around the courtroom.

Mom walked out of the courthouse with Tinkey. It was sunny out. Tinkey figured it was a lot brighter than wherever Dub had been led. He had a million questions swirling like dust devils in his head. Some big. Some small.

"Did you see Dub's attorney, that skinny little rascal go and talk to that woman? That other attorney, the prosecutor? Are they supposed to be friends, Mom? Shouldn't he be a little pissed at her? She's trying to kill Dub. They got the lethal injection down in Rawlings. I don't get it. Why they talking all friendly like that?"

"Now I reckon it's just done that way, hon. You know, they work together all the time, I suppose."

"Ahh, all-righty, then…do you know when I can visit Dub?"

"No, we can check I suppose." They both spun and reentered the courthouse.

That's when Tinkey got the notion someone was giving him the eye. He looked around quickly and realized his feelings were correct. Tiny little boar pig eyes, pushed into a fat face, were aimed at him. Detective J.W. Gacy loved to fish, but his face never grew accustomed to the outdoors. It was always windburned. Gacy was standing in front of a gal at a counter while squinting at him. He held his right hand high promising to do something truthful. To tell the whole truth and nothing but the truth. Tinkey approached him and slowed down some upon bumping into the cold squint.

Tinkey figured once again his dad musta been right on the mark about watching out for the law. This detective sure seemed to be shooting him an entire load of ill will. He was glad his mom missed the whole deal. It would have upset her to think someone had somehow come up with the notion that her son was a scumbag. That was the look, though. No mistaking it. Scumbag. Nothin' but a scumbag. Tinkey would have to be careful. Near as he hated to admit it, at times, Pa was right. Sometimes the law can decide to make things difficult.

CHAPTER 10

RIGHT FROM WRONG

"FOLSOM PRISON BLUES"—JOHNNY CASH

After jumping on a burger and fries, Tinkey hit for a corner spot in the cafeteria. He had picked up a brochure on the way to school and fully intended to know a thing or two about court. Dub stayed in jail after being arraigned. He had to sit behind bars, in the Natrona Detention Center. All of the different courts and words used in them were completely foreign. Tinkey realized that no way on god's green earth was he going to help his buddy if he didn't figure out the lay of the land.

Sheila finally spotted him after surveying the concourse a great deal.

"Why ya sitting here all on your lonesome? You okay, honey?" she asked, in a completely disarming voice. He wanted alone time, but the tone of her voice pushed him back off that mood.

Sheila leaned towards Tinkey to hear him better. "I picked up this brochure this morning. It's got all the stuff that Dub has to go through. Stuff like preliminary hearings, then a grand jury deal, pretrial stuff and then finally the trial. It takes a lot of time. Lawyers talk with words like *voil dire* and the judge gets after them if they act up in court."

"Where did you come up with that lawyer stuff?" Sheila was carefully scrutinizing her food, moving pieces around with her fork to make sure everything was up to snuff.

"Down at the Circuit Court for Natrona. Other courts are in the place, like Municipal Court. That's just for speeding tickets and stuff. I got this thing and aim to straighten all this legal mumbo jumbo out in my head." Tinkey was saying it but wondering if it was at all possible. Lawyers had to go to school and had to study a bunch and even talked Latin once in a while. He thought some on how cool it felt to say voil dire and wondered if saying it made lawyers feel important. Probably not. He thought over the word and concluded it was probably like any other word used by folks. After a while its novelty would probably wear thin.

Sheila glanced between her food and the brochure as she expertly pushed unworthy food items to a designated spot on her plate. One was a shriveled up pea and the other was a chicken nugget that was the wrong shape. At least that's what Tinkey concluded as he smiled towards his own plate. He'd already told her a million times what Dad told him when he didn't clean up his plate. 'Problem with you is you ain't never been hungry'.

Sheila carefully nibbled some before pronouncing the nuggets gross. "God this is disgusting. You study at all for Trig? We got that coming up in fifth hour...ya know?"

"Ahh, shucks, babe, let's finish up. Can you go over it quick? I can pull it off, maybe sit next to you."

Sheila helping Mister Responsible with remembering a test! That was a first. He had always been yammering on about nailing math scores so he could get through engineering school and drive trains around. Sheila couldn't make sense out of why one would need to know math to drive a train. Tinkey had looked into the matter and was convinced he was correct, though.

Tinkey found out in short order criminal justice involved a lot of time. Entirely too much time, according to his figuring. If the court could just get its act together and mix things together on the same day, like preliminary hearings and grand juries, Dub could get back to school. The cops, witnesses, and anyone for that matter had to tell the truth in court or else it was contempt or even perjury. This was a big deal to judges. If they caught on anybody was lying his ass off in court, then it was perjury. Yeap, that's the word. Perjury. Near as Tinkey could tell, once they fetched the limp dick detectives into court, things could get back to normal. It irked him to no end that Dub had to sit and wait, and wait, for a date when the next court thing was going to happen. He missed prom, though there was probably worse things on the prairie than not having to dance with Butterface. Courts should giddy up and go so innocent folks didn't have to waste time sitting in jails and detention centers.

Dubs was going to be granted the privilege of visitation. Tinkey wanted nothing more than to hang out, do some ball busting, and make everything a-okay with Dub. He owed him that much. He always looked after Dub. Dub would have had his back, that's what friends are all about. Besides, Dub would feel pretty good just knowing Tinkey was studying up some on how courts worked. Yeap… it'll feel mighty fine to tell old Dub he'll be out before long. Besides, Dub was innocent; those cops wouldn't know the truth if they got bitch slapped with it by the Statue of Liberty herself. The truth would come out in Circuit Court. Graduation was coming up and it was bothersome to Tinkey that the court didn't seem much interested in letting Dub graduate.

"Mom, just why does the court take so long to get on top of things? It's not fair, near as I can tell. If Dub goes and misses graduation, how you suppose the judge'll feel? Bet that wouldn't set well with him. Huh?"

"Courts and laws and everything are pretty complicated. That's why there are so many lawyers running around. They do all kinds of stuff. Civil things like getting folks married. Why…I think a judge is a justice of the peace. Anyways, you sure been a good friend to Dub. Some folks done got him convicted already, but not you." Mom was proud of a son who was turning out as she figured any son should.

Tinkey thought some, inhaled, then slowly let out his breath, still thinking. "You know, you are innocent in this country until proven guilty in a court of law. Why there so many folks already figuring Dub went and committed murder? Don't go and make a lick a sense to me no how. Near as I can tell, you're innocent until the cops are in the paper claiming you did something. Then folks want to get to the hanging even before court commences."

He poured over the brochure, dug into any book he could get his hands on and hit the computer. Over and over he considered torts, retainers, and malfeasance. He's thoughts were forming a barrier against unfairness. He considered different angles on how he'd prove Dub innocent. Dub in a jail cell. That thought was crushing, so he liked to fill his thinking with legal words. It commandeered his thoughts. It feed him the hope he longed for. He wanted to have everything be as it should be in his world. The court was proving to be completely ineffective in providing any common sense relief. The detectives, cops, or whatever seemed to be really good at getting away with anything they wanted. Tinkey figured the shit would hit the fan if he and Dub could just hang on. In court, the truth had to come out.

"Mom, should I be like nervous or something about meeting up with Dub? I've been a waiting and a waiting and now I get to wondering some. I don't know what all I'll say. Should I tell him I don't figure it'll be long before this damn court puts him on the docket? You figure he must know he's innocent until proven guilty beyond a reasonable doubt? Anybody could have snuck that four wheeler out of the garage. *Anybody*. That's where the judge will get on top of this, they really smart. I just can't be so sure that the court will look in on it before graduation. You think he'll havta go to summer school?"

"Well, my word, you've done plenty of thinking on this. You just tell him the truth. You best let him know you'll put some time in with him to get his studies in order come summer. Yes, that's what you'll do."

"Yea, yea…but what about seeing him? It's just plain downright scary. Don't know why but it is. It's scary I gotta say."

Mom looked at her not so little boy and felt a surge of pride. "You just march in there and do your duty. You are just plain a fine young man and mother is proud of you. I was with my momma when she was a fighting cancer and it was scary. You go see Dub. There was no how I was anywhere near comfortable in that hospital. It's normal I expect to feel like you're a feeling."

Tinkey approached the Detention Center. Somehow that's what the people of means seemed to call it, whereas folks around town just called it jail. Oh, they had other names for it, The Crowbar Motel, Hoosegow, and Slammer. Tinkey was thinking of it more as the Detention Center than the Jail as he approached it. He provided his name by way of a dry throat, and then he had to wait. The legal process seemed to be more about waiting than anything else. Hurry up and wait, then wait some more. After a while he was directed into an area where he sat on some kind of stool facing thick glass. His heart was causing a rushy noise in his ears as he sat in silence.

Then he saw him. The sadness was inhuman and seeped from Dub's eyes. He seemed to be struggling in the depth of sorrow.

Thoughts screamed in this silent, pitiful place of a crushed spirit. Where once Rogers pounded bruises, now this hollow grayishness loomed. It all seemed to amount to nothing but a heap of suffering.

The pain shared between the boys stopped time. Dub approached as was his manner. He was stooped forward as if to hide the plain truth he was tall and gangly. His face was heavy, his hair ruffled. All over him he bore the marks of hardship. He reached out with one foot and planted it all at once. Then he hauled his entire body up toward the planted foot, before doing it all over again. Tinkey was transfixed until he realized it wasn't the place that was crushing them. It was the circumstances. He looked from Dub, before he commenced with the sitting process, realizing others were smirking. Prisoners, or inmates as they were called, guards too, seemed to be laughing and joking around. Everyone seemed to have different reasons for smiling. Shared stories, or perhaps hopes of a scheduled release from incarceration. Then he spotted Detective Fish enjoying the moment entirely too much. He was leaning across a counter staring at Tinkey.

"Dub...Dub..." No other words came out.

They stared some. Neither talking, neither thinking, but both breaking under the constant strain of a fading hope. Then Tinkey held his fist to the thick glass and Dub responded in kind. He bumped the glass with his fist.

"I'm going to...you gonna get...out. They got a Preliminary coming up next." Then his grief welled up and ran down his cheeks.

Dubs' tears flowed, too. "Out of here...w-when...w-why... Tinkey?" His face was more pitted and wrinkled than his age demanded.

No answers arrived with the tears. Tinkey felt the blackness pouring into his soul, blackness aided by a smiling detective who seemed to revel in their grief. All the pain and suffering folded into the moment, branded a single notion in Tinkey's thoughts. Something had to give.

Silence stole the time allotted to them until Dub was directed to the same door he had come out of. He never looked back. He never smiled. He only plodded back from where he'd came, with nothing but worries and he weight of a system pulling him down. The detective smiled, the door slammed shut, as the sunlight forced Tinkey's eyes shut. The tears had disappeared. Tinkey wasn't sure when, but he knew they had stopped. He had to do something, anything, because nothing wasn't an option. It was all wrong, he had no idea how, but he was going to do something. He was going to break Dub out of this mess.

Graduation was approaching. Sheila had her heart set on a nursing program. She wanted to take up her studies anywhere Tinkey landed. He'd always been pointed towards Kansas City and getting certified for operating trains. Only recently he'd started pointing out that he figured he'd make a pretty good cop.

"Why you want to be a cop? Are you sure? Are you going to still keep at it after Dub gets out?" Sheila didn't figure Tinkey would ever give up his train on the brain deal. For as long as she could remember, it was always about running coal trains around the plains. Now everything seemed to be about cops. How they arrest people, how stupid they are, and how he could do it better. But was that enough to make a guy stick with a career? She'd always known she wanted to be a nurse.

"Well, that preliminary hearing is scheduled a full month after graduation. I'm all for sticking around Casper. I can't get on the force until I'm twenty one. I can start volunteering; I can do some criminal justice training over in Douglas."

"Casper College has a two year nursing program. That'll work for me, but you ain't going to go and change your mind on me... right, Tinkey?"

Tinkey said, "no, no, I have to stick around here for Dub. He's going to miss graduation. He'd do the same for me. I wanna help him some. After that hearing he can get back on track. Besides, I can try and get on a track gang with the railroad until I'm old enough to cop. I don't do drugs, yeah; I'd be a damn good cop. I'd be better at copping on my first day than them assholes Gacy and Fish. I know Dub is innocent. I know them detectives set him up. They didn't see Dub driving away from Rogers place that night."

"How do you know? Why would they lie?" Sheila asked softly.

"Because I just do. You do too. You know Dub wouldn't go and hurt a flea. We both know that Rogers should be dead. He was an ass. Ain't right to do what he did. No way is it ever right to knock a woman around…or a kid. Never—NO—how." Tinkey knew his friend didn't do it.

They didn't get to sit together at graduation. They were on the football field and there were plenty of folks milling around the stands and track. Tinkey stretched his foot as far forward as he could, without making contact with the girl in front of him. It was crowded. The superintendent said too much and was followed by the principal and class president. Tinkey's thoughts were as far away as possible. He was thinking of Dub hanging on bars for another day, doing what he'd done the day before. Waiting.

Finally, the day they'd waited for. The judge was going to consider the evidence and throw the case out. Tinkey figured a couple of questions would set the record straight. Questions like how drunken detectives couldn't of seen anything they claimed to have. It was plenty dark out and they'd been drinking and were a ways off in a car. Another thing, how the key was left in the four wheeler in an unlocked garage. Anybody could have jumped on that four wheeler. Dub was tricked into what the newspaper kept calling the confession.

The lawyer was making plenty of money and should be able to set the record straight.

Fish and Gacy were talking in whispers, glancing around as if it was imperative that they keep the conversation quiet. They approached the prosecutor and shared friendly gestures. The defense attorney slipped over to the prosecution's table and leaned into it saying unheard words before they all laughed. Tinkey had gotten used to it. All this back slapping and grinning wouldn't piss him off as long as the defense got it right. He'd waited for what felt like a life time for today and knew it felt even longer for Dub. Sheila sat down next to Tinkey.

"Wow…you came?" Tinkey really liked her, and his voice showed it. Sheila was glad she had come. She knew all about wishful thinking and was worried about Tinkey. Sometimes folks go off and do something you'd never expect. They get worked up and lose it. Dub was getting messed with pretty good. He could've gotten riled up and just cut Rogers without thinking on it. Be pretty hard to have to see him using his mom for a punching bag. Was Tinkey right, though? Dub always seemed to be harmless. But why not call the cops? You can't just cut a throat like that. It was just gross thinking about it. She hadn't ever been in this courthouse. It had a little divider between the folks that came to watch and the lawyers. At least that's what she figured they were. They had on suit and ties and a mess of papers and books on a table in front of them. The two detectives that Tinkey didn't care for were standing and leaning over the divider. There was a high wooden place with flags towards the front of the room. Otherwise, it was pretty quiet in the place.

Dubs walked in and purposefully headed towards one of the tables. The smaller man next to the prosecutor marched back to Dub. The small man looked to be whispering a shady conspiratorial thought for only Dub's ear. Dub's eyes were staring into the carpet as the little guy continued to whisper in his enormous ear. Sheila knew he had no idea what the little man was telling him. She also got the feeling; the little guy was talking to Dub because talking seemed to be what he was supposed to do. She was trying to figure out how it felt to be Dub when she was startled into the present moment.

"All rise." Chairs and scuffling bodies were heard around the courtroom.

Sheila automatically rose along with Tinkey and everyone else in the room. Then the judge walked in and sat down and told everyone to please be seated. Other people were walking around, carry different things and acting important. Dub had sat down and then the state called its first witness. It was one of the Detectives who swore to tell the truth. His conversation, after saying who he was, caused Tinkey to stiffen. The *Casper Star-Tribune* reporter was busy writing on a pad. The detective was going on and on about clearly seeing Dub running to a four wheeler and fleeing the scene. Sheila rubbed Tinkey on his thigh. He'd just told her a couple of days ago the detectives would have to say the truth and told her what he figured the truth was. It wasn't nothing like what she hearing now.

Two more detectives were called to testify and one added the fact he that got a confession freely from Dub. The Judge ruled the matter would proceed to a grand jury. It all happened in a blur. Sheila dreaded having to talk this over with Tinkey. He wasn't going to take this well. She had felt him stiffen. He was just looking through folks. What if the cops were right? she wondered. They had been sworn to tell the truth. She figured the best way to go was to let Tinkey do the talking.

"Did you hear them in court?"

She knew who he meant without asking.

"Did ya? Running. Dub never runs nowhere. It was dark out. How in the hell could those cops go and see anything? They didn't, that's how!" Tinkey clenched his teeth. "That lawyer, he don't give a no never mind on whether Dub goes and gets kilt over this. It's a game. You see them laughing and stuff?"

Sheila was glad she opted for keeping her thoughts to herself. She never could remember Dub running, though, and it did happen at night. It was dark at Rogers' place out there on the outskirts of town. At first she figured the cops had it right. Then she figured Dub wasn't acting right. Now all of a sudden she figured Tinkey had it right. What would it mean for her and Tinkey if the law didn't start figuring out just what happened? She wanted everything, more than anything, to work out for her and Tinkey and…Dub.

CHAPTER 11

TWO DOWN
"PSYCHO KILLER"—TALKING HEADS

Some headed off to college. Some just hung out. His first summer out of school was about the same as every other summer. He stuck with Shorty's. Sheila was looking towards the future more than he was. She was working at the Garden Square Assisted Care Center and loved it. His plans had to be put on hold for matters of the heart. Once he figured out how to right the wrongs landing in Casper, Tinkey figured there'd be plenty of time for a future that included Dub, a railroad career and Sheila. Nothing was spinning in the right direction as of yet though.

Visitation had gotten easier. Dub never did much talking but did sparkle some in the eye on occasion. Classmates fell off the Casper portion of Wyoming to pursue futures including more schooling, the military or whatever.

Tinkey clung to his hopes, only to have them disappear into the wood chipper of the trial machinery. Lawyers would lope into court, strut and stretch some, and talk. They'd kick up a good fuss that never amounted to a hill of beans. Nothing made a lick of sense to Tinkey. Everything about the prosecution was wrong. The defense seemed to wallow as hapless as a steer done went and got stuck in quick sand. None of it was going anywhere. The judge could never get the lead out. He'd just lolly-gag into court and have everyone fawn over him. Nobody gave two hoots for how long an innocent guy was stuck in jail.

"Yo…Dub, Grand Jury time. They'll set this matter straight. So all-righty then, my man." Tinkey had built up hope on plain, common folks setting the record straight. He refused to listen to another voice in his thoughts. It whispered into his torment about nothing ever being right again. It said that Dub was gonna die, and he wasn't going to be able to do a thing about it. Dub was going to feel the prick as the poison-loaded needle slid into his vein. Then he'd just float away, knowing his life was taken away so unfairly. Tinkey pinched his nose between his index finger and thumb and squeezed until the voice quit taunting him.

"All-righty then…you 'bout have enough of this already?" Tinkey let his eyes wander past Dub up and down the gray walls.

"Ma-ma-mostly nothing, not a lot to do-do in here ya know." Dub stopped choking out words.

"Is your lawyer waking up yet…dude?"

"He a th-th-thinking we g-g-gots to plea bargain some. He f-f-figures it my decision but we gotta say I'm guilty so to get the d-d-death penalty to go way. Judges can d-do that."

Tinkey's vacant stare turned into a blow torch of a glare that seemed to be capable of delivering burns. "Look, you didn't do it. Goddammit. You ever tell that li'l bastard to shove it up his ass and just do his fuckin' job already?"

"Well he-he says I should do a p-p-p-plea and maybe fetch a l-l-life deal and not d-d the death penalty…he say it'll b-b-be a r-r-really good thing."

"That's lame, my man. You didn't do nothing and you know it. So all-righty then, what am I missing?" The voice in his head started whispering urgently, no matter how much Tinkey talked. He ground his molars, together but the whispering continued. 'How are ya gonna to deal with the legal folks?' 'How are you rein Dub in?' 'How are you going to right these wrongs?'

"It j-just izzz...I expect. Didn't ask him why." Dub pushed himself up in a mechanical fashion, spun towards the guard and was swallowed up in the dark hallway. Tinkey stared into the darkness without seeing it.

"Come on, let's go, Tinkey. Time to haul ass outta here." The beer bellied guard was wearing a plastered on smile in a disarming, I'm your buddy, don't give me any trouble, sort of way.

Lethal Injection. Wyoming sometimes killed folks. They belt you to a gurney. They slip a needle into your carcass. You get sleepy, real sleepy, your eyes shut and in ten, fifteen minutes you're ready for your last car ride to the cemetery and a dirt nap. Phenobarbital is the poison. It does its work painlessly. Well, who in the hell would know that, Tinkey wondered. Rawlings is where they killed innocent folks, or at least some of 'em were innocent. This time it would be different. Tinkey didn't have his thoughts in order just yet, but he was working on it.

Shorty's seemed to always be busy. After the system gulped Dub down, the paper, TV and radio people forgot. They were busy chasing new stories. Forgotten. Dub, Rogers and the big murder had somehow became just a memory, being replaced by tornadoes, car accidents and drug busts. Some folks had it figured ol' Dub was already down in Rawlings. Lives had to be lived. Acres of pizza had to be choked down and kids soccer games watched. As days drifted by, more and more of Dub seemed to slip away. Life just ground on, leaving all mistakes in its wake.

A new fellow had taken over for Dub in the kitchen. Tinkey liked the kid enough. Couldn't hold a skinny kid accountable on account of Dub. Cops, judges, lawyers, beer-bellied bailiffs, and jurors were a different story. They were in the profession of justice and had a duty to get it right. Tinkey thought it over and over while a smile slowly worked its way onto his face. A duty to get it right was what they had. If they didn't get it right, why then it was high time to do something about it. The smile indicated helpless tormenting whispers were being stampeded out of his thoughts by something new. Resolve. A determination to stop the silly little men in their aura of self-importance.

"Tinkey…wudja c'mere a minute?" Fish was sitting alone in the bar while Tinkey was stocking ice. Tinkey walked in and hadn't noticed him in the cool shadows. "I toleja Dub did it. I seen it, my own eyes. So he did the crime, now he gots to do the time. That's how it works, pal." Fish was nursing a beer that had given up its foam.

"I suppose you could think that. I don't know what to think is all. I knows what's right though. I want everything to be right is all, Mister Detective Fish." Tinkey was shaking his head slowly and staring at the floor.

"Yes-er-ree, y'll know wutchamacallit might get put down for what he pulled out there at Rogers' place. The attorneys are discussing it. They want to plea bargain it down to life. Yup, that's what our justice system boils down to…but I told 'em. I don't want any damn plea bargain. That's what I said. Ain't right. Rogers dies and Dub don't care nothing but how to save his own hide."

"Yes sir." Tinkey was saying as he walked back to the kitchen. "I'm a gonna be a policeman, ya'll know. All-righty then…time to be a getting back to work." Tinkey wanted to figure cops out and figured he'd study up on them some. He wanted it all to be like he knew it could be. It was on him to figure out what needed doing was all. The smile pulled his mouth across his face and lifted his spirits into something resembling hope.

Rattlesnake Hills was a whole lot of sand, rocks and patches of scrub brush. The Sweet Water River meandered towards the east. Tinkey was all on his lonesome as he picked his way around the rocks poking here and scratching there with his trusty stick. The sand had a crunch to it as he walked. He had a pair of gunny sacks tucked under his belt. The sky to the east looked as if it was splashed together from a set of water colors. Crimson red faded to orange and then yielded to a deep blue that was erasing the stars. Suddenly Tinkey heard a telltale buzz.

The three-footer was buzzing its warning and sliding back away from Tinkey. It kept its diamond-shaped scaly head pointed towards him but did not strike. The rattler slid its head back over its coiled body and then squeezed its coils back towards the head all over again in slinky fashion. The deadly buzz of the tail would slow some before it started up again. Its muscular body was covered in black and brown scales. It had a forked tongue that flicked out of its mouth, tasting Tinkey's presence. Its eyes were yellowish, sinister orbs slashed by the slit of a pupil. Tinkey tapped in front of it, and the snake struck instantly.

As he worked the snake up with his stick, he tugged one of the sacks out from under his belt and shook it open. The snake struck again but found nothing to pump its poison into. "Ahhh, you are an ornery bastard. We'll get along just fine, you and I." Tinkey pinned the snake's head into the sand with the end of his 'y' stick. "There—there." Tinkey said in a soothing voice that had absolutely no effect on the seething reptile. The poisonous beast wrapped its muscular body around the stick. With heart pounding and beads of sweat getting caught up in his brows, Tinkey did not want to do what he did next. He reached for and seized the serpent behind its head. The snake felt rough and was easy to hold onto. He peeled and pulled the slithering body from its grip on his right arm. He carefully played the snake out until it went from frantic to an exhausted twitch. The snakes rattle end was carefully lowered into the sack before Tinkey was absolutely certain he could drop the entire creature into it. When he felt the weight of the snake hit the bottom of the sack he quickly tied it off and realized he hadn't exhaled for some time. He allowed himself that luxury only after he laid the bag down gingerly.

The second snake was harder to come by. It took many miles of dusty strolling always aiming for the next boulder or rocky ledge. The sun had fallen towards the west before another snake was dropped into its bag. Tinkey hadn't eaten. He hadn't even given food a thought as he had continued on his rattler expedition. The wind blew some as he wiped the dust build up from his brow. Snakes caused his eyes to feel like they needed no blinking and demanded he whisper to the silent countryside. His tormented thoughts relaxed some with his activity. Highway 220 got him pointed towards Alcova. Before getting there, he pulled onto gravel, which was more a cow trail than the minimum maintenance road the state of Wyoming had declared it.

The road had been washed out and contained pot holes that caused the bagged passengers on his truck bed to buzz angrily. He didn't put much stock into partnering with nasty rattlers but was glad he had. The buzzing reminded him he was doing something. It was about time someone got them varmints for getting after Dub. Determination pushed him towards doing things he never knew he could do.

An ancient wire fence was his clue that he had arrived at a certain spot on the endless prairie. He pulled towards the side of the trail as if it was necessary, picked up his dangerous cargo and followed the fence to a mostly dry rotted, caved in line shanty. In a prior life he had spent plenty a night hanging out in the old shack. It was a perfect spot for high school innocence to lose some of its luster. He stepped up onto the creaky boards and entered the facility. He tugged an old closet door off of its last remaining hinge and laid it across the entry. The kitchen door hung in place, though he had to shoulder it shut. Perfect. Nice spot in the country for him to leave his partners. Wasn't a soul around that was attached to any ears. Any amount of screaming would be lost to the endless sounds of the prairie.

He heard the steady buzz that pulled him out of his slumber into the yet to be hot morning. He missed the alarm on his first swing but found it the second time around. Up and at 'em he thought as he swung out of bed. He knew he had a nightmare but couldn't remember it. Today could be the day. He'd have to be snake patient and only strike when he was sure. Absolutely certain. He'd seen how those critters do their killing on *The Discovery Channel*. The snake, in a blink of an eye, got its fangs into something and spit its load of poison out. If a snake wasn't in the mood, for whatever reason, it could hold off on the spitting deal. It could just dry bite and not inject poison. That wasn't acceptable as far as Tinkey was concerned.

He landed on the kitchen chair, realizing mom had beaten him into the kitchen and was already putting the finishing touches on some pancakes.

"You missed supper, honey. School run late?"

"Yeah...I got a test coming up in my Criminal Investigations Class." Mom always said if it was necessary to lie, then something was wrong. Oh, how right she was, he thought, as he lapsed into more lying. He'd get his business in order before too long, then put an end to it. He hoped so anyways. He didn't like the feel of his mom's eyes while he was dodging the truth.

"Well, you going to be home tonight?"

"Steak special tonight, Mom, be home late unless I got to go over the test with the guys. Don't worry none," he said automatically while picking up speed for the door.

"Oh, I won't worry none if you promise to be careful." She never turned around from rummaging in the cupboard. "How you fixed for insulin?"

"I'm good. Thanks, Mom. I should be good for the week."

He tossed his ten-speed in the back of the pickup and headed back towards the shack. He didn't want to be late but couldn't figure out a better way to get ready. He thought over his Criminal Investigations class and how easy it all came to him. He hadn't missed a day. Couldn't. Something might come up that would help Dub. He gorged on the police sciences. He had to know. Fingerprints, self-incrimination, DNA applications, the whole deal. He was hungry.

"Sheila, where are you? I got a test, man. Come on…Christ." It was crazy he thought, when he was late, how come Sheila always managed to be even later? He pushed the truck door open, but Sheila was headed down the stairs, two at a time. She trotted across the yard, brushing her hair.

"We got to haul ass, babe."

"Yea, sorry, didn't see you pull up. Why ya so late?"

"Alarm didn't go off." First Mom, now Sheila. Lying had become a way of life for him. Two down, and he was thinking he wasn't even in school yet.

"You waiting on me after your last hour?"

"No, gotta work. I'll swing by on my way home…tonight is snake night."

"God, gross…Tinkey…how about steak? Tonight is steak night."

Tinkey laughed the slip off.

Tinkey was always full of questions. Criminal Investigations was just the start. He was going to enroll in Constitutional Law come winter. Most of the others in his class thought it sucked when compared to Tactics or Investigations. Not Tinkey. Anything about courts and cops. He wanted to know it all. His burning interest pushed him to the top of his classes. After racing through his test he headed to Shorty's. One question regarding legal procedures, bugged him and he promised himself he'd look it up to make sure he understood it. That was the only question he had about the test, figuring he aced it.

Steak night was on. Seemed like every cowboy brought his gal in for a bite. Some of the cow girls had started ordering chef salads, which were harder to make up than a club steak. The guy that took over for Dub was good. He was fast and picked things up quickly. That all made it easier on Tinkey. Before they knew what hit them, the dinner rush was usually over. Tinkey'd be mopping. The new guy would be wiping up in the cooler and taking care of the counters.

"Later for you unless you have anything else for me to do."

The kid knew his place. Tinkey appreciated it. He was also still in high school and figured Tinkey was old. "All-righty then, see you around, buddy. I'll lock down the kitchen."

Tinkey watched him disappear into the evening. He then laid back into his thoughts realizing everything was about to change. He walked out into the lot after locking the door and looked for the vehicle he knew was parked there somewhere. He'd slipped back towards his pickup and had to hang out for who knew how long. It had to go according to plan. He fished around and doubled checked everything. Fish usually only hung out in Shorty's on Tuesdays. He'd have his steak, some beers, and talk shop before heading home.

Tinkey slouched down in his truck but was in no danger of falling to sleep. Not tonight. He was on, not as much as he had been with the snakes, but he was on. His teacher had gone on and on about how the rule of law made the American Judicial System the best in the world.

Tinkey had pointed out nothing is perfect, including the law. The professor had gotten the last word in as professors tend to do. He had said something about the American System of law being the worse until it's compared to any other system in the world. He might have laughed along with his classmates, but he knew. He was the keeper of secrets only he could do anything about. Tinkey felt the cold steel of his pistol in his jacket pocket. It was a .38 caliber Smith and Wesson with rough wooden handles. It was a six shot. It would do.

The door swung open and Gene, Bill, and Fish stood in the bug-infested yellow glow of a single bulb over the door. Laughs broke out and hands delivered farewell back slaps as final farewells were exchanged. Gene worked for the street department and was a pretty good guy. Bill was retired from something. Tinkey stared, realizing the time had come and he hoped nothing would mess it up. Dub had waited long enough. Waiting another week would be like waiting forever. It would be worse than waiting. Gene walked off before turning and waving, then jumping in his truck to hightail it home. Fish was laughing and pointing at a backward-stepping Bill, who also turned and jumped into his car and pulled out of the lot. Great. Luck seemed to be the order of the evening, at least for Tinkey.

He quit thinking it all over and wondered how he'd know when to do it. Then he just slipped out of his truck and it almost seemed like he was watching himself approach Detective Fish.

"Say, Detective."

Fish turned. "Oh, it's you. What now? More crap 'cause Dub didn't do it?" Fish got in his Bronco and rolled down the passenger window to hear what Tinkey had to say. He spun his head slowly towards Tinkey while raising his eyebrows.

"No, not that at all." Tinkey spun and hoped the lot was as dark as it appeared to be. It was getting to the point where he couldn't back out. "Let's keep your hands on the wheel." Tinkey kept the pistol close in towards his body as he pointed it at a suddenly very interested Fish.

"Whoa...kiddo, what's this? Why, you're just plain being un-neighborly."

"All-righty then, head down 220, so as we can talk some." Tinkey pulled the door open and slid into the truck. "Or else, I'll blow that empty hat holder off. Got it?" Fish was staring down the barrel of the gun. He'd never done that before. His predicament was catching up to a brain that did not believe what was happening.

"You don't a need to have that thing pointed at me, Tinkey. You and me, we both on the same side of the law. Ain't that right...*boy*? So what's this all about...*son*? You going into law enforcement, you're out at the college. Ain't that right? So what? Has this got something to do with Dub?"

Tinkey suddenly snatched Fish's Glock from its shoulder holster. He had Fish unarmed quick as lighting. They had practiced that in Police Tactics.

"Slow down, here...turn ..." Tinkey didn't want him to miss the turn. Fish had to look hard before realizing there was a trail or something to pull onto. They bumped and bounced westward before Tinkey smiled and had him stop. "Look, Fish, you've been a good cop. I don't want you making like a superhero tonight okay? So I'm a gonna snug up your wrists some so as we can have us a right nice conversation. I ain't a planning on a doing you any harm."

Fish was too pissed to be afraid. Tinkey was wondering why he ended up lying again. Fish was unarmed, roped, and all on his lonesome before he knew it. His angry thoughts fought it out with humiliation. If his fellow officers found out a green horn went and got the drop on him, he'd never live it down. Never. They'd laugh him off to the Laramie Mountains.

"Now...now, we a gonna take us a little stroll is all, over yonder. Pert near a perfect evening for us to a...be a...spending some time together. Hoo-wee! What a night…Huh?" Tinkey tugged Fish towards the old shack from the end of the rope binding his wrists together.

Fish couldn't bury the 'fuck you' glare that was burning out of his eyes.

"Get along little doggie—get along." Tinkey sang to a cop on the empty prairie. Fish opened his mouth but then slammed it shut before any dark fuck yous escaped. He was the cop. He called the shots. He strutted around town…so how'd this squirrel jack him up? Little bastard would pay…every dog has its day.

Fish stomped up into the shack working as much of the anger out of his bones as possible. Tinkey secured him tightly to an old oak pillar that had long given up its decorative luster. He then went to the caved-in, dry-rotted, mouse-piss, stunk-up kitchen and gazed over at two gunny sacks on the floor. He moved with purpose. He had looked over this scene again and again in his mind. He slid a baby food jar from his trusty fanny pack. It had nylon pulled over its top, secured in place with a wide rubber band. He quickly dumped the inactive, stiff, snake onto the floor, causing an immediate, angry, buzz.

"Boy, there a snake in there, son? Be careful now, you hear?" Fish concentrated on the buzzing, not wanting any harm to come to his captor. That would put him in a pickle. Tied up like he was. "Goddammit, boy, you a-hearing me?" All he heard in return was the steady drone of the gusty wind. Fear finally pushed the anger from him. "Oh, come on, please…" Without effort he whined, in a tone, about like folks tend to do when they'd been handed a ticket for doing thirty-five in a thirty.

Tinkey didn't take notice of the whiny little voice. He had pinned down the snake, picked it up carefully, and slipped the fangs into the nylon fabric. He'd seen how they do it on *The Discovery Channel*. Milk the venom outta the nasty critter. Sure enough, it worked. Thick, yellowish drops pooled in the bottom of the jar. He felt the swollen glands and slowly squeezed the gunk out of them until it stopped squirting onto the side of the jar. The snake had wrapped and unwrapped itself around his arm tightly. He topped the collected poison off with the next snake's venom. He then injected himself, later than usual, with his insulin and promptly filled the syringe with the fiendish, killer spit. He slid in quietly behind Fish, who was struggling against the ropes. He froze up as if he was a lawn ornament upon feeling his pants leg being pushed up from his ankle.

"Boy…boy…boy. You listen to me. Stop this please and let's talk. That's what you say this is all 'bout is talking. So why you sneaking around behind me? What are doing with my leg—huh?"

Tinkey held the syringe up, admiring the poison. He tapped on the side of it before slowly pushing it into Fish's whitish calf. The skin resisted and was pushed into an indent before the sharp point plunged deeply into surrendering tissue. Then it was time. Tinkey pushed on the plunger and watched as the liquid disappeared into flesh.

"Kid, what the fuck…that stung. What are you doing? My leg is burning up."

Tinkey refilled the syringe. After all, Fish couldn't survive. Besides, snakes always leave two fang marks. One wouldn't do. He slid the needle into Fish where he figured a second fang mark belonged. After dumping the load of nastiness into Fish, he slipped back into the kitchen and snagged his fanny pack. He walked up towards a bluff, feeling a surge of gratitude for having pulled off what he did. He was pleased that his reptilian friends had come through for him. Tinkey was leaving them high and dry without any venom and watched them crawl off into the sage brush.

"Ahh, fuck, what'd you go and do kid?" Fish struggled against the rope and had his eyes firmly closed. "Wooow, it burns, c'mon kid,

I never." He was talking in a whisper really quickly, as if he wanted to save energy in the face of losing precious time. "Kid, be careful now...I heared a snake back there...don't want you a getting hurt any. Listen, kid, what's this about? My leg's on fire."

Time was racing on. The full moon had pushed up from the eastern sky until it glowed brightly down on the Wyoming countryside. Tinkey wondered if it would be landing behind the western horizon before Fish went to where ever sleaze ball cops go after putting in there last day on earth.

"Look, I never done you any wrong. Thought we were out here to talk. You weren't a gonna hurt me any, right? So look, why my legs on fire? Why? I feel I'm a gonna puke my guts up? What the hells going on?"

"I'm mighty sorry I hadda go and pull this stunt, Fish. You done wrong, though. Okay?"

"How? How you go and figure I did any wrong, is all I wantta know?"

Tinkey stepped around him and spoke slowly. The story, penned up inside him for what felt like forever, stampeded out. Only after every word of the truth was regurgitated did Tinkey lapse into silence and some kind of peace. "Pretty easy to fuck with kids when you're prancing around Casper with your badge, isn't it? You screw with kids, don't you, Detective Hamilton 'Albert' 'Ubby' fuckin' Fish? You said yourself you wanted Dub to get lethally injected. Best be careful for what you wish pal 'cause you been injected for crimes against kids. You in the court of...Scott-fuckin-Tinkersley now. Whoeee...allrighty then! You also been charged in Honorable Tinkersley's court for impersonating a cop. Give you a lethal injection for crimes against teenagers. Yessiree, you a gonna smoke a turd in hell, Detective—*sir*. How does that bite ya?"

Fish's breathing was becoming labored. The fire appeared to be spreading all over him. Sweat rolled down his face. Before long spit bubbles appeared in the corners of his mouth. The leg started swelling up to where it looked like it'd pop. A filthy blackness took the place of the initial redness around the punctures. Yellow paste and sticky black tar started oozing out of the holes that were being pushed into slits by the swelling. Tinkey could actually smell the gruesome process. Fish had soiled himself and his breathing was no longer regular. He'd stop all together, and Tinkey would get the notion he was done for. Then he'd snort and gurgle again. Tinkey had had enough, but wanted to make sure Fish was really on his way before he cut him loose. He found it hard to believe a healthy dose of rattlesnake juice could do in a big bad cop so fast.

After a couple of hours it was evident that rattlesnake saliva was indeed nothing to mess with. Fish's face had swollen up, and his spit had changed color as it dribbled down his chin. He'd make squeaky, whiny, whistling sounds and started appearing too tired to breathe. His eyes were out of focus and not blinking. Fish's breathless spells started lasting longer and longer, threatening to put an end to the breathing all together. Tinkey dragged himself up on legs that had fallen asleep and carefully put weight on them until the needling sensations disappeared.

Fish collapsed full force to the floor after being untied. His wrists weren't bruised from the ropes. Tinkey positioned his legs and carefully went over the area. He had never been near the place without gloves on. Nothing was left at the scene. Lighting was in the sky. If it rained it would only help with the problem of tracks. He snapped on his fanny pack for the bicycle ride back to Casper. He swept a Russian thistle behind him, erasing his tracks. The scene was as he wanted it to be. He was learning plenty in his law enforcement classes and was excited to put the newly acquired knowledge to good use. He hiked his way all the way to 220, but not before slinging Fish's keys away from the Bronco. Perfect. He then headed to where he had ditched his bike along the highway.

After duck walking up towards the highway, Tinkey peeked down the road, making sure the coast was clear before pushing his bike up onto the pavement. Gee whiz. His own brand of justice had been carried out. Tinkey got on his bike and pedaled back towards Casper. Adrenaline carried him quickly from the scene. He was smug in the knowledge that improving law enforcement wasn't all that tough. He had stuck to his plan and carried it out without a hitch. Or had he?

CHAPTER 12
ANOTHER ONE
"COP KILLER"—BODY COUNT

"Yo, Dub…ya hear? They went and found Fish deader than road kill! Whoee, pal. He was hanging out in the Old Shack. Nobody knows what it's about. Cops ain't saying much pending the investigation or whatever. The counter crowd is a-talking plenty. They a sayin'…snake bite…dude. He was up to no good. He was supposedly out there all on his lonesome. Yeah, right. Probably drugs…I mean, who knows? He was always hittin' on the country girls. Didn't bat an eye as to whether they married or not. That's it, a pissed-off hubby probably caught up to him. Who knows? One thing for sure… dude…his lying days is long gone. Can't hurt. In court I mean. What your lawyer's thinkun'? Huh."

"Lawyer said they still g-got Gacy. The confession is taped. Wa-we still g-gotta take the plea I'm a expecting."

"Whoa…say what? You mean to tell me that lying bastard is six feet under and they still got a case against you? No way! Ain't right no how in my book. He's the sonofabitch that went and jammed you up."

Dub pulled his stare up to look into Tinkey's eyes. That meant something. Order of their visits usually consisted of a whole lot of staring at the floor and throat clearing. Then it happened.

"Ya-ya-you know what a lawyer and an a-apple have in common?" Dub stared at Tinkey, who was too startled to keep his jaw from going slack. The Dub from the past had finally showed up. "They both l-look good hanging from trees." Dub laughed.

"All-righty then…why in the hell did you confess? Why? Why did you go off and say all that stuff on the tape, Dub?" Tinkey and Dub sat in silence. Tinkey wanted to know. "Dub…you couldn't go and kill nothin' is all I know. So why in tarnation you'd say it? That you did it?"

"I'm tired inside, p-p-places y-you know, whu-where s-sleep can't find it none. Tired, like way down in my b-b-bones. Them there d-d-detectives went and said what I should say, so I said it is all. Didn't figure there'd be much harm in s-s-saying it. Somebody went and kilt Rogers, so why they don't get the real, f-f-for sure killer? is what I wants t-to know. Cops got schooling. They l-look at e-eve-evidence is all. Right?"

Tinkey had thought and thought about this. It just didn't add up. No way detectives should go and want to put words in a fella's mouth. He hadn't had the Interviewing and Interrogation class just yet, but felt he already knew better. People don't just go and say they did something when they didn't do it.

Dub was looking up from the floor where his face was pointed. "I-I went and said I-I did it. Hadda. T-they l-let me know how to say it. La-like cutting his throat 'c-cause I got to figurin' ma…" He rubbed his hair as he started to get up on his paddle sized feet. He continued to dig his fingers into his hair, rubbing in circular motions.

There it was. He went along with it because of his ma. Always protecting her. Rogers laid low then Dub got to talking and made it so easy for the cops to look good solving a murder. Fish is dead and it still can't be right. Gacy couldn't find his hand in a snow drift. Now he's the copper gonna keep messing with the truth? Well at least the dim wits weren't gonna get on top of Fish and his death. If they're so stupid they'd nail an innocent feller, then they probably too stupid to ever figure out what really happened in Old Shacks.

"Sit back down, Dub, *please.*"

"Near as I can t-t-tell…hashing this over ain't g-g-gonna maa-make a lick of difference."

"All-righty then, Dub…why'd you bring up your ma? What's she got to do with this anyhows?"

"Well—*she*, ahh, I d-didn't want them there detectives g-g-getting after her any—"

It started making a whole lot of sense. Tinkey was none too happy with what became so clear, so fast. Dub was a taken' care of his ma again and that screwed everything up. She probably had an alibi, but then Dub had to be the hero. Who wouldn't take care of their kin, though? That's what good folks do. But Christ, Dub's good intentions were really making it hard to straighten this mess out. She was the one that should've put an end to Rogers and all the whup-ass he was a puttin' down on her and Dub. It was plenty stupid is all. How could Dub ever reckon his ma could go and cut up Rogers? He didn't know, so how'd Dub come up with his story? What did he say, the detectives told him? They told him what to say to land on death row. Is that what good police work is all about?

"Dub, did you say the detectives told you what to say in that confession?"

"Well, ya-yup…t-they sure-sure-ly did."

"Why ain't that on the taped statement, then? Don't make a lick a sense."

"Oh y-ya it does. They took a b-b-break is all. Fish wha-was really f-fine and da-dandy 'til I says what he wanted to h-hear. He turned off the recorder, ta-took a-a break so he could s-scoot and get me aaa c-coke is all. Then Mr. J. W. g-ga-got me caught up on what really happened. I didn't rightly know what to say as to-to how m-ma, I mean m-m-me, how I kilt Rogers. I'm plenty glad he d-dead, Tinkey, you know?"

Deputy Beer Belly started approaching them, making the "come here" gesture with his index finger. Dub started positioning his feet under him.

Tinkey remained seated, mauling everything over. Another jailer startled him out of his thoughts by putting a hand on his shoulder. The jailer smiled and winked, asking him if he wanted to spend the night. The joke hit Tinkey as more funny than the jailer ever figured it could. He walked towards freedom realizing some would figure, he should spend the rest of his days in a place like this.

They had been going over serial killers in class. Criminal Psychology. Two down and how many to go? Tinkey didn't know, but he didn't exactly take kindly to the notion of killing again, even if he had to. Guys become soldiers and do plenty of killing, picking up medals and stuff for killing. No one goes and calls them serial killers. Dogs go and get to biting folks and they gotta be put down. Sometimes, things just gotta be taken care of.

> don't know if writing can straighten it out in my head any i thought it was better but it ain't how much more I gotta do to make it all good and stuff? near as i can tell it aint no better not yet it aint better   Dub bugs me is all

The unexpected demise of one of Casper's finest was big news. Everyone was talking. They were recalling him, Officer Fish, as being a wonderful officer who somehow always just wanted to help good ol' folks out. People were crying about it on TV. The town started bracing for the funeral. There were plans to have horses, bag pipes, and probably a bunch of crying cops. Tinkey didn't share any of the anguish. He just couldn't understand how nobody, but nobody was setting the record straight. He'd heard the rumors about Fish and his womanizing. Folks said he was horny enough to fuck a pile of rocks if he thought a snake was in it. Now everyone was making like they were big-time friends of Detective Fish, how he gave his life doing right.

The professor entered the room solemnly. He was wearing an expression usually found only in a casket. "Listen up everyone, police work is always, first and foremost, about being involved with the community. The Casper P.D. is going to need assistance regarding the arrangements for Detective Hamilton Fish. He always helped out around here. So we should do something for our brother in blue. Anyways, sign up on the sheet out in the hallway, if you're interested."

Everyone in the class seemed interested in volunteering for the event. It was a good way to start putting together a resume, and besides, everyone wanted to be a part of it. Great feelings came with being in the middle of something everyone was talking about. The instructor had explained the need to be involved in the community on the first day of class. Stuff like rodeos and parades, though he never mentioned a funeral. Tinkey wanted to work with and get to know real, honest to goodness officers. Good way to look good where he might end up working someday. Near as he could tell, the Casper P.D. was going to be hiring more officers real soon. He didn't see any other way around it.

The funeral was big-time. A sergeant was at a fenced-in area where all student volunteers had been directed. They all wore yellow and purple jackets designating them as Law Enforcement students. Tinkey was assigned to a place in the rear of the church and told not to let anyone wander into the basement. He entered the church and slid along a wall waiting for his eyes to adjust to the dim lighting. It was the proper thing to do, look tired and blue at a funeral even if you weren't. He squinted and hung his head low like everyone else seemed to be doing. After spotting the stairs he stood in front of them stiffly, with his hands locked behind his back. His expression didn't change.

The funeral director arrived with several assistants and they positioned the gray casket perpendicularly to the door. It was opened and a flower arrangement was placed 'just right' on top of the casket. A table with pictures on it had been arranged next to the casket. Tinkey noticed that Fish was laid back with his head sunk into a satin pillow. His stiff fingers had a rosary folded around them. He looked a lot better in the casket than he had tied up to the post. Tinkey heard the wailing before he saw them. A plump lady dressed in black approached the casket. She was holding a hanky over her face and wailing. "Why, oh why, did it have ta be Albert?" Tinkey could see her shoulders heaving as she slumped in front of the casket, a tall skinny fellow rubbing her back. She turned, noticing Tinkey.

"Oh, thank you, young man, for taking time for O-F-F-I-C-E-R..." but then shook her head and put a hanky over most of her face. "Did you know my Ubby? Didja? Huh?"

"He was a good man...ma'am, I'm just glad I got to be a part of his life. It was because of him, you know, that I got involved in police studies." Amazing, Tinkey thought, he couldn't even go to a funeral without having to lie a little. In a church. God knew, though. He knew Fish belonged in a really hot place. But the other half was true enough. Fish was, in fact, half the reason, he got involved with police work. "Yes, he certainly is in a better place with the angels." The heavy-set woman hugged Tinkey hard, thanking him for taking time for her Ubby.

The service, once started, went on and on. Tinkey spotted Detective John Gacy up towards the front of the church. He seemed to be commanding attention, or so it seemed to Tinkey. The media were asked to be respectful of the fallen officer's family and to be low key. No cameras, flashes, that sort of thing. Preacher Rypenski tossed a ton of kind words out for the fallen member of the police department. The words didn't impress Tinkey at all. Christ, he thought, what would happen if a really good officer went and got his ass bit by a snake? It was amazing to be a part of the spectacle. Nobody seemed to be concerned with adultery landing an officer in hell. He'd heard the rumors plenty. Mom had said it was all just about being polite. Tinkey concluded it wasn't nothing but a whole heap of nonsense. Then it 'came' to him. He couldn't go through anything like this again. It would have to be different. If he had to kill again, he'd see to it that it was a 'complete kill.'

Nobody gave him any problems, everyone preferred to stay out of the church basement. People were being 'funeral' polite. The entire crowd shuffled out the door for the cemetery to plant Fish once and for all. Tinkey was forgotten, as everyone hurried out of church, hell bent on not missing anything. Tinkey hung out in the empty church.

"Man, oh man, can you believe he was a cop all that time, then steps on a snake? Ten-Four!" a fellow classmate and volunteer asked Tinkey.

"Just goes to show you, ya just never know when a snake is gonna mess up your plans. You ever see that Fish in any classes or helping around the school?" Tinkey asked.

The classmate cast glances around, ostrich-like, eyes too big for his face, with a whisker here and there. "Nope, but I heard the Professor say he done did that."

"May be he was just stupid. I mean, who dies nowadays from snake bite? You'd think he'd a got his butt to the hospital, wouldn't ya?"

Ostrich boy just looked at him while sucking air into his mouth. "You need a Ten-Ten? I'll watch both our posts—" He let his offer hang, while his head bobbed in pigeon-like fashion.

Tinkey considered the offer from the skinny lump of ignorance. He wondered if Fish sprang out of such stupidity. Perhaps it's a survival of the fittest deal and Fish damn sure wasn't fit near as Tinkey could tell. Killing someone just because they're stupid isn't right though. It's when stupidity and authority are smashed together that dying can become necessary. Kinda like a horse that breaks its leg. Can't do anything about it once bad things happen. There plenty of good cops around, but somewhere, there has to be the worst cop ever. That's the bad stuff gotta be culled from the herd. Fish was shot up with a little old snake spit cause he earned it, plain and simple. All this crying for Casper's fallen hero was a waste of time in his book. Almost like citizens needed a good cry like they had to water lawns at times.

The killing could have been better. He knew it. He screwed it up again. When you finish off an ignoramus, you got to let people in on it. They got to understand some of the whys. Save a boat load of Kleenex.

After the grieving members straggled back to the church, he found his place again. Tinkey knew practice makes perfect. He figured he didn't have to be to awful hard on himself. Fish was a dick. Not the detective kind, but a real, honest to goodness dick. He left a family plenty upset. But, then again, even dicks have friends and family to cry over them. Executioners aren't crying and carrying on. Nope. They're just doing their job. He figured he'd get better. He had to. Besides he was learning. He was just doing his duty was all. A sly, smile started working itself up onto his face before it dawned on him and he squashed it.

"Scott Tinkersley…I appreciate it. Thanks for being here today. Means a lot." J.W. Gacy! Impressive. He approached Tinkey with his hand extended.

Tinkey stepped back before catching himself. "Why thank you, sir, thank you very much. It has been my honor. It really has, Detective Gacy."

"Well once you got away from that Dub character, I gotta say, you've done alright by yourself." Gacy patted him on his shoulder and thanked him again while they both headed to the parking lot. "I didn't expect you to change your colors, but I guess you coming around and understanding law enforcement. We officers. We're family. We take care of each other."

The friendliness sparked a question Tinkey was burning to ask. "All-righty then. Why'd you go and coach Dub? He told me so. While Fish was fetching him a soda you was getting' in his face…tellin' him what you wanted to hear. Reckon that's what…coercion? near as I can figure."

Gacy snarled a reply as Tinkey realized how he'd asked the question. "Goddamit…prove it…bet it ain't in the taped confession. Christ…Dub is gonna get his comeuppance. GET OVER IT!"

The blank numbness accompanied Gacy's words into Tinkey's mind as he decided then and there. It'd be better. One more, but it would be complete. Training and experience make for one kick-ass cowboy who'll git 'er done. He wouldn't leave Casper in turmoil this time. He'd see to that. The good citizens would know, is all. He should have thought of it with Fish.

Mom's friend had her house burglarized in broad daylight.

"Tinkey, I'm so glad you're going to be a policeman. We need all the help we can get. Can you imagine? I never. It's shocking. Why…what's becoming of Casper when folks have to go and lock their doors?" Mom's friend, Judy, had rotator cuff surgery and was on medication. She had stopped by and was sitting at the kitchen table.

Tinkey looked startled. "What did the thief or burglar get away with?"

"Not much. They dumped some things over. I suppose they were looking for jewelry or money. Who knows? And just think...it was during the *day*. How did they even know a body wasn't home? They checked the bathroom and took my medication, for this shoulder. You suppose they needed it?"

Tinkey appeared to be thinking, as he was tapping a pen against his front tooth.

"No, it's drugs to them. They get high on that stuff. Them there painkillers is called Hillbilly Heroin, no need to a worry any. I don't expect they'll be back."

"Oh, dear me." Miss Judy held both hands over her heart. "Why I never, my name's on the jar. Can I get in trouble or something?"

"No, you aren't going to get in trouble, Miss Judy, but if the burglar gets caught with them pills he'll be in trouble, big-time. The police listed the drugs as missing, isn't that so?"

"Oh, yes, they did, and a detective even came over. His name was Detective J.W. Gacy. He said they'd try and solve the crime. That's what he said."

Tinkey smiled, said he had to get going, jumped up, and bolted for the door.

The grand jury had handed down an indictment for a capital offense. The lawyer had told Dub they do this all the time. It's just a formality, so it was completely expected. The prosecutor gets to say and do anything he wants. The rules get tighter during the trial in front of a criminal jury. He still advised Dub to consider the life without parole business. This had upset Tinkey. He was afraid Dub would simply do what was asked of him. Justice seemed to trample anybody unlucky enough to have the cops get after them.

He kept clear of Gacy as much as he could around the station. While doing ride-alongs, he always listened and was always polite. He'd been warned that a 'certain' detective didn't care for him, and he was on a short leash.

Shorty's was a place offering wonderful opportunities to acquire tidbits of info regarding what Gacy was up to. Gacy was married once, though it ended when his wife got sick of the drinking. The divorce led to more drinking until finally Gacy took the cure. He had actually earned a pin at AA for staying away from booze. He liked fishing down on the Platte and even spent time on the Columbia salmon fishing. He'd land in Shorty's on occasion, though he was never considered a regular. Patience was the key for the perfect execution of the execution. Tinkey liked how that sounded.

After months of nothing, something finally happened in the Walmart. Tinkey had been hauling ass to pick up some oil in the rear corner of the store when he spotted Gacy. His prey. He felt like a spider that suddenly detects a treat struggling on its web. His pulse quickened in anticipation of the wonderful opportunity he found himself in. He'd been waiting for what seemed like forever. He also still had his hoodie on. That was good. When you're seizing opportunities like Tinkey was, you didn't want to show up on surveillance videos.

"Umm...good evening, Detective Gacy, sir." Tinkey smiled shyly.

Gacy considered him with a grunt and muttered..."Need some six-pound spider wire. Then I gotta pick up some Preparation H. I feel like I had a barbed-wire enema, for Christ sake." He winced in pain, as if merely saying the word was reason enough to cause his hemorrhoid's to flare up. "Look, kid, Dub ain't on my agenda tonight. Okay?"

"Umm, I can help. I'll snag some oil and meet you up at the front of the store with the 'H.' I'm truly sorry, you know. I didn't mean it. I mean for what I said in the church. I want to be in the law enforcement family, like you said."

After checking out, the off-duty investigator and his hooded companion walked out the automatic doors into the cool Wyoming evening. The Walmart was up on a hill overlooking the fairgrounds. They walked slowly towards Gacy's Chevy pickup. Tinkey wondered why he hadn't spotted it in the first place. He promised himself to be more observant in the future. He'd be a better cop if he was more observant.

"Have a nice evening, sir. You going fishing, I bet. Heard they're hitting down by the yard." He was hoping that would be enough to ping Gacy's interest. The detective seemed to clearly want to catch fish that involved as little driving as possible.

"Kid…thanks…have a good one." He was distracted by the roaring fire raging under his beltline.

Tinkey smiled and walked away from his prey. Gacy carefully positioned himself behind the steering wheel. It was taking some time. Tinkey trotted to his truck and got in, with time to quickly scan the contents of his fanny pack. Everything was in order as he waited for Gacy to pull out. Now if he just took the bait, why everything could get so much closer to being right again.

Gacy slowly pulled out of the lot, making sure to miss the pot holes. Tinkey gave him time to get out into traffic, figuring he knew where he was headed. No use in alarming him. Next piece of the puzzle that needed to fall into place was to have nobody else down by the river. There was a walk path from the parking area that went up over the tracks, before dropping down to the shoreline. True enough, the river had bushes and tall grass along the banks. It was still in town though. People could be around. There were always trains running, night and day. A large yard was located along the Platte surrounded by a community that had sprawled around it over time.

Gacy drove slowly into the lot avoiding bumps and pot holes. He was taking the bait. Nice. Gacy fetched his pole, tackle box, and soda then started his struggle towards the river. Tinkey was scanning the area, it looked clear. Tinkey unzipped his fanny pack and put his latex gloves on before fishing the Smith and Wesson out and putting it in his hoodie pocket. After this, he snapped his pack on. He walked downhill and across the controlled intersection towards the river. He could see the setting sun coloring the Wells Fargo Tower bright white.

He knew the terrain well. It took no time to catch up with Gacy, who was staring down his pole tip. He watched from a smattering of buffalo grass. It was already pretty dark when Gacy cranked his line in. "Fish biting…my ass." Tinkey heard the mumbling.

"Huh, Detective Asshole…"

"What didja say?" Gacy spun and saw Tinkey in a combat stance with the Smith and Wesson pointed at his chest. "What the fuuu—"

"Hands out, we got some talking to do. I don't want you pullin' any superhero stuff. Got it?"

Gacy smirked. "You're fucking with me, good one."

Tinkey produced a loop of nylon rope. He was thinking it was his modus operandi. He learned that term in his law enforcement studies. A great modus operandi is what he was about. Just takin' care of business. He quickly placed a loop of rope around Gacy's wrists.

"Whu…this, this better be good. You asshole, you got a funny way of getting into the little ol' law enforcement family. This 'bout Dub again? I told you already buddy boy, he ain't no bedder then horse-maa-newer. Okay pal, I ain't got nuttin' else to talk to you 'bout." The contempt slithered out of his wet puckery mouth.

"Drink this, JW, or is it Detective Gacy tonight? Drunks tell the truth. Don't be stupid sir, bottoms up." Tinkey's icy stare revealed his determination.

Gacy, eye brows mushed down, took the Gatorade bottle and smelled it. "This ain't Gatorade, boy."

"Oh-yeah, c'mon, really. I'd be much obliged if you'd just down it, so we can talk some and then giddy-up outta here."

"I'm an alcoholic—huh. That your game? Fuck me up with a lit'le juice? Well, I'm bigger than that, you little worthless bastard." His hands balled up into fists and he suddenly stepped towards Tinkey, who quickly pointed the pistol at Gacy's face. "This on account of Dub...huh? Well I'm bigger than a damn bottle of whiskey." He gulped the Jack down, not realizing that it came with a wallop of Oxycontin for good measure. The booze bit into Gacy, and he was immediately reminded of how right liquor made things. It'd been a long time since he'd downed some Gentleman Jack. He had put his feelings for Mr. Daniels out of his thoughts, but he'd never forgotten. Love is a hard thing to dash from heart and soul.

The concoction took hold faster than Tinkey could've imagined. He watched Gacy gulp the entire bottle. The pistol had become heavy in his hands, as he wondered how long it would take. Gacy's face flushed, his eyes lingered on pleasant thoughts, and he choked out a tune. "Campfire girls, wontcha come ta play...come on out... and dance...the moons a gotta some light. Oh...I-got-a-tiger-by-the-tail." Gacy smiled some and wondered if he'd get to down another bottle for the little bastard.

"Up...up. Up and at 'em. Let's go." Tinkey steadied Gacy, as they started up the path from the riverside towards Gacy's dying place. "Buddy boy...I'm ahhh fucked up some. Whoeee." The words were all mashed together and gurgled through a lot of spit before escaping the mouth. Tinkey slipped Judy's empty bottle of oxy into Gacy's pocket. A reverse pick pocket. Tinkey figured if anyone happened to see them they'd figure he was just helping a drunk up from the river. But nobody did see them. It was dark.

He'd been pushing some Cheerios around in a bowl of milk when Mom was talking to her friend Miss Judy. She was plenty concerned about her upcoming surgery. He rode along to Judy's with his mom after the surgery. Perfect. He knew when his mom left the house to take Judy to physical therapy. He knew where the Oxycotin was. It was easy. Tinkey slipped into the house, grabbed the Oxycotin, and then tossed stuff around to make it look like a burglary. Then Gacy had actually investigated the burglary. Too good to be true. The paper would choke on this sordid tale of a cop done gone so wrong! His plan was working.

They only had to go so far, but it was a struggle. Gacy, mumbling and stumbling, was tugged in the right direction with the soft rope around his wrists. When they stopped, Gacy had to support himself against a bridge abutment.

"Boy, you ain't a bad boy is all I wannnna to say is all. You got moe of the Jack?"

"Shush now, and I'll get you some. We gotta wait. I hear a train a cumin'. You got anything to say on account of Dub?" Tinkey slipped the rope off Gacy.

"Who?" Gacy stuck his finger in his ear and wiggled it violently as if to clear his head.

A Burlington Northern locomotive, with ditch lights on, roared past them at the head of what looked like an endless string of hundred ton hopper cars. Tinkey guessed the maroon hoppers were loaded with wheat. The cars had compressed springs, indicating they were full. Tinkey heard the screeching brakes down the line as the engine fought the string of cars to a groaning halt. He knew the train would be shoved back into the yard where it came from. The big purring diesel's exhaust blew back over him and with it brought on memories of times long ago. He and Dub had spent hours enjoying the switching operations that seemed to go on continuously.

Gacy had no comprehension of the noises that were coming to him. He didn't hear the release of air from the train or the diesel revving up to push the monstrous cars back into the yard. He didn't hear Tinkey coaxing him forward, nor did he feel the push that landed him under the hopper car. Tinkey spun and ran down the trail to survey the vacated fishing hole. That was part of the plan. It was completely dark now, which was to his advantage. The trail was stomped full of shoe and boot prints from many fishermen but he was going to toss his shoes. He was going to get rid of his hoodie too. He was not allowing for any error.

He crouched, military fashion, as he rapidly scooted up the trail and heard the steel groan as the train started to roll backwards. He suddenly didn't like the idea of having left Gacy out of his sight. But he quickly realized he needn't had to worry. He stepped out along the sagebrush and crouched by the bridge. The flanged steel wheel, rolling on shiny rail, slipped evenly through Gacy with the ease of a knife going through soft serve ice cream. Gacy's head, shoulders and some of his chest rose slightly, while being neatly severed from his stomach and legs. It wasn't all that gruesome. A nice and tidy red line marked the place where the wheel had cut him in two. His head, face down, and chest were between the rails, and his stomach and legs were alongside the outside of the track. A blood splat from the wheel stained the rail over and over again as it rolled on. Meat and tissue had been squished onto the top of the rail and blood had spilled out.

Tinkey slipped from the scene by scooting under the bridge and trotting up the path. He had to get back to Walmart for his truck.

He didn't want to be too late for his law enforcement club's meeting. They were voting to see who was going to be president tonight. He figured being club president couldn't hurt his chances of copping someday. Just a little something for the ol' resume. He realized the Casper Police Department was going to be hiring soon, and he was kinda bummed that he wasn't old enough to apply yet.

CHAPTER 13
ACCIDENTAL DEATH
"TEAR IN MY BEER"—HANK WILLIAMS

A police car sped past him as he pulled into the parking lot. He had figured it wouldn't take long and it didn't. They'd found what he wanted them to find as soon as the engine backed clear of the body. It was certainly a better effort than his first go round. A complete kill. He felt proud of what he'd managed to accomplish and how he was making contributions to improve the police department. He yawed as he waited for Sheila. If Rogers could have amended his ways none of it had to happen. If the cops had set the matter straight he'd of not been late for his meeting. All he wanted to do was work on the railroad. He had it all figured out. He and Dub working on the railroad. He had Sheila. He got along with her better than anyone. The only time he got under her skin was when she was talking and he had other things on his mind. She'd howl some and he had to admit that he was getting worse. She didn't understand him though. He had a lot of things on his mind, like studying law enforcement and applying what he was learning. It took skill to kill. Anyone could kill someone, but a complete kill was different. No, anyone could kill, but not like him. He killed when he needed to. He would kill with skill. He was learning. It was an art. To kill completely—take the life as well as everything people thought they were. Destroy it all, and then apply the final touches to leave the cops scratching their nuts. Sweet.

She smiled and approached him bouncing her ponytail.

"Hey—"

"Hey back, we got to hurry. I can't be late. We're having our club elections tonight."

Sheila was talking about things and Tinkey was nodding and smiling at what he was hoping were the right times. This was his third kill and he couldn't keep his mind off of it. Would this make a difference for Dub? Did he forget something or was he going to get away with it again? Were the cops still as stupid as they had been the first two times? The thinking game bugged him. He wished he could kill like the lions on TV. They just killed and ended up dozing. He figured he'd thought of everything this time. Asshole John Wayne Gacy was a thing of the past. The discovery of drugs in his pocket would make for great reading in the papers. Yes! Gacy, the perfect detective, solving crimes while committing burglaries. None of that hero crap about how great a community servant he was.

"Hey…slow down. Something's happened down there on the tracks. God, there's like cops all over. See, right there, Tinkey." Sheila was pointing and squinting her eyes towards the lights.

Tinkey jumped back into the presence of Sheila. He had thought she had caught him again just doing the pretend game. "Yeah, something's up big-time. Maybe a train accident…"

"Let's go down there…come on…you could learn something about police work." She was squeezing his hand while leaning forward to see past him. "Think someone got hit by a train? There is a train stopped down there on the bridge. Yeap…I totally bet that somebody got hit by the train. The path runs down there to the river. Didn't you and Dub fish down there?"

"We gotta get to school." Tinkey was thinking it all over. He'd ditched his hoodie and shoes. He had worn latex gloves. No one had seen anything, as near as he could tell. "If I know this town…we're gonna know everything done happened down on that bridge before long."

"*Nooo*, come on, Tinkey. Let's go down there and check it out. Everybody's down there…let's go…"

Tinkey didn't think going back to the scene was a good idea at all. He didn't like it. It wasn't in his plans but now Sheila'd gone and got herself all in a lather. "Really, come on, I'm like serious…god you're no fun now that you're in cop school."

"Okay already. Christ, I'll pull over, then."

It was tricky getting across the street. Cars were slowing down and everyone was checking out the tracks. Tinkey had Sheila by the arm and directed her to the path. They worked their way down towards the scene. Things came into focus as they got closer. Yellow tape was tied around a lit up area. The train was stopped, shining its bright lights on the scene. It made the final approach to the police tape easier.

"God, that light is bright." Both Tinkey and Sheila said it together and then laughed before the solemnity of the event put an end to it. Several people had heard their approach and turned towards them.

"Tinkey, a fisherman is up on them tracks, dude. Train went and backed over him. They got that blanket, like, totally covering him. Why they cover him up like that? You go to cop school. You know, right?"

Tinkey leaned into the whisper…"it's to keep gawkers from getting too grossed out. You know, like us."

Sheila stared on, speechless.

"Tinkey, over here…come here." One of Casper's finest was motioning for him. He had met Tinkey while giving a demo up at the school about arrest techniques. Tinkey gave a quick look around and slipped under the tape and approached the uniformed officer.

"Can you get your ass up to the street and help the M.E. down?"

"Yes sir!" Tinkey was no longer uncomfortable as he suddenly realized he was a part of the action. He knew Sheila was going to be mighty impressed with her Tinkey. He turned and told her and some of the listening public he'd be right back.

After getting back to the scene with the medical examiner, Tinkey was left to kinda hang back as the officers approached the blankets tossed across two lumps on the tracks. Tinkey cocked his head toward his shoulder and listened in. One of the uniforms pointed and said it was Gacy. The M.E. knelt down and touched the head before straightening up.

"Accidental death…looks like he didn't wanna wait on the train. I'll make a blood draw and you boys can get him out of here. How you fellas doing?"

There was no answer, but the investigator turned towards the M.E. "Think I can collect his personal affects? I gotta head to his folks' place over towards the refinery."

The M.E. glanced at the investigator. "John wasn't a drinker. I'm thinking I smell alcohol here. You photograph the scene already? I want to check that Gatorade bottle over there." Investigator Dean Corll nodded up and down to the question. The examiner gently picked the bottle up with two fingers towards the bottom and opened it. After smelling the opened bottle, he capped it quickly.

"Whiskey. He couldn't've been back on the sauce for long. Just seen him at our last meeting. I know the Fish deal hit him hard, though, really hard, guys."

The examiner made a quick blood draw by pushing a long syringe between ribs, piercing the heart. Tinkey had to look away.

Corll knelt next to the bottom part of the torso and checked the pockets. He held up a wallet and dropped it into a plastic bag; he also found a comb and keys. When he checked the jacket, he discovered the pill vial, and scanned it quickly, before palming it and dropping it into his own pocket. He then pulled his empty hand out of his pocket and looked slyly to his left and right. He spotted Tinkey and smiled quickly and finished up his search. Tinkey couldn't look away. The sight of the pill bottle discovery was the culmination of a very grand evening. His plan had worked out after all. The officers zipped Gacy up in a body bag and had to hose off the scene with a pumper truck.

"Well, I guess you're one of us now, boy. You always visiting your friend in the jail...didn't catch your name." Corll smiled in spite of what his duties had just required he perform.

"I'm Scott Tinkersley, sir, and thank you for letting me help out here tonight." Tinkey was getting the feeling he'd be one of the best officer's ever on the Casper Wyoming Police Department. He knew there were several officers who were getting up there in age and besides, they were dropping like flies so far. He wondered why the state had a minimum age requirement in the first place. Seemed awful unfair to a guy who was under twenty-one.

"We need to chew this over some. Why don't you walk with me back to the road? Can your gal pal manage on her own?" The detective wanted to talk to him. Tinkey figured it would be really interesting to hear him out. He was just a first year law enforcement major after all.

"Now, Scott Tinker—"

"Just call me Tinkey. That what everybody calls me, sir."

"Okay, Tinkey. Now that you're one of us sometimes things happen that are better left unsaid. Just because you think you heard and saw things don't mean you can go shooting your mouth off all over town. We have to respect Officer Gacy, we surely-surely do."

Tinkey felt very much like he'd arrived. He smiled and cleared his throat…"Oh, yes, sir, you mean about Gacy getting intoxicated and falling under the train. Oh yes, not a soul. He was on pills too—" and immediately wished he hadn't gone that far.

The detective spun on him and said in a low menacing tone that only kept getting lower…"you open your fucking mouth over any of this and you'll have to dig a size twelve outta your ass. You gotta know what the code of silence is all about, pal."

Tinkey stared numbly at the path and followed the silent detective back towards the road. Sheila had been just ahead of them and spun when he approached her. Her feelings about Tinkey were all over her but she suddenly stopped. She stared into him realizing he was plenty upset. She felt guilty for having dragged him down to the tracks. It had been her idea the whole time. The rest of their night was mainly silence and hugs in front of an unwatched TV.

"Tinkey…honey, wake up." Tinkey was rolling away from his mom's voice until his memory put his situation into focus.

"Yeah…yes, Mom…what?"

"Another detective died. Last night. Down by where you guys always fish on the Platte." Mom was focused in on the story. "He was that detective we were interviewed by…about Dub. Oh, dear…I can't remember his name, but we met him. You'd know him. Um…was his name Gacy? He's the cop who talked to us."

"Yes, mom, that's the name."

"He was drunk and fell under the train?"

That comment slapped Tinkey wide awake. "How didja know that, Mom?"

"Why lordy, y'all know this town. Gossip, gossip, gossip. Whatchoo want for breakfast? We can talk some over fettles."

Somehow the town had it all figured Gacy got drunk as a skunk and fell under the train. Tinkey thought really hard on it. Would Corll think he was shooting his mouth off? That he couldn't keep his trap shut? It just didn't make sense to him how stupid all the cops were he was running into. He had midterms coming up. Dubs finally had his trial coming up. It seemed like forever since he'd landed in jail. A year and a half is forever when you're young. Dub's ma had started running with another fella and they carried on 'bout like she and Rogers had, though he hadn't heard of her running around at night in sunglasses. Not yet anyways.

The news was reporting that Casper had lost yet another one of its finest. It stung. He had put so much work and planning into killing Gacy properly. He'd done everything right. Everyone was talking about how terrible the death was. Gacy had fallen under a train and had been sliced in two. Fish getting killed like he had, musta been too much for good ol' Gacy. He fell off the wagon and landed under a train. Folks were feeling mighty sorry for another one of their fallen heroes. Tinkey wanted to puke.

The funeral was going to be another humdinger. Tinkey had had to sneak into a house and get the painkillers. He had dreamt up a perfect, complete kill, and then Corll hides everything. Corll had put the vial in his pocket and ditched it. No one was talking about the drugs, no matter what mom said about gossip. They were doing a toxicology test, and they weren't going to come clean with the info. Tinkey knew he had put enough Oxycotin in the whiskey to knock a horse off its hooves. He had left the vial in Gacy's pocket so the dimwits would know what to test for. Is this what it's really all about? Do cops always take care of their own? Is that what Corll meant? The code of silence? The truth only matters if the cops figure it matters? The blackness was in his heart and soul. It had eclipsed any lingering shine of hope. It had established permanent residency in Tinkey, with the officers of the law paying the rent.

Tinkey was bracing for the trial. Finally, months had somehow added up to a year and some before…Dub was going to have his day in court. Fish and Gacy were gone.

Tinkey sat behind him after the bailiff had escorted Dub into the courtroom. The community of Casper had lost plenty of interest in Dub after he'd spent so much time in jail. The room wasn't even full. Some media, some people crying before court even got under way. Tinkey figured the mourners had to be some relatives of Rogers. Dub's ma had shown up with her new boyfriend. He wore beat up horse shit smeared boots with a hang dog expression. His shirt had holes but was tucked in. Tinkey waited for her to stop whispering to Dub before he made his move.

"Dub…what does Gacy dying have to do with today?"

"My attorney, he s-says that he gonna g-go and argue ta-to get it out of c-court. That t-t-tape the detectives went and said was m-my idea. My lawyer, he says it's good those two r-r-rascals are laid in their g-grave. He didn't go and say i-it but it's what he meant. W-what's the d-difference between a lawyer and a v-v-vulture? The law-lawyer gets free-f-frequent flyer miles."

The joke was great. Not that it was funny. It just felt great to hear a joke from Dubs. He was somehow surviving in jail. Tinkey figured he'd have gone and cracked up by now if he had to sit in a cage and watch the sunrise through bars.

"So all-righty then, Dub, your lawyer can spring you out of here?" Tinkey felt like he did when he'd spot Sheila headed his way. She always made everything 'Tinkey' better.

"Well...yeah...I figure that's what h-he went and meant."

The prosecutor entered the courtroom from the side and talked with the folks who were all worked up. She was wearing an expression that said she was feeling their pain. Tinkey watched her lean towards the crying folks, whisper something, and nod towards Dub. The prosecutor was putting on quite a show.

The room was silent 'cept for the shuffling of papers to the accompaniment of the flap-flap of tired ceiling fans. Tinkey was wondering what must be going through Dubs mind. He was on trial for his life. The prosecutor already had told the court that she wanted to kill Dub. The prosecutor had used a whole bunch of legal words and numbers about why the state would seek the death penalty. Tinkey smiled as he realized the prosecutor was probably squirming plenty on account of two stone-cold detectives and a case that seemed to be unraveling. His mind drifted across thoughts of him and Dub hanging out again. Camping, drinking, and tearing around. They could even get back to Kansas City and get going on railroading careers.

Dub's attorney finally strolled in and sat his case down on the table opposite the prosecutor and nodded at Dub. He then meandered over towards the prosecutor and got going with the chummy talk. This annoyed Tinkey to no end. He wished the attorney could hate the prosecutor just a little on account of what she was trying to do. She was all about murdering Dub no matter she kept harping on and on that it was the state that was going to do it. Tinkey didn't figure the prosecutor had no business speaking for the state when she was so dead wrong. Whenever he was around the prosecutor the blackness seemed to glow even more darkly.

"All rise."

Tinkey jumped up as Dubs and the rest of the crowd got to their feet.

The pretrial was a whole bunch of legal mumble jumbo with the lawyers standing to discuss motions and act angry. Tinkey couldn't quite figure it out. Were they friends or not? He liked to hear Dub's attorney using a voice laced with anger. May be Dubs had a chance after all. His attorney was presenting a motion to suppress evidence based on the fact no one could actually state it was an authentic recording. The prosecutor was hopping mad over the motion referring to prior actions in the proceedings. Tinkey figured he had it right when he started seeing the courtroom as some kind of Big Top full of clowns. The judge took the matters the attorneys had been talking about under advisement and disappeared through a door.

CHAPTER 14

MORE AND MORE

"SYMPATHY FOR THE DEVIL"—THE ROLLING STONES

Tinkey swung by the jail and dropped money off for Dub. He didn't figure he'd get to hand deliver it. It wasn't during visiting hours and the jail staff followed most of the rules religiously.

"Howdy, Tinkey, you old scoundrel. How's it hanging?" Beer-Belly Bailiff asked with a smile.

Tinkey smiled, knowing he was building on a great chance to get hired by the Casper Police or Natrona Sheriff's Department. Detective Corll had even been plenty friendly with him after chewing him out. The detective had gone out of his way to let the others know that Tinkey was a good guy. Someone who could be trusted. It was so easy, Tinkey thought. All he had to do was keep quiet about a certain officer who could've burglarized a place for some Oxy, got drunk, and fallen under a train. There was more to copping than meets the eye, for sure. He knew he couldn't call Corll out for ditching the painkillers. The vial was, no doubt, long gone. The intoxication level was no big deal. It wasn't criminal or anything, so, nobody would be raising a stink. Now that Gacy had met his maker, he wouldn't be in any courtroom spewing out lies. His life had been cut short when a train sliced him in two which could only mean good things for Dub. Or so Tinkey hoped.

After yucking it up with Beer-Belly for a while, he headed for Sheila's place. They both had class. He never had a problem with any of his law enforcement classes. He was always totally focused and willing to push himself if he didn't get something. Laws, tactics, and criminal procedures galvanized his attention resulting in 'A's. Everyone figured him as a natural, high achieving and future police officer. Nobody, not Sheila, Dub, Mom or anyone realized the growing disgust his increasing knowledge of the profession was resulting in. The more he learned, the more he knew that policing wasn't for him. He didn't like the feeling that slipping into a uniform somehow made a person better than the rest. The whole Casper's Finest deal. Once Dub was sprung, he was done with law enforcement. It was that simple.

"Oh, there you are sweety, my little police-see…" She squeezed his thigh as she fastened her seatbelt.

"Naw, I reckon that being a cop isn't for me."

"Why you taking the classes then? Huh?" She thought he was joshing her.

Tinkey drove on and lowered his voice. "I don't know. Cops are always standing in front of memorials. Looking like heroes and stuff. But I've seen 'em lying and cheating. Screwing around. You know, I just couldn't be one thing and then act, like, I was all high and mighty, is all…I reckon."

"Well, you wouldn't have to be like them guys, then."

"Yeah, I know, but what kinda life is it where you havta hang around with guys like that? You know, fellas that are always hiding what they are really about. You know they have a word for it.

Professional courtesy is what they call it. That's why cops don't get speeding tickets or anything. Then unions and city attorneys are always covering up for cops. They call that Data Practices. I mean, law enforcement gives me that feeling like ya have, leaving ahh porta-potty, on a hot day. You know, that grossed-out feeling. I'd like to stick to running trains around Wyoming is all. I'd like to work with regular folks who aren't always you know, pretending to be something they ain't—perfect. Me and Dub can do it, too. I just know it."

Sheila had started talking plenty lately 'bout how so and so had gone off and gotten married. Last weekend they had gone to another wedding, and Sheila had been maid of honor in Butterface's wedding.

"Well…what about us?" she blurted out, but Tinkey was already springing from the car, hollering that they'd be late if they didn't get a move on.

Dub missed prom, graduation, and now some weddings because he was all but forgotten behind bars. The judge couldn't have cared less that Dub was locked up and left without much hope. Only occasionally did the regular old cooters mention Dub while sipping coffee at the counter.

"Do the crime…pay the fine. Tinkey there, you used to be a friend of Dub, didn't ya? What da ya think…son, put him down? He ain't nothing but a waste of taxpayer's money—*right?*"

"Everybody innocent until proven guilty in a court of law is what they say in my Criminal Law class. I figure Dub is good enough to deserve his day in court."

"Whoa, kiddo…you sounding more like a lawyer every day." Everyone burst out laughing, with one exception.

Tinkey slipped into his usual front seat in Criminal Psychology. He had kissed Sheila good-bye in the hallway and realized it wouldn't be long before she was the next Tinkersley. Today the class was going to discuss some real scary folks called serial killers. The instructor entered the room and talked with a couple who had a question about the dates of upcoming tests. It bugged Tinkey that half the class always seemed more hung up on tests and scores instead of what really mattered. Serial killers were a lecture subject that could crunch hours into minutes.

After clearing his throat the instructor said, "Now, the Federal Bureau of Investigation defines the term...serial killer as...'a series of two or more murders, committed as separate events, usually, but not always, by one offender acting alone or, including the vital characteristics, a minimum of two murders.' Often, a sexual element is involved in the killings, but the FBI states that motives for serial murder include 'anger, thrill, financial gain, and to gain attention.'"

Tinkey's spine straightened, while classmates were busy taking notes. Two or more murders in separate places by one guy. Anger is the motive. Am I angry? Yea, I'm pissed at the judge, at how long the legal deal takes, at dead, snake-bitten, and drunken dicks. I can't stand mechanics who are women beaters. That's three, but I'm a soldier, in a fight to make it right is all. I only kill 'em when they need a good, complete, killing. Okay—okay, not sure how Rogers happened, but it did. He messed with me first and it happened before I could think on it much. Fish, tricky Fish, he didn't go and interrogate Dub at all. Nope. He set him up, is all, and now he's dead. Gacy? He figured Dub was guilty and told him what to say to make sure Wyoming could do him in. That ain't how I've been a learning to do police work. An investigation is supposed to uncover the truth as it is, not as the detectives or cops think it is.

Ted Bundy, he's a serial killer. Rogers had more in common with him than I do. Ted beat woman. I don't. Nope, there are some real weirdoes out there killing folks, but I ain't one of them. Besides, if the cops did their jobs I wouldn't have had to take care of Rogers in the first place. I'd have never figured cops out if it wasn't for Rogers.

"Yes Tinkey, do you have a question?"

Tinkey's eyes were furrowed as his thoughts kept getting in the way of his words. "Let's see now. If a soldier kills someone one day, and then more on another day, he ain't no serial killer. He's just a hero—*right?*" The class erupted in laughs for reasons Tinkey didn't get.

"Well, killing in battle is sanctified. I'm thinking your inquiry is more directed towards a discussion based on philosophical grounds."

Tinkey swirled a pencil around in his hair not following the instructor's response. "Well, okay…what 'bout a guy that hasta kill cops cause they're gonna kill somebody? An innocent guy, how about that?"

"Now Tinkey…A person is authorized to kill another person in self-defense or in the defense of others, but only if that person reasonably believes the killing is absolutely necessary to prevent serious harm or death to himself or to others. If the threatened harm can be avoided with reasonable safety, some states require the person to retreat before using—"

Tinkey butted in, "I get it, then. Sometimes you might have to go and kill a cop if you're defending yourself or a friend or something—right?" He thrust his pencil towards the professor, in a fencing motion, as he said each word. "Stand your ground."

"No, no. That's not it. You seem to be considering unlikely scenarios. In the event police officers were in the commission of a homicide you'd best be advised to report it. If you start taking action in events involving justice, taking the law in your own hands, then you'd be what's referred to as a vigilante. Vigilante justice is rationalized by the idea that legal means of law and order are nonexistent or insufficient. Vigilantes typically see the authorities as ineffective in enforcing the law of the land. These individuals often justify their actions as necessary and good."

Tinkey nodded to indicate he was agreeing with the professor. His classmates were getting restless because the subject had gone from serial killers to something far less interesting, vigilantes.

"Well, now…we are getting off the topic here. I think what you're discussing is vigilante justice. That's not acceptable. There are checks and balances in place to address misbehaving police officers. Now, let's consider the case of Albert DeSalvo…"

The professor launched back into his lesson plan. Tinkey had heard enough of the ideas dished out during the exchange to satisfy his means of thinking. He was no serial killer because he had no legal recourse. If he didn't do something about what he knew was wrong, Dub would pay with his life. He was only about making matters right. He had plans. He was going to marry Sheila, finish up the Dub matter, and work on the railroad. He was saving for a diamond. He was waiting for the Dub mess to clear up. Then he and Dub could head to Kansas City for schoolin' before his wedding.

Tinkey swung by the jail. He and Dub went over their future. Dub thanked Tinkey for the cash and asked about Shorty's. More and more waitresses and others had moved on while he sat in jail. Casper was changing while Dub was stuck, lost in front of gray walls and unbending bars. He knew his ma was running with another man. She came and saw him.

"What does your lawyer think of the motion? Can the judge get your butt outta here? I wonder if you could've afforded a better lawyer if you'd be out of here. This is wrong, Dub. You don't even hunt cause you ain't no killer. Only thing you'd probably kill is a snake. Ain't that right? Even if a snake went and helped you out some, by nailing Fish. Can your lawyer say that in court? That you're non-violent?"

Dub just stared at him. "Judge already ruled. Next thing I-I-I do is have a jury s-selection and then fine-finally my trial. T-the judge called m-m-my tape ad-admissible. Wyoming is g-gonna as-ask to go an-and have m-m-me kilt if the jury says I-I'm guilty. I'm mighty t-tired, Tink-Tinkey. I-I c-can't make hide nor hair of any of this. All I just wa-wanna d-do is ha-hang s-some with ya out by the P-Platte. You knowed that t-time you hollered s-snake. I'd give 'bout an-anything t-to have you pull that s-stunt a-a-again. It's mighty powerful l-lonely in this ha-here place. I-I'm tired is t-tall. Really t-tired all da-the t-t-time, issss all."

"All-righty then...heads up, dude. Come on, Dub, stay awake, fella. We come this far and we gonna see this thing through."

"I'm m-mighty o-b-liged to you, Tinkey. I'm plain g-glad to call you my f-fu-friend. Lots of friends wouldn't s-stand by folks like-like me in a j-jam like this. Ain't no-nobody from class swing by. Hu-how folks go-gonna t-treat me if I find a way out-ta here anyways? I-I d-don't know. They saying in jail...I get out of her-here there are guys onna outside g-go and string me up. You n-n-know I didn't go an-and hurt Rogers. You n-n-know it Tinkey?"

"I know, I know. I only wish I could conger up a notion as to help you out is all."

"You going to c-c-cop school. Tinkey, can't you figure out w-who really c-cut up Rogers?"

"I know you didn't do it, Dub...but so far I gotta tell you, I'm plain buffaloed as to how to prove you didn't do it."

The bailiff approached while swinging a large set of keys around in his hand. Tinkey's visit was over.

The trial date was set for autumn. Tinkey did so well in his law enforcement classes that he was on the Chancellors List. He knew several cops and a deputy and continued his ride-alongs. Sheila was wondering just what she was getting for Valentine's Day, as if she didn't know. He had asked his mom for help on that business, and she delivered.

"This was your grandma's ring. She loved you and just look... how lovely...it is. Of course if Sheila doesn't take a liking to it, you can surely get another setting. But your Grandma is smiling down on you, son," Mom said, "and she's mighty proud of how you've turned out."

"I don't know, Mom. Sometimes I wonder on just how I've turned out. Dub in jail. Me and him were gonna run trains. Now he's locked up in that place." He pointed in the direction of the distant Detention Center, "I figure I belong in train engines with Dub. More learning I put down about them cops, the more I know I don't wanna be a one of 'em. Sometimes, Mom...I just wonder. I got it figured right, them cops are just plain folks like anyone. Then they get to believing they are a cut above us. Special in their uniforms with medals and badges and stuff. That's when they get in trouble, when they start believing their own bullshit. Oh, sorry, Mom."

"Oh, dear, but you got a lot on your mind. You'll make a wonderful policeman, just you don't worry about that. Dub, he couldn't do any better, finding a friend like he has in you. God works in strange ways, the parson is always saying, he surely does...son."

"Well, thanks, Mom, for the ring, I mean. Well, for the talk and everything. Thanks. I got to get to work. It's steak night. See ya." He grabbed his keys and almost forgot to kiss his mom good-bye in his mad dash for the door.

The courthouse was a lot busier than Tinkey had come to expect. News cameras were sitting around on tripods. News gals were putting makeup on, and some were wandering around with microphones looking for anyone to pounce on. Tinkey arrived early, not wanting to get stuck out in the hallway to watch everything on a monitor. A news station had even made it up from clear down by Cheyenne. After so many days and nights in jail, Dub had landed in the middle of a three-ring circus. Tinkey thumbed his way through his Criminal Law book to hide the fact the court proceedings were so near and dear to him.

"Excuse me…sir. You know the defendant…would you please be so kind as to comment for me?" He looked up into an incredibly beautiful face, all dolled up in makeup.

"No, I don't have nuttin' to say." Thoughts were screaming in different directions threatening his orderly thinking.

"Was he a good friend? Did you think he could go and do something to have him…you know…like end up here today?" Another reporter leaned over the first one's shoulder. "Do ya think he's remorseful for what he did?"

"He didn't do a thing, I tell ya. It's a case where a fellow is locked up for doing what the cops says he did, but he didn't. I know that much. He's a good guy is all I know." Tinkey felt like his mouth had gotten away from him so he shut it tightly.

The prosecutor showed up in a bright red dress, made up about as much as the reporters were. The makeup didn't have the same results on her looks as it did for the reporters, though. Dubs was dressed up about as good as he could get dressed up. Tinkey got to thinking he should've picked him up a suit or something. Didn't look like his ma had come through for him. Tinkey realized the court wouldn't get much done today. That's not the way they operated. It would just be more throat clearing and paper rustling, but with cameras this time. He was right. After the judge took his seat and everyone else sat down, both lawyers ended up in front of the judge whispering things. More crap, Tinkey told himself in an almost audible voice.

Just then, Sheila changed places with the cowboy sitting next to Tinkey.

"Hi'ya…"

"I thought you hadda work."

"No, silly, I took off. Is that the best clothes Dub could come up with?"

Tinkey nodded his head. "I know, his ma was supposed to get him something better than them rags. May I'll hit Kmart for tomorrow."

"Kmart? I think I'd better help you out."

"Thanks, Sheila."

"Oh, come on, Tinkey. You ain't alone. I'm with you and Dub. You know that."

"No, I mean here, thanks for being here for me today. I love you, Sheila. Lots. Will you…do you want to get…you know—*hitched?*"

She was speechless and just looked at the ring that was revealed after his fingers relaxed from the fist that had been clutching it tightly.

"Well, I never…where? how? yeSSS." Her voice rose into a louder whisper while saying yesss.

Tinkey surprised himself. He never figured this was the place to ask Sheila. It just happened. He was scared. He was happy. He hurt and he felt better.

"All rise."

"Well, I figured it was high time I make you my fiancée is all." He wanted to get away, but couldn't. Dub clung to him and he clung to Sheila. It worked. It made it better somehow.

The lawyers took turns walking around the courtroom asking the same questions over and over again. Have you already formed an opinion regarding my client's guilt or innocence? Do you believe in the death penalty? Have you ever been charged with a crime? Have you ever been in an unfortunate domestic incident? They just kept it up and up until finally the judge called a recess.

"Can I tell folks we're engaged?" Sheila cooed through a sweet smile.

"Wha...oh, yeah...why not, Sheila?" Tinkey hugged her out in front of the courthouse as a warm sun shined on them. That's what freedom, in the forever west of Wyoming, with Sheila, felt like. They'd have to figure out what and where to eat. Choices, choices and more choices to be burdened with. Dub didn't have any of the problems freedom offered. He didn't have the hug of a gal, sun on his shoulder or a choice on eating arrangements. Pig bologna is what he was munching on. Tinkey could remember him saying he'd never ever eat pig bologna if he got out. He said just the thought of it gave him a headache between the eyes. He was living under fluorescent lights, swallowing pig bologna. No way, no how, could Tinkey come to grips with how it musta felt to be so innocent, yet so incarcerated. How could he ever make it up to him? He had no idea. He was bound and determined to figure it out. Killing didn't seem to be the answer. Rogers died and caused the mess in the first place. Then, two lying-assed, tricky detectives only made it worse. Nothing seemed to be helping though. Tinkey hoped he didn't have to go and kill again, what, with plans for getting married and all. Shit could happen though. Who knew?

The blackness slipped up next to the happiness he was feeling for Sheila. Getting engaged wasn't the answer to the black thoughts in his head and on his soul. It was her, the prosecutor with her sharp words and finger pointing. She didn't know a thing. Tinkey was the only one that was certain about how wrong she was. What gave her the right to act like she cared so much about Rogers? How much were her antics costing Dub? Why did she strut around? Why did she love being the center of attention? Was she trying to blow herself up bigger than she really was? Tinkey thought about her ruby red lipstick and what a waste it was. It's like he'd been told once, you're wasting lipstick, if you put it on a pig, because, it's still a pig. His black thinking was pushed aside by a question.

"What are you thinking about?" Sheila had flashed him her warm smile, figuring he must be thinking about what married life would be like.

"Oh, nothing. Nothing at all." Tinkey smiled and wished that was the case.

CHAPTER 15
THE PEOPLE OF WYOMING
"KANSAS CITY"—LEIBER AND STROLLER

The trial finally got under way. Tinkey was relieved. Dub hadn't been done in by any plea deals. The prosecutor was responsible for that. She was prancing around claiming no deals would be made in the interest of public safety. Tinkey told Dub he shouldn't take a deal because he was innocent. Dub's attorney thought otherwise which had spooked Tinkey. He knew how Dub just kinda followed orders.

Tinkey rubbed his temples during her opening remarks. He realized he could end it all right here by standing up and emptying a gun into her, the judge, baliff. The works. Bang, bang and it'd be all over. He smiled on his grim thoughts about how good it would feel, to let them know, he just didn't have to take it anymore. He'd waited long enough for folks to figure it out. By god, I could just blow 'em all away. That'd show 'em!

Sheila picked up a pretty good suit for Dub. Actually, Tinkey paid for most of it, but she chose the colors. The clothes just kinda hung on Dub, though. Tinkey hoped the spiffy suit would help out. Their future, trains, laughs and a life under the Wyoming sky was riding on the trial. If they found Dub guilty, they'd pay, he thought. Dub was innocent after all, and Tinkey knew it.

After a whole day of having the would be jurors fill out questionnaires and answer lawyer questions the court adjourned until Monday.

"Jeez, nothing ever gets done in court, Sheila. We graduated like forever ago and Dub, he's just plain rotting away in the slammer. Nobody cares. Ya…know? This whole court deal is a waste of time near as I can tell."

Sheila leveled her eyes on him. "You and I care; we're doing what we can."

He cared enough to put bullets in the whole bunch of them. He could see himself standing up in court and hollering 'I fuckin' did it, you assholes' and just start banging away.

"Have you ever thought of what'd you do if he, you know — " Sheila was digging around for something in her purse.

Tinkey leveled a steady glare into her. "If he what?" He spent a lot of time keeping the word away from his thoughts. "Look, we don't have to talk about this anymore."

"Well, like if he's guilty and they do what they say they're a gonna do. Then what, Tinkey?"

"He's innocent, babe. They don't find innocent people guilty. They can't go and kill 'em, if that's what you mean. That's why we have courts of law."

"I'm just worried 'bout you is all. I know Dub and you are like brothers or something. I want him out of there. Ah course I do. What if he don't…you know…get out? is all I'm saying."

"He has to, babe. The court's'll get it right. They have to. I've had criminal law you know."

"Will listen Tinkey, I'm worried. I don't know if the court deal gets it right all of the time. What about OJ? Huh? Folks always a talking about how he got away with murder."

"Dub ain't OJ!" Tinkey thought about shooting the courtroom up again. That would take care of it, once and for all. Dead lawyers don't lie. He slouched down rubbing his face.

"Well, look, Sheila, anything can happen, I suppose. But I ain't gonna set around and let them dick with Dub. I've about had it! I mean it! The same old thing! Every! day!"

Sheila looked at him and shook his shoulder. "Come on, you've done everything you possibly could. Now we should pray for him and hope for the best. I don't know what else we can do."

Tinkey suddenly sat bolt upright, letting his hands fell to his side. It came to him. Yes, he could do it.

Sheila stopped rubbing his shoulder. "What? What are you thinking about?"

"Oh, I'm not sure." But he was. He seen it flash across his mind. He was going to put a stop to this court business once and for all. He had to. It was Dub's only chance. He should have seen it all along.

"Okay, okay. I'm with you Sheila." But he wasn't. He was already trying to figure out which gun to use. He had to get the dynamite and knife. The trial was going to end.

Later that night, Tinkey dug his journal out.

Two lying cops gone. Rogers history. What's a fella got to do to right wrongs? i hate it I surly do Dont know there any other way to make things good   I am a trying Sheila got it thought out, maybe she got it wrong   Tinkey&Sheila

He lay back on his bed with his arms behind his head. The only way he figured he could stop it was with a gun. Dynamite also. Killin' with dynamite couldn't be any grosser than punching a knife into someone's throat. That memory still lingered. Disgusting. The snake and train stopped two detectives dead in their tracks, but not the trial. A gun and dynamite would put a stop to the trial once and for all. As he tossed and turned, sleep finally overruled his troubled mind.

Mornings always seemed to come on too early. He ate Mom's pancakes, rolling his eyes towards the ceiling and chewing slowly. After breakfast he headed to Sheila's. She always looked pretty in the western sunshine.

They went through the motions of being together. She was discussing an upcoming nursing exam and he was thinking about how he was going to put an end to Dubs trial.

Detective Corll had managed to cover up for Gacy. Tinkey smiled as he thought about how it would be over soon. He finally had the answer.

"Look, Tinkey, you haven't heard a thing I've been saying. I now…don't worry. You got a lot on your mind."

Tinkey sat up and checked his watch. "Oh, God, I gotta motor to work. Love ya, babe."

The lawyers spent the morning getting a jury seated. Waste of time, Tinkey figured. Sheila had said she'd meet up with him after her test. Tinkey told her she didn't have to show up, but she insisted.

"Dub, your attorney like the suit?" Tinkey leaned over the partition during a recess.

"He-he a-a said i-it can't h-hurt."

"All-righty then. Look…my man…how ya holding up? Are you okay…Dub? This nightmare is going to be over soon."

"Didn't fig-figure you for no c-cop, Tinkey. Why you wa-wa-wanna be a c-cop a-any-a-ways? Look what they d-did to me, T-Tinkey. They went and lie-lied for no g-good reason. No whu-way they see me getting on the…four wheeler. I hated R-Rogers, but-I didn't kill him none. You naa-naa-KNOW?"

"We've been over this a thousand times, buddy. I ain't gonna be nothing but in a train engine with you. Got IT pal?"

"S-some a-a time I-I figger I-I-I-only goin' ta Raw-Rawlings fo-fore one a thing…"

Tinkey didn't want to hear Dub talking about the death penalty. He quickly reached over the partition and rubbed his shoulder. "Look, man, you're going to Rawlings to run *t-r-a-i-n-s*. We got some schoolin', Kansas City, then off we go. The big units! I'm telling ya this court thing is going to be over before ya know it."

Beer Belly Bailiff approached Tinkey. "Come on, Tinkey…no contact with my prisoner, you know the rules, buddy."

The jury was picked. Next came opening statements. It didn't matter because surprises were in the offing. After waiting so long, another month or two didn't bother Tinkey. Gun, dynamite, lots of details hadda be worked out. Besides, who knew, perhaps the jury just might get it right. He doubted it, though.

Prosecutor Toppan waltzed around the courtroom telling the jury she was going to present evidence proving that Dub was a cold-hearted murderer. She'd stab her finger at Dub. "You'll see there are attorneys on both sides of this matter. You'll also hear about why this is such a serious case, we are talking about a homicide. Nobody should take a charge like that lightly on either side. This was a very extensive case conducted by a very capable Casper Wyoming Police Department. There is one victim in this case, Mister Glen Rogers, who was lost to his family." With this comment Toppan stopped, and her eyes landed on different members in the audience who until now had been all cried out. Now some of them got weepy all over again. Nobody was crying for Dub. Tinkey took a deep breath.

Tinkey was concentrating on the words she was tossing around but his mind locked onto…heinous, cruel and atrocious. He was wondering just what church she attended. The whole notion of 'judge not lest thee be judged' seemed to have escaped her. It was clear she was enjoying herself. She walked around the room, then would suddenly stare at Dub. Tinkey stared back at her on account Dub's gaze was driven into a piece of paper on the desk in front of him. Tinkey relished the idea of ending her career. He sat just behind Dub with Sheila and his mom.

"This whole case just plain sucks. I'm glad it's ending soon. I can't take this anymore."

Mother was startled. "My lord, Tinkey, shush." She shot sheepish glances around the courtroom and was relieved that nobody had noticed.

As court ground on Tinkey made a mental note to pick up bullets. He had to decide on the right gun. He figured he'd use his dad's forty-five caliber Glock. He'd already picked up the knife and ditched it in his trunk. He had to remember the pen and paper.

"Listen to me, son. Talking in court is breaking the law. You can land in jail for contempt. That's what it's called, son. Contempt. So you just hush in there." She pointed to the courtroom as they were standing in the hallway during a break.

Tinkey cleared his throat. "I'll shush, Mom. I gotta hit the bathroom, insulin." He couldn't help but smile over the 'breaking the law' for talking in court deal. Not considering what he was about to do.

After returning from the bathroom Tinkey's mom hugged him. "Look, honey, Mom knows this whole thing has been hard on you. If I could make it go away I would dear."

Tinkey looked down on her. "It'll be over before long mom, you just wait and see."

Pictures of the crime scene were shown to the jury. Tinkey watched as their eyes would widen upon encountering so much gore. Several of the members actually were casting glances toward Dub. It seemed like the prosecution had showed the jury a million pictures before it was time for another recess. The prosecutor had indicated her desire to play a taped confession to the jury. After the defense argued against it, because the officers who had taken it had passed away, the judge ruled on the matter. The confession could be played in its entirety.

The recording was started and then stopped in order to adjust the volume. It was restarted and was easy to hear in the courtroom full of hushed spectators. Everyone seemed to be pulled towards the voice of Dub, answering the questions in his dead pane style. Tinkey remembered how the detectives had gotten the confession. Oh yeah, they stopped the 'confession' to get him straightened out on the facts and how to say them. If the pictures weren't damning enough, Dub's voice was even worse.

The reporter was going on and on about the trial. It was the lead story. Everyone in town seemed to be talking about how they 'just knew' Dub did it. A lot of folks kept some of their thoughts to themselves when Tinkey was around. They all seemed to know, full well, for some reason, as to how he felt.

> i know journal how much Dub didn't kill nobody even if they needed it / i know how wrong things can be even if nobody else is knowing / I know i got a plan / I know how stupid everything gets / gotta be smart / everything well be good again

CHAPTER 16

DYNAMITE
"SPIDERS & SNAKES"—JIM STAFFORD

Tinkey could remember from days long past how some critters landed in the varmint category. Once there, then it seemed like they required killing for one reason or another. When just a kid of nine or ten, he had gone with his dad and some others out to a prairie dog town and blasted away. It was a blood feast enjoyed by all with one exception. The others had concluded that he was just a bad shot. 'Hell kid, you keep banging away and you bound to hit one by accident.' But he didn't kill nothing by design or accident.

He remembered it well as he watched the prosecutor strut her stuff in front of Dub. She was making all kinds of motions and legal arguments about how she thought things had to go down. People around Casper had even gotten to talking about how she belonged on the bench. How she was keeping the prairie safe for decent folks. Tinkey made it a point to keep his mouth shut. No point in letting on how he concluded killing the human animal was far easier than killing innocent critters. Pronghorns ran around raising young and avoiding trouble. Snakes even hit the trail whenever possible. Spiders ate flies and mosquitos. Now, the human animal, that was a different beast all together. After he had his accident with Rogers, it was just a punch; he'd forgot about the knife, people started messing up. Then they somehow became the easiest animal to kill, Tinkey realized with a start.

Tinkey headed to class and landed in his chair.

"Now, class, let's consider how the homicide trial is going. We all know our very own Tinkey has been sitting in on it. Now, you personally know Dub...w'all know that."

"Yeah, I do, I know him from back in school. I know him really... really good."

One classmate from the rear of the room spoke up... "How does it feel to have a killer for a friend?"

Tinkey, spun towards the voice. The instructor chimed in, "Now, we all know Dub is innocent until proven guilty of the crime." The instructor crossed his arms and leaned back, looking over the class. "So what we mean to say is how does it feel to be friends with someone who has been *charged* with homicide."

"I figure, I know he didn't go and kill nobody. That's just the way it is. So I would guess that's the best answer I have for you."

Another class member confessed to following the case in the papers. "The papers reported, Dub admitted to killing the mechanic because he wouldn't fix his Honda. That's what they're saying in the papers and the papers have to be right or else they'd get sued."

Thoughts and words froze up in Tinkey. He just sat until the classroom somehow got empty except for the teacher.

"I didn't mean for that to happen, and I apologize for it. You okay?"

Tinkey looked at him and started putting words together, somehow forming a question. "Innocent people land on death row all the time. If Dub is innocent until proven guilty, why he gotta rot in jail? None of this is actually making any sense to me — you know."

"Well…now…I know this whole thing must be a terrible thing for you to go through, Tinkey. I'd like to think most folks on death row belong there, though. We're a civilized country after all."

Tinkey thought some on this and got up from his desk. "We're *sooo* civilized, why there all them folks getting out of jail on account of DNA? Why so many of them had to sit behind bars wondering when our *civilized* country was going to get around to killin' 'em? Huh?"

The instructor scrunched his face up, scratching his chin, mumbling something towards Tinkey's back as it stomped down the hallway.

After what had seemed like an extra-long evening of night classes, Tinkey was glad to be in his truck. He drove with a purpose before parking. He slipped his journal out from under the seat and dotted down ideas that needed to be put in order.

what if i'm doing stuff thats wrong? / i don't feel right killin but what else can i do anyways? / do stupid people need to die? / if your writing wrongs does it make it right? how in the hell do you write wrongs???

Upon his arrival at the front of the boulders he knelt and pried some of the smaller ones loose before checking his flashlight. It worked fine plus he had the necessary spare in his pocket. His stick poked and prodded into the darkness as he crawled and wiggled his way around the rocks before finally standing up in the cob webs and dampness. A sly sorta smile snuck up on him as the thought of Dub smacking his head, years back, came up. Dub deserved another shot at anything. There was absolutely no reason what so ever for him to be sitting in jail.

Everyone always talked about bats flying around spooky old mines, though Tinkey couldn't remember ever actually seeing one.

Spider webs were a fact of life, and he had to keep pulling them out of his hair, trying to feel if spiders were crawling around on him. Finding the rock concealed entrance wasn't any problem. He'd been over it and over it in his mind. He put the flashlight in his mouth and shimmed up towards the stones without hesitating. He was being methodical. He wasn't afraid of the loneliness the dark, dank, mine offered up. Determination crushed his fears.

The dynamite was still packed in the long forgotten crate. It was still leaking deadly paste and would, if done properly, blow Dub free. He carefully placed ten red sticks from the wooden crate into a burlap bag he had brought along and then tightly wrapped them up. He picked up some ancient blasting caps and fusing. They'd been laying on the dirt floor of the mine and were badly rusted up, but, again that didn't matter. He handled the bag with care and ignored the webs and a spider that zigzagged in a confused manner across his face. He blew at the spider with his pursed lips but continued to devote his thoughts to the burlap bundle in his hands. Rattlesnakes were constantly mentioned as permanent residents of old, abandoned mines, but again, Tinkey couldn't recall bumping into one while crawling around tunnels. Perhaps it was just to put the fear of god into kids, so they'd keep some distance from holes in the ground. He knelt on the cold dusty dirt and carefully nudged the burlap forward inches in front of his face. He had to forget about spiders and snakes as he worked the dynamite forward with his hands, followed by his wiggling body. It wasn't long before he was standing under the stars, slowly exhaling. He brushed spider webs and dust off and felt around for any moving creatures on his body.

The road seemed to have somehow developed more pot holes on the return trip. Tinkey eased the truck at under a walk speed back towards the black topped road. He stared hard into the night hoping not to bump into anyone. It wasn't long before he was back on 220 and headed towards Casper with his precious cargo.

"Order up," Tinkey hollered before spinning the wheel and reading the next order. Work provided him with the necessary time to plod slowly into his plans. He could see what needed to be done in his thoughts. He had carefully pulled his flannel coat over the dynamite and jumped out of the truck, bumping into a waitress standing in the lot.

"Christ, Tinkey…it's like totally freezing out here, and you decide to leave your coat in the truck? I mean, really."

"Whatever, think it's gonna be busy tonight?"

"I hope not, the cook's probably gonna freeze to death before he gets to the kitchen. What you cover up in there anyways?" She leaned towards the passenger side window, but it was plenty dark in the cab of the pickup.

"Bait, don't figure worms belong in a kitchen."

"Yuck!" That did it. She had pulled her collar up over her mouth and half ran, half walked, towards the restaurant with a laughing Tinkey blowing past her and opening the door.

"Age before beauty." Tinkey motioned with his hand for her to enter.

Between orders he got to thinking on how much lying he had to do. He took care of Rogers, then Fish, followed up with Gacy. No one was the wiser for it. Dub didn't have a clue as to who really did Rogers in. He actually thought his ma could've done it. After the last burger was fried, he quickly cleaned up before heading to his truck.

After starting the truck he made sure the coast was clear while zipping up his coat. He then cupped his hands and blew a steady breath into them. He remembered to put on latex gloves and then picked up the coil of fuse that had been conveniently crimped onto the blasting cap. Perfect! He slid the corroded metal into the stick of dynamite and bent down towards the floor and started a crumpled hunk of newspaper on fire but he blew it out quickly.

Now it was time for the drive to the judge's place. The icy wind blew on. Tinkey figured he couldn't have picked a better night for his nocturnal activities. Nobody with any sense would be out on a night like this. It was up to him to put the brakes on a system rolling towards so many wrongs. He didn't have a clue cold temperatures made his precious cargo even more dangerous.

After parking Tinkey looked around and then slipped into the shadows of the neighborhood with his dynamite and burnt paper. A dog yelped in the distance and he heard the wind rattling branches overhead. He was standing next to the judge's house and its gas meter in short order. He had already scoped out where the meter was. He carefully cradled his stick of dynamite onto the burnt piece of paper on the meter. Perfect. Tinkey quietly headed for his truck.

It was late, it was cold but he was on a mission. He headed out of town driving along the river southbound. He kept going, driving clear past Alcova before turning westbound for some slowed-down very careful driving. He headed clear up the canyon he knew was surrounded by brilliant red walls come sunup. He stared and worked his way along more of a cow trail than proper path for a truck with nine sticks of dynamite as passengers. Tinkey had to be completely in the moment. What he didn't know was how unstable ancient dynamite becomes. It even becomes more unpredictable when it's chilled. By now Tinkey's passengers were plenty cold and the trail was loaded with gullies and pot holes. He could've driven on the moon and encountered fewer craters it seemed.

His intended destination was Tower Pass. It wasn't nothing more than sagebrush and rocky formations. His truck landed hard in a pot hole blown over with dust. Tinkey was able to breathe again only after waiting to see if he was going to get ripped apart by exploding dynamite. His state of mind, fear fueling panic, was making it impossible to think of nothing but what he was doing. The truck had rocked to a stop on creaky leaf springs and shocks. Tinkey whipped sweat out of a stinging eye and cast a glance at the dynamite. "Fuck" he murmured before letting his foot up off of the brake and allowing the truck to lurch forward. 'Fuck' he thought again as he slowly, so slowly rolled towards the pass.

He wasn't making much time but was relieved to still be in one piece. He reached a sandy turn around and slowed to a grateful stop. He checked his flashlight and carefully walked around the truck to retrieve his cargo. "Careful, careful," he was saying as he worked his hands under the sticks, cradling them as carefully as a newborn baby. He walked with his back to the wind into the darkness, knowing he had no further than thirty or forty feet to go. He couldn't see it but knew it was there. Once he had concluded he had somehow missed the brick pile completely it took shape in the darkness.

"Careful now." Tinkey worked and mouthed words as he gently wedged three sticks of dynamite into a crack between two pieces of cement. Must have been the steps to a now long forgotten line shack near as he could tell. He left the top of the sticks exposed. He snapped up a tumble weed and crammed it in place over the dynamite. "Allrighty then," he told himself as he crab walked carefully, so carefully around the brick pile planting sticks of dynamite here and there. His hands were freezing in the wind but he was almost done. He discovered latex didn't keep fingers warm at all. If he had to freeze up his fingers some and avoid leaving fingerprints, then so be it.

He stepped back and forced himself to look over the job, blowing warm air into cupped hands. Perfect. He finally beat a hasty retreat towards his pickup with its functional heater. He shone his flashlight around and was pleasantly surprised by how fast his tracks had blown over. Wyoming wind storms were good for something after all, he figured.

Tinkey hadn't forgotten to set his alarm. He had to pick Sheila up for church before eating brunch with her family. He bounced up to the front door, singing *Zip-A-Dee-Doo-Dah*. They were looking for a place of their own but weren't in much of a hurry with the cost of school and all. Tinkey trusted her about many things, except one. He'd never be able to come clean with what he did with some of his free time.

"Come in...come in, Tinkey, the ladies are still getting gussied up." Sheila's dad was forever in a good mood. He enjoyed Tinkey's company and always spoke proudly of him around town.

Tinkey stepped into the house, smiling, and tried to hear something about breaking news on the radio. It turned out to be impossible as Sheila ran up and bear hugged him. Then her mom started carrying on about being late for church as she turned the radio off.

"How'd work go last night? You have a hard night? It was plenty cold, suppose most folks stayed home."

"Yeah...it was plenty dead, I reckon."

"Come on kids, come on, let's get a move on." Mom was hollering.

Tinkey and Sheila got in the back and her dad drove. The radio wasn't on, and Sheila's mom was all worked up over a new Pope getting voted in. Tinkey couldn't have cared less but nodded and even asked what he looked like.

"Whoa, lookit down yonder. Why there's a ruckus going on down by the judge's place. That's his house — right?" Sheila's dad was staring down the street at a crowd mostly standing around squad cars. Mom raised her voice to get his attention back on driving again.

Once in church, before the priest made his appearance, there was a lot of talk going on.

"A bomb was found at the judge's house. Why I declare, it's them there terrorists is what I'm a thinkin'."

"You don't know such a thing. Weren't no fire trucks down there!" the woman's husband reminded her.

She sat straight up and leaned towards him. "Well, I do declare. I heard it clear enough. There's a bomb down there. Probably a foreigner doing a dirty deed is what I think. I heard it clear as a bell...I surely did. The world is a getting mighty small. I hate to think of what's going on in this little old world of ours. Folks just aren't going to church enough. That's what I think."

"Oh, please. No reason to get all worked up." Her husband rolled his eyes.

On the way to brunch, after services, everyone peered down towards the judge's place. The police were all piled in down around the house. After sitting down for brunch, Tinkey finally heard what he knew all along. There was a bomb found on top of the gas meter near the Chief Judge for the District's residence. The bomb hadn't gone off because the fuse wasn't lit right or something. Stuff like this had never happened in Casper. Everyone was in a tiss.

"I'm scared, Dad...no one would want to blow us up would they?" Sheila didn't like talk of bombs interfering with her nervous rabbit-like nibbles.

"No, fact is...that bomb was meant for her, she's a lady judge, that much I know. Crazy people running around this country. Not like when I was a youngster, why folks had a certain respect for law and order. Near as I can tell, this isn't nothing but some wacko trying to be a big man by blowing up a lady. I never met her, but I've heard it told, she's a mighty fine person...all I know," Dad drawled.

Tinkey cleared his throat, "All-righty then…I bet it's someone, somehow gone and lost respect for the law. I bet that's what it's all on account of."

The media fed the starving folks tidbits of info. A bomb squad was handling what was being called an improvised explosive device. The bomb consisted of a very old stick of dynamite. It was done up in a very primitive manner. The reporter was droning on that the dynamite was older than years or something and was weeping its nitroglycerin. Tinkey shushed his mom and moved closer to the T.V. as the reporter continued her story. She finished up by saying the police were very pleased no one had been hurt. Cold temperatures contribute to accidental explosions because it makes dynamite entirely too unstable to mess with. If the dynamite had gone off on the meter there could've been an enormous explosion.

Tinkey realized he'd gotten lucky. He and Dub had a blast with the stuff over the years. They never treated it as anything more than fun and knew next to nothing about it. He thought some on the bumpy road and crawling out of the old mine with it. He found it near impossible to keep his mind off dynamite. What if he'd gone and blown himself up? If he'd gone and got killed what would've happened to Dub? Sheila? What would folks think of him? He only had to deal with dynamite one more time to make it right. Besides, he didn't have to get anywhere near the stuff.

CHAPTER 17

GOOD-BYE, BITCH

"I WANT TO KILL YOU LIKE THEY DO IN THE MOVIES"—MARILYN MANSON

Tinkey leaned back onto his headboard while aiming his pistol at a picture of God. He knew he was getting closer to where he had to be. He recited the Lord's Prayer. He'd put together plenty of learning and it wasn't all in school. He had the answer, wishing it hadn't taken so long. It was so easy. Now it'd be smooth sailing? He could've just blown Dub outta jail from the get-go and not had to kill so much. The P.D. had benefitted, though. He knew one of the guys that had gotten promoted and figured he'd do a great job. At least he'd be better than old Gacy or Fish.

Killing Rogers had sure changed everything. He went from worrying about tests and getting to work on time to hunting humans. It wasn't easy. People were as tricky as he'd overheard hunters claim elk were. He remembered being little. He remembered the warm dirt. Mom had scratched a furrow in the ground and he dropped a seed about every half an inch into it. After some weeks he returned with mom and stared into the beauty of the exploding colors being mobbed by bees. Mom picked some of the flowers and smelled from them deeply. He recalled bygone hopes and kindnesses. Now he realized the human community had did away with everything. It had to be stopped, and he was the plug. He had to stop the water from drowning the flowers. He had to protect the flowers, the hopes and kindness of things.

Prosecutor Jane Toppan acted if she alone was the answer. Death penalty? She was on record saying Dub had earned the right to be put to death. Earned the right? Toppan had been raised by God-fearing parents. Missionaries. She had left God behind, picked up a law degree, which somehow provided her the opportunity to judge and condemn. She was talking up a storm on T.V. Old goobers at the counter were even talking about how Casper needed her as a judge.

"Why, Tinkey, son...you going to cop school and all. You a right nice feller near as I can tell. You wouldn't go off and kill nobody, no how. That's just facts of life, son." The old-timer pulled on his suspenders, looking like a fat, smug toad leaning into the conversation with a really broad lipless grin. "Just a waste of taxpayers' money... to go and pen him up down in Rawlins. That's the way it be. Not the way I want it to be, mind you. No, siree. Why he had his day in court and was found guilty. Now that prosecutor, she a sharp gal, yessiree, she claims Dub a needing that *death penalty*. That's what she been a saying. He's guilty 'cause the jury decided he is."

The words had hammered Tinkey like a woodpecker pounding on iron wood. Individual words had landed on his eardrums but hadn't ended up in sentences. The court condemned Dub to be put to death by lethal injection. The judge went on and on but Tinkey's ears refused to cooperate. The judge had sounded like a recording being played at a really slow speed. His Honor's words were groaning on and on in a slow, steady, cadence. Dub's eyes had become empty things. The skin on his face was gray and looked to be losing its hold on the bones. His body had sagged, threatening to fall like a lighting-struck tree on the wide open prairie.

The prosecutor was still showing up on the nightly news proclaiming how justice had been served. She had no idea she'd be serving up a healthy dose of justice soon. Real soon. She was going to get it right the next time around. She wouldn't even need to be backed up by a jury getting it wrong. Nope, she'd get it right the second time around with just a touch of help.

Tinkey spotted Sheila looking for his approach from the boulevard. He returned her wave with a smile. She looked worried, hurt or some*thing*. Dub probably got to her. He swerved next to the curb and jumped out giving Sheila a hug.

"We'll be okay. We'll get through this, babe," he whimpered while avoiding her eyes.

Sheila was clearly upset as they both sagged onto the curb. "Look, you don't have to you know…marry me. But I—"

Tinkey filled the void of silence when she couldn't continue, "What is it? Wyoming wants to kill Dub. The jury sucks. They're dead wrong. I'm bummed out, too."

"I'm going to have a ba-baby, our baby, Tinkey. I just can't… can't…you know…end it or anything. I can't give our baby away. Not no how neither…like in adoption."

"What are we going to do?" Tinkey asked.

"Well…I'm gonna have our baby, but you don't havta do anything. Oh…you're all I've ever really loved but I'm not going to like trap you or anything."

"A baby? Now, how did that—" He stopped talking so his thoughts could catch up to his mouth. Sheila's shoulders drooped in the silence. "We're engaged, we're going to get hitched up anyways.

Let's just do it quicker is all. I'd never do anything to our baby like an abortion. That'd be murder and we ain't murderers…Sheila." He reached for her hand and squeezed it.

"I know you're so right for me…I hadda make sure is all. I know you'd never go and hurt anybody is all I know." Sheila believed in his goodness.

As they discussed a future and whether it contained a son or daughter, the sun was threatening to touch the western parts of Wyoming. They talked on into darkening shadows about their brightening future.

He knew where she lived. He had taken to hanging out in the park where she took her mutts for walks. She did this every day, rain or shine. Tinkey figured it was this or she'd have a mess on her carpet or lawn torpedoes in her yard. On clear blue sky days a lot of folks took to walking their dogs. Fortunately cold days pushed aside warm ones and rain rolled in occasionally. Then the crowds of responsible pet owners dwindled in the park. He'd wait for the cold, rainy days to deliver up the moment he needed. When the time finally arrived she was huddling under an umbrella, leaning into the wind, dogs in tow. Tinkey strolled up alongside her. He clearly gave her a start.

"Jesus Christ! I didn't see you. Just as well kill somebody as to scar 'em half to death…"

Tinkey was smiling evenly. "All-righty then!" His mask of happiness was clearly just that. "We need to talk is all. I gotta clear my thinkun' if ya don't mind…*ma'am*." His politeness irritated her.

"Yeah, you're that fella from court…Dub's friend. You got a problem, I suppose, with how it went down…huh?"

"Look…we have to talk is all…why, don't we hit for your car, *ma'am*." Tinkey pointed as Toppan veered away from him, tugging her dogs in a new unexpected direction.

"Kid...you need to talk to a shrink, not me," she said, glancing over her shoulder.

Tinkey caught up with her and opened his coat. He had no problem keeping pace with her..."Look, I couldn't ever put a bullet in you...but then again, maybe I could waste one of your pups. Which one, lady?" He displayed the pistol by pulling his coat even farther open.

"Look, you little prick, leave my dogs out of it. I don't have to put up with this. Got it?" She leaned into him, releasing a shower of tiny hot spittle droplets.

Tinkey cocked the gun, hoping he'd only have to point it at one of the dogs for effect. "You won't talk to me, then, it's only fair...I guess...to you *know*." He carefully aimed as he nervously smiled and narrowed his eyes. His thoughts raced as he realized he couldn't shoot a dog.

"Don't—Don't...put that thing away. Now!" She lived with only her two dogs. They had clearly, long ago, became more than mere pets to her.

"We have to talk. I have to tell you things. I promise I'm not going to shoot you. I wanna show you somethun'...please." When he said 'please' it sounded like a guy pleading for his first kiss.

"Okay...settle, I don't wanna lose Tanner or Taco because you're feeling like a big man with a gun. You wanna talk or what? Just lose the gun. Don't want to see you have an accident with that thing." She had raised her hand and was slowly lowering it parallel to the ground.

Tinkey pulled the coat back around him as they quickly walked towards her car. She loaded the dogs into the traveling crate and Tinkey only then slipped into the front passenger seat. He figured correctly she'd never leave her dogs in his company. As she slid in behind the wheel he pointed towards the street.

"That way...lady...and don't be stupid."

While heading out of town she failed to dim her lights for a car that flashed her several times.

"Look, goddammit, lady...you're aggravating me plenty...or let me guess, you forgot to dim the lights. You got anything else in your bag of tricks? Should I just shoot one of your mutts now? Which one?"

Her voice was low and steady. "Okay then, no more tricks, I promise. Scout's honor. No more tricks. Okay?"

"You always babbling on and on...on T.V. That make you feel important or what? How come you barfing up lies all the time? How it feel to kill an innocent guy? Yeah...Dub is big-time innocent." The questions had bubbled up out of him like water out of an artesian well.

"Look." She paused while considering her thoughts. "I presented the evidence to a jury. I followed legally recognized judicial procedures or did you miss that? Is it just possible your buddy boy killed someone and you can't accept that tiny little bitty fact? A jury decides guilt or innocence...not a prosecutor. You should've picked that up in your classes by now."

He heard her words noticing she knew he was going to school. She just didn't get it. What was the use? Talking to her made about as much sense as talking to one of her dogs. He leveled his voice into a statement having realized the futility of asking questions. "You just strut around like a banty rooster is all. You just playing your part. You wanted to be Missus Big Shot. Maybe a judge...huh? You don't care at all about someone missing prom, graduation or anything. You ever ask those dipshit cops why they figured Dub did it? You ask how boozed up they were or anything? Yeah. They weren't feeling no pain, I tell ya. You ever ask? You ever wonder? No, you're just happy you won. That's all it is. Just about you winning, no matter Dub hasta die. You one miserable bitch near as I can tell."

Toppan stared straight ahead and squeezed hard on the steering wheel after swallowing hard. Tinkey didn't expect an answer knowing she could never admit to herself what being an attorney meant to her. How could she live knowing she quit listening to her parents' God? As they drove on they didn't encounter much traffic. They had left Casper on 220 heading south.

"Look, you're his friend. I know you're upset. How can I help? I'm concerned. This was very upsetting for all of us. But Rogers..." He couldn't believe how easily lying came to her. Maybe they teach it in law school, he figured.

"Turn here, here" —he pointed towards the west— "drive to the end of this road, it's bumpy, take it easy."

She turned and headed west on the bumpy kinda road or trail.

Tinkey picked up the conversation where he had left off. "Okay, my dear Watson...you know why I'm convinced you want to kill an innocent guy? It's really simple. Really. Take a stab at it—*why?*"

"You ain't planning on doing anything stupid now, are you?" she whispered quickly.

"If you didn't act so heartless, just think, we wouldn't be here tonight. Riddle me this, Batman, do you know why I know Dub is innocent? COME ON ..."

"Don't hurt me."

"STOP...STOP!" Tinkey spun towards Toppan. "Nobody could've shut you up in your beloved court of law. Oh...you ain't so full of piss and vinegar when you're all on your lonesome? You can't even answer one simple question. Cat got your tongue? Nope. Now you just wanna know if I'm going to do something stupid. Well, let Simple Simon ask you, one-more-time...*lady*...do you know why...I *know* Dub's INNOCENT?"

Toppan opened her mouth but left it at that.

"You played that tape over and over. You showed them the pictures. You got what you wanted. Didn'tcha? Oh, God, you turned it up. The tape. Is that a trick you learned in law school? Aren't you something? You must be proud of yourself. Do you have any idea why I know Dub is innocent? It's hard, isn't it, to convict an innocent man? Any attorney can nail a guilty guy. But innocent, that's where the going gets tough. Well, looky here. I have me a little notebook for you to commence with writing in on how you stuck it to an innocent fella. Start writing…NOW!" Tinkey snapped his fingers repeatedly while thrusting his hand towards her face.

While she sat back in the seat looking at the paper, Tinkey slowly voiced the sentences he wanted written. She couldn't figure out the direction of his thinking but wished she wasn't alone with him. Tinkey was throwing her a strange smile, not of happiness, but the one born of bad intentions.

"Oh, goody-goody, let's see if you can't fix up a nice to-do list! Yes-yes. Put in there how ya had the knife and ditched it. Put in there how ya killed Rogers. You needed a big case, a murder to float your boat. Put that in there. Number them. Put it in there that. Yes… yes, do it. Or wait…write it up like you lawyers do. Use words like homicide, murder weapon. Yeah, murder weapon. Lordy…how's it gonna feel for you to be in the hot seat? Oh, we gotta talk about how you a want to be Judge. Yeeehaa…here comes the JUDGE!" Tinkey laughed while using his phony little schoolboy voice with a mask of innocence plugged on his face.

"Well, now, let's write up how you went and left that stick of dynamite at the Judge's place. Put something in there about how you had it figured Dub's case would get you made a judge. Put something in there about knowing all along Dubs was innocent. Write up how you next hadda kill a judge to pave the way for your lit'le *pro-mow-tion*.

Yessiree, here comes the Judge. Ha…put it all in there so as we can haul ass outta here already."

The darkness had fallen around them. The dogs whined and made digging motions with front paws as they sensed uneasiness from their master. There had been a shift, a move from control to an unknown they picked up with their canine brains. They resorted to quiet yips as if to demand a proper order to their world again. They wanted to hear strength from their master but none was forthcoming.

"You see…I'm only here tonight cause I'm righting wrongs. That's a notion new to you, I expect. You a big-time lawyer. If you were even half as good as you think you are we wouldn't be here tonight. You see, you're the lawyer. Oh excuse me, I mean *pro-see-cute-her*. So you don't ask the right questions, you don't do nothing but get innocent folks found guilty is all. So whaa-laa, heeeere's," Tinkey screamed, "JOHNNY," causing Toppan to scream and her dogs to bay loudly.

"Are we done, you gonna leave me be, Tinker?"

"Tinkey. Don't call me Tinker. You don't want me mad now, do ya? You see that brick pile over yonder? You gonna run over there and I'm gonna vent. I'm going to unload this here gun and then drive off. You can walk back to your life of shame for all I care. You never did venture a guess as to how I know Dub is innocent, but all-righty then. Go! GO NOW!"

Toppan leapt from the car. She sprinted clumsily behind the brick pile.

Tinkey smiled as he took careful aim under the tumble weed he knew hovered over sticks of righteousness. He used the door as a prop. He squeezed the trigger, not wanting to pull the shot. The first shot slammed into the tumble weed pile with only a ringing sound coming from the ricocheting bullet. The wind was howling and it started to rain.

Toppan huddled into the bricks after hearing the shot. Her thoughts raced as she mumbled into the chilly air for it to be over. She didn't want to hear the gun again. Then she wanted to hear the car start. The only sound she heard was the howling wind punishing the prairie. Was he coming for her? Should she run? She knew she didn't want to hear what he had to say. She had a pretty good guess what it was. It would make it worse. He'd have to kill her if she knew the truth. Then a deafening roar and bright flash suddenly stopped her worries and ended everything about her in a split second. Her battered chest cavity and some viscera splattered back across the scrub brush in a helter-skelter fashion. Some of it would no doubt provide breakfast for a hungry coyote or two.

He straightened up as he got out of the car to survey the carnage. He thrust fingers into his ringing ears, vigorously shaking them, up and down as he waited for the ringing to stop. After the wind had blown the dust cloud from the scene enough blood splatters and chunks were present announcing the prosecutor had argued her last case. He left the to-do list on the seat. Perfect, he thought as he dropped the knife from so long ago onto the seat with Rogers dried blood on it. DNA was truly a wonderful thing and it certainly was going to be righting a big assed wrong. He had kept his word also; he had not shot her. Perhaps his lying days were over.

He walked across the cold lonely prairie knowing he had done right. Nine sticks of dynamite had moved a huge hunk of the brick pile. Plenty of the bricks had pounded onto the car he was in. The windshield was even shattered. The dogs hunkered down, looking around, wanting to run. To get away. It had taken him two shots to get the dynamite to cooperate. He had talked some with the dogs, not wanting to leave them, but knowing he had to. After slipping out of the car, he trotted quietly into the peaceful evening, putting distance between himself and one helluva death scene.

As he was moving down the trail he stopped and looked back into the landscape illuminated by dimming headlights. Her tracks were the only ones they were going to see in the freezing mud. He was very careful to stick to the worn path. This would be pretty hard for the cops to cover up. Not with the ATF in town investigating a dynamite incident already. The pages of notes written in her hand, would certainly get the law enforcement hounds pointed in the right direction. At least the direction he wanted them to take. The knife, the DNA on it, the dynamite at the judge's house. Well, now, this just might be a happy ending after all, he thought.

EPILOGUE

Staring towards the top of a prison wall was about all she wrote. No way. Not in a million years did I see this happening. Then it's all gray, cloudy and getting darker and here I am.

Dub lumbered out of the prison gate towards Tinkey. So much had changed in his couple of years of lost living. Tinkey smiled at some guards strolling towards their cars and nodded his head. What do you say to a guy that's been through as much as Dub? Do you jump right into the wedding he was going to be best man in? He already knew about the baby that was on the way. Do you mention it's high time they hit for Kansas City to get after their dream?

Tinkey wasn't the same fellow who'd tried to do something right and then see it all go oh, so wrong. Life changes a man. Tinkey was getting married and becoming a father. Once he thought of only hanging out on the North Platte with Dub. Then the human animal reared its ugly head, changing everything.

Why wouldn't he consider a profession in law enforcement? He'd done well in his classes, and was well regarded. How could he come clean with them? How could he tell folks, the more he learned, the more it disgusted him?

The reporters were jumping up and down on how she'd done it. She'd made a simple bumpkin out to be a murderer and gone and went and got him the death penalty. They were saying she'd done it all to look good. If she didn't have an accident with the dynamite she'd gotten away with it. It was plenty cold that night she was playing around with the stuff. That makes for unstable dynamite. She was no doubt, going to blow up another judge, so she could get her promotion. No doubt about it, she'd kill to be a judge. She'd killed Rogers already, what was another judge gonna matter any?

He tried to remember most of the stuff correctly. He might've forgotten something or added some other stuff but it would be on account of an accident. He had done it. Scott 'Tinkey' Tinkersley had righted wrongs.

Dub lumbered up to Tinkey and stared wordlessly.

"So you hear? That prosecutor done gone and set you up. They, the cops, have it figured Toppan did it. They got all kinds of evidence...man. Knife was in the truck, Rogers' blood on it, everything. They call that a misprision of justice or something...Dub. Them cops had no idea what they saw that night! Witnesses always a getting it wrong."

"G-g-gawl dern i-it...I-I-ma right glad ta-ta be out ah-that place. I knowed I never done any of that. T-tanks to you, Tinkey...I got out of there."

Dub and Tinkey hugged into the next several minutes of their lives, as a well-fed coyote dedicated its song to the American west.

Made in the USA
Charleston, SC
01 February 2014